SINFUL SHADOWS

JADE WILKES

Editor: Havoc Archives
Formatting & Cover Design: Disturbed Valkyrie Designs
Blurb: J.D. Midnight

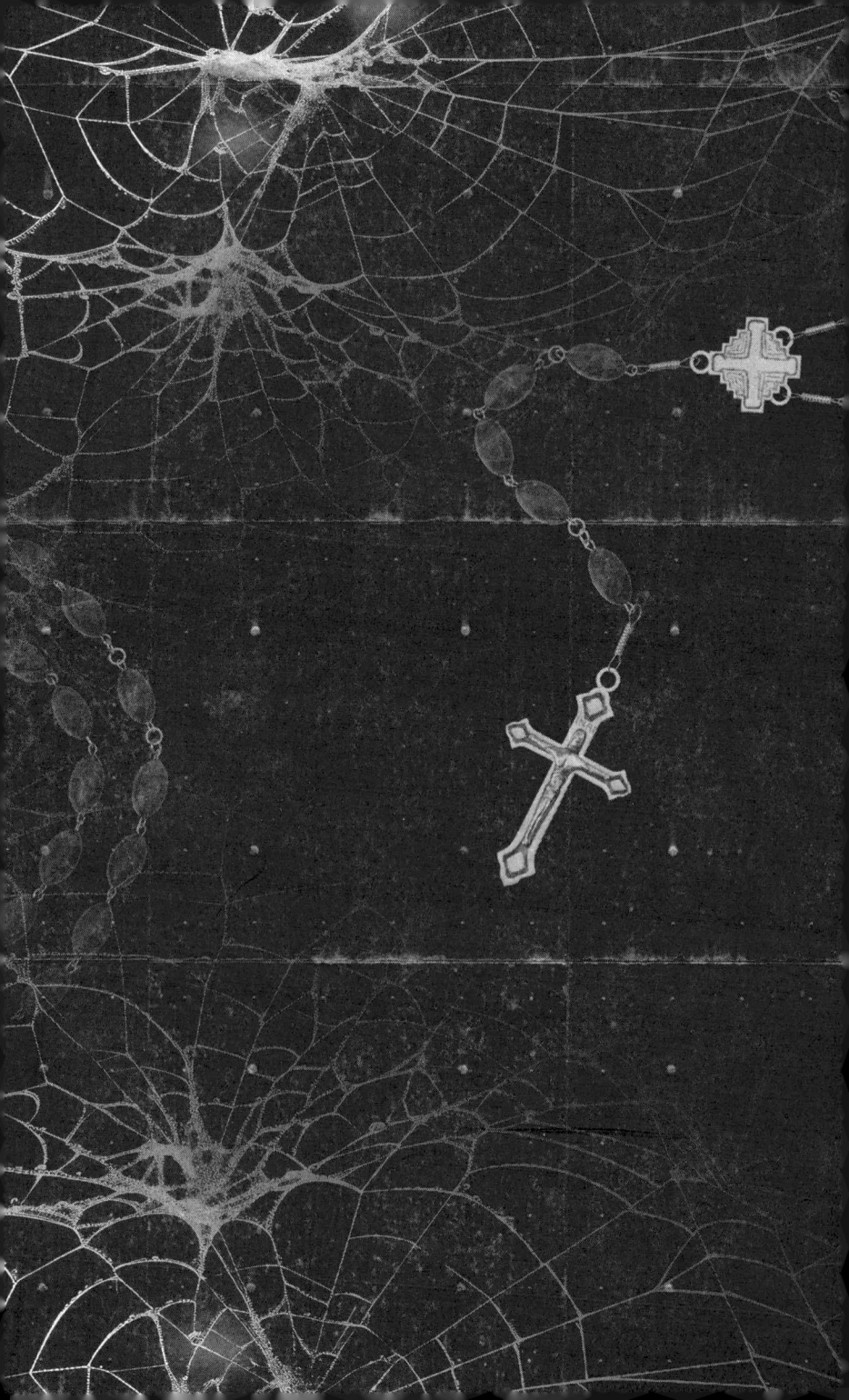

CONTENTS

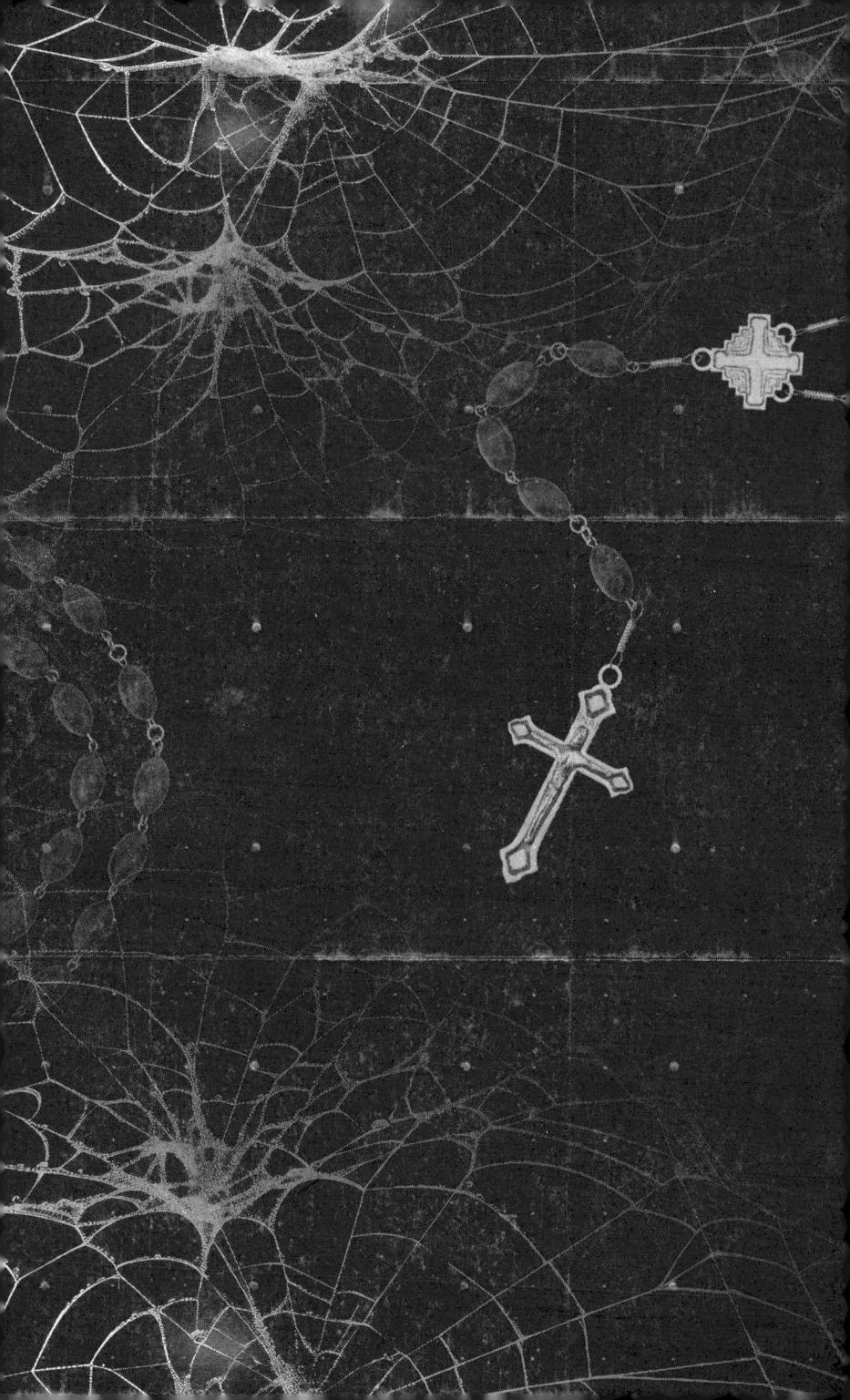

Author Notes

Please visit www.jadewilkesauthor.com/contentwarning for the complete list of content warnings.

If you do not like fast-paced books, this won't be for you.

PLAYLIST

Jeepers Creepers - Slayloverboy
Psycho Killer - Talking Heads
Devil in Her Eyes - Bryce Savage
Halloween Never Ends - Diggy Graves
Medicate Me - Rain City Drive, Dayseeker
Just Petrend - Bad Omens
Hey Ya - Sleep Token
Miracle (Church Verison) - Ellie Goulding, Calvin Harris
Thrown Down - Fleetwood Mac

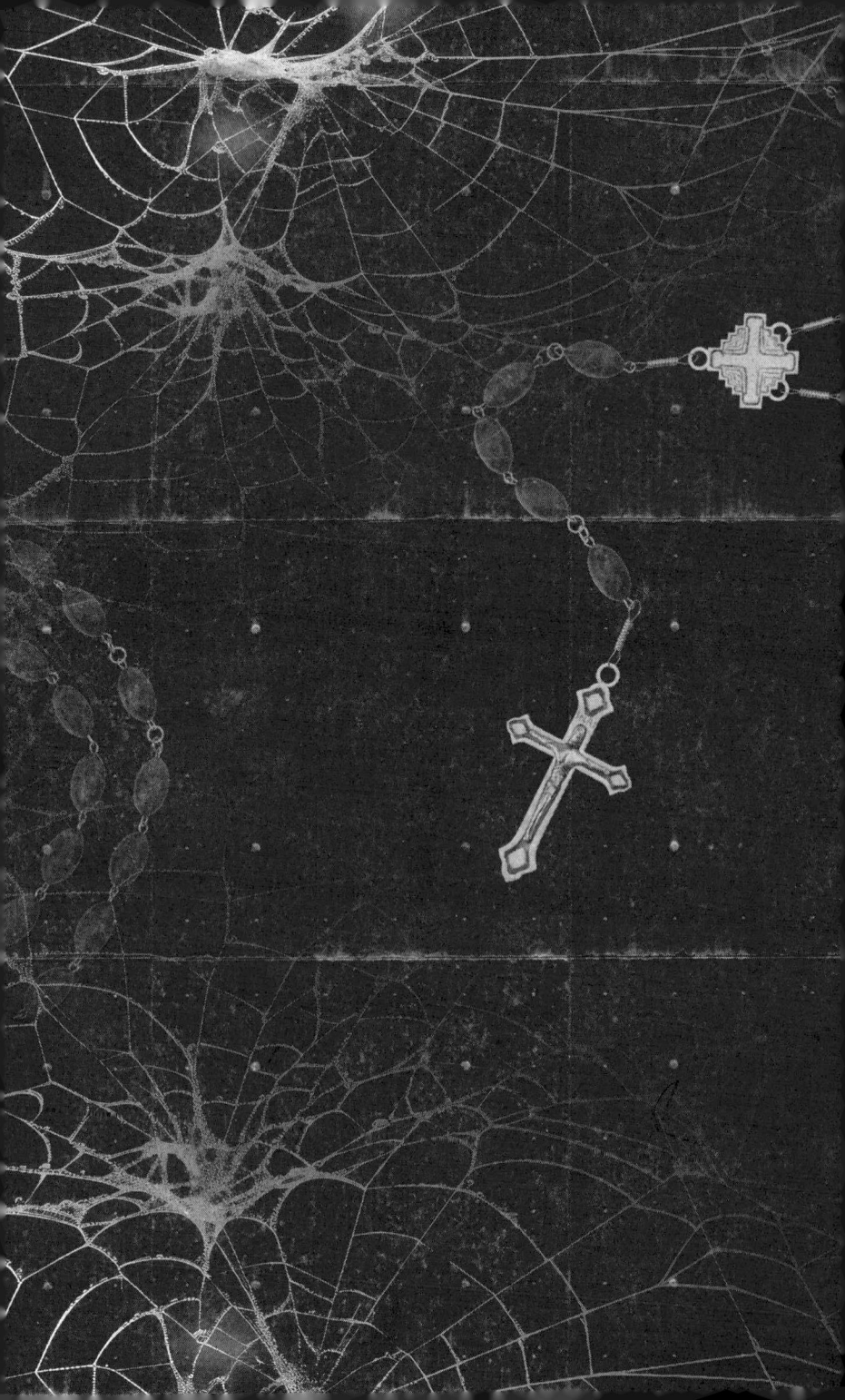

This is for those who are scarred by their past.
I know you crave nothing more than to be truly seen—just once.
You don't need a hero.
You need someone to walk through hell with you and not look back.

CHAPTER
ONE

HILLY

Moving in with my mother has been the best decision I've made in a long time. Trust me, I make some dumb fucking decisions. It all started when my mother discovered my father in bed with one of her close friends, Sara, eleven months ago. The betrayal left her utterly devastated and broken. Who wouldn't be? After the shock and pain, she felt lonely and abandoned in the home they shared for years.

Around the time my father was cheating, I had just finished college and was living with my friend Nadine in a downtown apartment.

Although my mother had not paid much attention to me when I was growing up, she stood by me during my darkest moments—when I lost myself to drugs and alcohol. I felt deeply obliged to be there for her.

Returning back home was not easy, though. My addiction had shattered my self-worth, and I had grown to love independence. I was very apprehensive about giving that up.

Since my parents' split, my mother focused all her attention on me, a change which put me on edge. This proximity felt alien, almost unnerving. The very thing I'd yearned for as a kid was suffocating me. But as much as it made me uncomfortable, I couldn't bear her suffering. I just couldn't leave her to deal with the heartbreak by herself.

Halloween was approaching fast, and the weather started changing—leaves fell and the wind began to carry a colder bite. My mom and I spent so many nights talking and sometimes crying. I gradually began to see the change in her, and having me around seemed to be working. We got into a routine, which brought some normality back into her life. We would watch movies on the couch, snuggled in blankets with hot chocolate and cinnamon buns. When the weekends came around, we would take strolls in the local park and talk about new prospects in life.

Halloween was one day away and it was a cold, gloomy Friday morning. Mom and I were on our usual walk. She stopped, her arm linked with mine. Her eyes sparkled, shining with excitement and jitters. "Hilly, I have something that I've been meaning to tell you." She gave my arm a gentle squeeze. "I've been seeing someone. He's really nice. I know that you'll like him as well."

The pieces fell into place, and a smile creased my face. No wonder she had become cheerful, and dinner with her "friends" occurred a bit too frequently. Now it all made sense.

"Oh, really? So I guess you haven't been having dinner with friends?" I squeezed her arm softly. "You kept that quiet. Tell me about him."

"I'm sorry, but I wanted to get to know him first. His name is Richard. He's kind, smart, and a hopeless romantic. He has a couple of children. I haven't met them, but he speaks highly of them."

"Well, it looks like he's making you happy."

"I've fallen head over heels for him, Hilly. He's truly swept me off my feet," my mom stated, biting her bottom lip.

"How long have you been seeing this Richard guy?"

"A little over three months. I should have told you sooner."

"Mom... It's fine. It's nice to see you happy. When do I get to meet him?"

She turned toward me, a smile washing over her face, and she released me from her grip.

"He's invited us to stay at his place this weekend." Her voice was filled with excitement.

It had been some time since I had seen Mom that happy, and I was still half-hearted about accepting as I hated meeting new people.

"Yeah. That sounds nice. Well..." I started, being very careful. "I told Nadine I would go to a Halloween party tomorrow night. You don't mind if I still go with her and return later in the evening?"

"Is that wise? Being around alcohol?"

"Mom..."

"I'm sorry." She tried changing the subject. "Richard mentioned something about his son going to a Halloween party."

I sensed that my mom needed to meet Richard's family, but the thought of it was unnerving. I wondered what he and his children would be like.

We continued our walk amidst the cool autumn breeze, feeling it brush across our cheeks, and listened as the leaves crunched under our feet. There was a woodsmoke and earthy smell in the air. I could see in the distance that people were getting their homes ready for Halloween by putting out pump-kins of various sizes and hanging orange and purple lights. I loved Halloween because that's the one time of year when all the decorations go up, and everything seems just a little bit more mysterious. I was utterly addicted to the thrills and spooky vibes.

TWO AND A HALF YEARS AGO

I lay on a couch, the lamp's weak illumination casting wide shadows on the dirty wall. People were sprawled out—some slumped in corners half-naked, others on the floor. There was an odor of sweat and alcohol. The broken table in front of me was a jumble of drugs, including crumpled foil, crushed pills, and empty glass bottles. My heart sank just looking at the sight of it. *Why the fuck do I do this to myself?*

My head felt dizzy like I had just come off a rollercoaster ride, and the room spun as I tried to focus my eyes.

I glanced right, and regret quickly washed over me. My arm was pinned under the neck of some guy I didn't even know. My instinct was to draw back, to try and slip out of there as fast and quiet as possible, but the thought of waking him made me cringe. I'd rather bite my arm off than have that conversation. God knows who he is—it must be some random I found at the club last night or something. When I was too high or drunk, I ended up in situations like this—not able to say yes or no to sex, waking up next to some man I didn't know, letting them use my body, trying to piece together the night before.

Suddenly, my phone vibrated in my pocket. I pulled it out with one hand, squinting at the screen. Multiple text messages from my mom. Panic set in as I imagined what she must be thinking, unable to reach me.

I texted her back, telling her a location where she could pick me up. Within a second, my phone buzzed with her reply. She must have been anxious to hear from me. Slowly, I slid my arm from under the guy next to me, and he stirred, hunching slightly in his sleep. I froze, holding my breath, hoping he wouldn't wake the fuck up. I really didn't want an awkward morning-after conversation. I slowly stood up and tried to balance myself. I felt heavy, stumbling around in search of my heels. The floor was messed up with empty bottles, clothes, and other items from the night before. I finally saw my heels close to the door, lying halfway under some crumpled shirt. I bent down to pick them up, wincing at the sight of my feet. They were cut up, bruised, and sore like I had walked barefoot across a broken glass. *How did they get like this?* I held my heels in my hand, too tired and sore to even think about putting them on. I looked around the room one last time.

I turned and walked out, taking a deep breath, with my heels swinging in my hand. It felt like each step I took was branded by the night, which I wanted to forget. What I left behind in that room wasn't worth holding on to. *Get me the fuck out of this place.*

The morning air hit me like a cold slap. The only thing I could remember was the street name, and someone named Mitch giving me free drugs.

As I strolled along the curb, I saw reflections of myself in car windows. My dark brown hair had become frizzy with tangles. My makeup ran down my face, and my clothes were stained. I looked like a wreck..

I turned a corner, and my mom's car was up the road, sitting and waiting. She looked all around, no doubt for any sign of me. My heart sank at how much I put her through, waiting anxiously for me to turn up each time.

I could feel her eyes on me as I walked up to the car, taking in my messy appearance. I knew she had questions I didn't have answers to, or maybe ones I just didn't want to face. I opened the passenger side door and slid in.

"Oh, Hilly..." My mom sniffled, tears in her eyes.

"Can we talk about it later? I just wanna go home." I buckled up and avoided eye contact. "Oh, and please don't say anything to Dad."

I looked over at her, trying to gauge her response, but she gave me an awkward closed-lip smile. "I won't. He's gone away for the weekend on another business trip."

My father had traveled every weekend for business over the past few months. The house grew quiet, bit by bit. It was wearing on my mom, being alone so often. It didn't help that I was out every weekend, disappearing into the night and letting any man use my body for their own needs. I've never thought about how my mom must feel, sitting around in that quiet house all the time, waiting for my dad's next call or for me to stumble through the door.

Mom drove down the road, and the air was so thick with silence that I could choke. I could feel her wanting to say something. I swear I could almost hear her thoughts, the words she was struggling to keep inside.

Finally, she broke the silence. "Hilly, I don't like this," she began, focused straight ahead on the road. "I'm picking you up every weekend at strangers' houses." She stopped to take a breath. "I can't just pretend this is okay." Her voice broke as she continued. "Your feet are cut, and I can smell you—the alcohol, the smoke, everything." She swallowed back another sob. "It's just breaking my heart to see my little girl like this."

I didn't know how to reply, so I looked out of the window. She was right. I knew she was right. But knowing it and doing something about it were two different things. But there was something sadistically ironic about the way my mother seemed to take a sudden interest in me, as if she had just discovered that I did, in fact, exist. Growing up, I was almost an afterthought, just a shadow that occasionally appeared and disappeared.

Maybe that's why I started drinking. A way to fill the void, to numb that unending ache of being unseen.

CHAPTER
TWO
HILLY — PRESENT DAY

I HAD MY WEEKEND BAG ALREADY PACKED AND READY TO GO. I WAS JUST waiting for my mom. I could hear her humming and shifting around down the hallway, putting things in her bag. I could tell she was in a good mood. She probably was thinking about Richard because he was all she kept talking about on the walk home. She'd gone on and on about him—how considerate he was, the dinner they had planned for tonight. Sweet, yeah, but after the first few minutes, I found myself tuning out. Hopefully, I wouldn't have to put up with an entire car ride of conversations about Richard. I think I felt this way because I'd never been shown pure love before, and it scared me. I sat down at the end of my bed and was going through my bag one more time when my phone buzzed with an incoming text.

JAMES (FATHER):

Hi, it's been a while.

ME:

I know…

JAMES (FATHER):

How are you?

ME:

I'm good.

JAMES (FATHER):

Good. Well, me and Sara are fine.

ME:

What do you want?

JAMES (FATHER):

I was going to call and tell you, but Sara and I are going out for dinner soon. Sara is pregnant!

What an asshole. I stared at the screen. He hadn't checked in for months, but I knew his game—he just wanted to let me know about his new family. He didn't actually care about me, and he never had. He was always too busy with "work" and left my mom to pick up the pieces all by herself, dealing with me at my worst.

I flung my phone onto the bed. What would be the point of responding? He didn't deserve my words, or even my fucking anger. I didn't have the heart to tell my mom about this either. She was finally happy. Something inside me really wanted things to work out between her and Richard. Just seeing her smiling and hearing how she laughed when she spoke about him is something that hadn't been seen in such a long time.

My stomach started to twist. I didn't know why, but it was there, nagging. Whenever this hit me, I'd reach for my angel cards. They'd become a source of comfort to me, a way to seek guidance whenever everything else felt uncertain.

I plucked the deck from my desk and knocked on it three times, a ritual that I had taken up because of my belief that it helped clear any residual energies. I shuffled them, the sound of the cards sliding against each other. The dark purple illustrations and symbols fanned out before me as I spread them on the bed.. I closed my eyes for a moment, taking a deep breath before I opened them again, letting my intuition guide my hand.

I always pulled out three cards for the past, present, and future. With a deep breath, I upturned the first card, and my jaw literally dropped as I read what it said. *Let go of the past.*

The words made me chuckle bitterly. Letting go of the past —something I'd tried to do so many times. Still, the memories clung to me, unrelenting shadows that refused to release their grip. I wished I could forget so many things. Like how my mom and dad hardly gave me attention growing up. All the nights that I let men use my body and pretended it was the only way to feel something, anything. When I came home every weekend bloodied and bruised, nights that left me literally scarred.

Then there was the intervention, when my mom and Nadine finally had enough and made a last-ditch attempt to pull me out of my downward spiral. They sat me down to tell me that I couldn't go on living like this, that I was destroying myself. The past card was right. Perhaps it was time to let go and stop letting the memories define me. I couldn't change what had happened, but I could choose not to continue being controlled by it.

I turned over the present card. *Steady progress.* I sat there for a minute, just soaking up the message. The cards were so right, it was almost freaky. Maybe because it was Halloween, and something in the air made everything feel a little more intense and connected to the unseen. Whatever it was, the card hit home.

A shiver ran down my spine as I took a deep breath and turned over the final card, the future. *Blessing in disguise.* I didn't know how to react, so I was confused and curious. *A blessing in disguise? What does that even mean for me?*

Was it something good behind something bad, or rather a

warning of things worsening before they get better? The card felt like a riddle to me.

My mom's voice snapped me back to reality, making me flinch. "Ready to go, Hilly?"

I hastily gathered the cards, carefully collecting them into a neat stack before tucking them back in their box.

Swinging my weekend bag from the end of my bed, I took a final look around my room to ensure I had everything before breathing in deeply and heading toward the door.

Stepping out into the hallway, I could see Mom was already waiting by the front door.

Of course, Mom talked about Richard the entire ride. Her babbling never stopped, and I could tell she was a bag of nerves. I nodded and occasionally said "Mhm" as my thoughts wandered. The world outside whizzed by in a fog of orange and red. Autumn had always been my favorite time of year. I loved the colors and just being able to snuggle up on the couch with a blanket.

My phone vibrated in my hand and snapped me back to reality. I glanced down to find a notification from Benny. We met on a dating app and had been talking for a few months. He was a decent guy who took an interest in me, always asking me questions. But I hadn't told him much about myself. I didn't know how to open up, and I always felt so awkward.

I could picture the conversation in my head: *Hi, I'm Hillary, but everyone calls me Hilly. I used to get so drunk I'd fuck a street light if it winked at me.*

Yeah, perhaps not.

Benny had been asking to take me out on a date, and I'd always find excuses to put it off. I did want to meet him, but I was just too anxious.

I'd never been on a date before.

I sat there, staring at my phone for a moment. *What do I do?* My mom still chattered away. I wanted to tell her about Benny and get her advice, but I wasn't ready for that conversation yet. In fact, I wasn't even sure that I was ready for Benny.

The car came to a sudden stop. Iron gates draped with cobwebs creaked open slowly in front of us.

We rolled onto a gravel driveway lined with thick, overgrown rose bushes. Their twisted branches reached out like hands ready to snatch us. A dark, towering mansion materialized ahead through the fog. Ivy writhed up the stone walls, curling around the windows in a fashion that seemed right out of some kind of old, haunting novel. It was breathtakingly beautiful, sending a chill through me. Its black façade was perfectly fitting for Halloween, and the atmosphere felt almost too real.

"Whoa. What does Richard do for work again?" I gawked at the mansion.

My mom wasn't surprised by the mansion's beauty. I guessed she had been here before. "Oh, I thought I said. He invented a dating app called Wickedy," she replied nonchalantly.

My heart stopped for a second. I could hardly believe my ears. That's the app I met Benny on. A surge of panic came over me as I scrambled to look for more details.

There it was, his name clear as day: Richard Northwood, developer. This was the same Richard my mom was infatuated with, the same man whose mansion we were driving up to.

A wave of sheer anxiety swept over me. What were the odds? Out of all the people in the world.

Skeletons hung from the window, ghostly figures on the door. It all resembled more of a haunted house than anything else, but it fit so completely with its dark style.

My mom had managed to pick out a guy with both money and good taste. *Well done.*

We both got out of the car, and the air was different here—crisp and clean. I inhaled deeply, letting it fill my lungs. Turning toward my mom, I sensed that she wanted to say something. It was as if I could hear her thoughts.

"Hilly..." she started. *Ah, that's what I was waiting for.* "Please be nice to Richard and his family. I know you can come across... uh... blunt."

I couldn't stop it—the eye-roll came out automatically on its own, and a little snicker followed.

"Mom, I promise to be on my best behavior," I replied as I got my bag out of the trunk.

"This weekend means a lot to me."

"I know it does, and I won't disappoint you. Promise."

Jesus, I had said that so many times in the past.

As mom gathered her stuff from the car, I saw something that made my heart skip a beat. In an upstairs window stood a dark figure, very still, almost a shadow. I blinked, trying to focus, but the figure was gone as quickly as it had appeared.

Fucking perfect. This place is haunted. I didn't know which was worse: spending the weekend surrounded by dead people or being forced to socialize with a bunch of new people.

I sighed and looked up again. Just an empty pane of glass stared back at me. I was reading too much into it, allowing myself to fall prey to the spooky atmosphere of the place.

As my mom and I walked toward the front door, it opened before we even reached it. An older gentleman stepped out, and I couldn't help but gawk. He was the embodiment of a silver fox: perfectly trimmed gray hair and beard against a crisp white shirt and tailored black trousers.

"Richard!" my mom called out.

That's Richard?

"Ruth," Richard replied as he bent down and kissed my mother on the cheek. Then he turned to me, his eyes warm as he opened his arms.

"This is the famous Hilly. I've heard so much about you."

"All good things, I hope." I stepped into the hug, and right off the bat, the smell of cigars and aftershave enveloped me—a surprisingly pleasant combination that suited him to a T.

I drew back from the embrace. "Your house is quite lovely, Mr. Northwood."

He waved a hand, dismissing the formality. "Call me Richard."

Without missing a beat, he took the bags from me and Mom. "Come in," he insisted.

We followed him inside, and I marveled at the stunning foyer. The high ceilings felt like they went forever, and the dark wood paneling made it warm and historic. This place was timeless, filled with dark antique furniture.

Richard laid the bags on the floor before turning to my mother and putting his arms around her waist. He got close and whispered in her ear, "I'm looking forward to you finally meeting Damon."

Damon?

"I'm guessing you've been here before, Mom?" I tried to sound casual. Richard released his grip on my mom's waist, and a knowing smirk played on his lips. My mom blushed. "A couple of times."

"Right! Let me give you a tour," Richard said, a little too cheerful. I followed him along with my mom across the mansion, and each room seemed more impressive than the last.

Eventually, we made our way upstairs. Richard stopped in front of a door, his hand on the doorknob. He flashed us a coy smile. "This," his voice was low with all sorts of playful mystery, "is where the magic happens."

Oh, fucking Christ! Not the bedroom!

I held back a loud groan, bracing myself for whatever was going to happen next. Richard swung open the door, and relief washed over me. It was an enormous office, not a bedroom. It was lined with bookshelves, and in the middle of the room were two huge desks directly opposite one another.

I let out a silent breath of relief and couldn't help but giggle a little at myself for jumping to conclusions.

A head jerked up from behind one of the computer screens and dark brown eyes locked with mine. The man stood slowly from the chair to reveal a figure that could only be described as striking. He stood tall, easily over six feet, and his brown hair, dark like a panther, was styled to look effortlessly messy and casual.

He was also clad in a tight white shirt—the top buttons were undone, revealing just a hint of sculpted chest. He sported a silver cross around his neck and silver rings around his fingers.

I was thrown off guard, so I shook my head, trying to clear my mind and focus on the situation. I forcibly kept my cool.

"You must be the beautiful Ruth," the handsome guy said, walking over to my mom and extending his hand. "It's nice to meet you finally."

My mom, trying not to blush, shook his hand firmly. "It's nice to meet you, Damon. Your father's spoken highly of you."

This is Richard's son? Fuck.

One corner of Damon's smirk rose higher as he slid his hands into his pockets and turned toward me, his eyes locked on mine. "And you must be my future stepsister," he stated in a cocky tone.

Stepsister? Yeah... That's too soon to mention.

Richard laughed.. "Aye, no talk of marriage." He nudged Damon with a friendly elbow. My mom joined in the laughter, clearly amused by the exchange.

"Oh, Ruth, let me show you this new painting that got delivered." He took my mom's hand and led her out of the office. Of course this piqued my mom's interest. She loved all things artsy.

I went to follow them, but I looked back at Damon leaning on the desk. "Well, it's nice to meet you." I held the door. "I'm sure this will be an interesting weekend."

Damon's eyes sparkled with curiosity. "I'm sure it will be. I'm looking forward to getting to know you better." His eyes moved from my feet up to my face, like he was inspecting me.

I joined my mom and Richard in the hallway, glancing back once more at the office door. I half expected to see Damon still watching me, but the door was now closed.

"Hilly, Richard is going to take us pumpkin picking later."

"As you can tell, I love Halloween. But I don't have any jack-o'-lanterns yet," Richard explained.

"Sounds like a great idea." I felt a twinge of awkwardness. At twenty-three, this seemed like a step backward into childhood, but seeing the genuine excitement in their faces, I couldn't say no.

A thought hit me. *I met Damon but not his other children.*

"Richard, you have other children, right?" I asked, turning to my mom to confirm. "Will I meet the others?"

Richard's expression changed as he put on a close-lipped smile. "I had a daughter." He avoided eye contact. "She passed away three years ago in an accident."

The hallway suddenly seemed very small, and my mom's

eyes filled with concern. "Oh, Richard. I'm so sorry. You never said—"

Richard politely interrupted her. "Ruth. It's okay."

I didn't know what to say, and I definitely didn't want to make that moment any more awkward than it already was.

"Anyway, here's your room." Richard opened the door behind him. "Feel free to freshen up and make yourself comfortable around the house."

It was a large bedroom with a huge bed heaped with fresh white linen, an armchair padded with plump cushions at a bay window, and a graceful wooden desk.

"Thanks." I entered and took in the details.

"If you need anything or have any questions, don't hesitate to ask. I want you to feel at home." My mom and Richard walked down the hallway, leaving me to settle into the room. I felt sorry for Richard losing a daughter, and many questions crossed my mind, but I couldn't ask them. I pushed it to the side and took a deep breath, wondering how the weekend was going to play out.

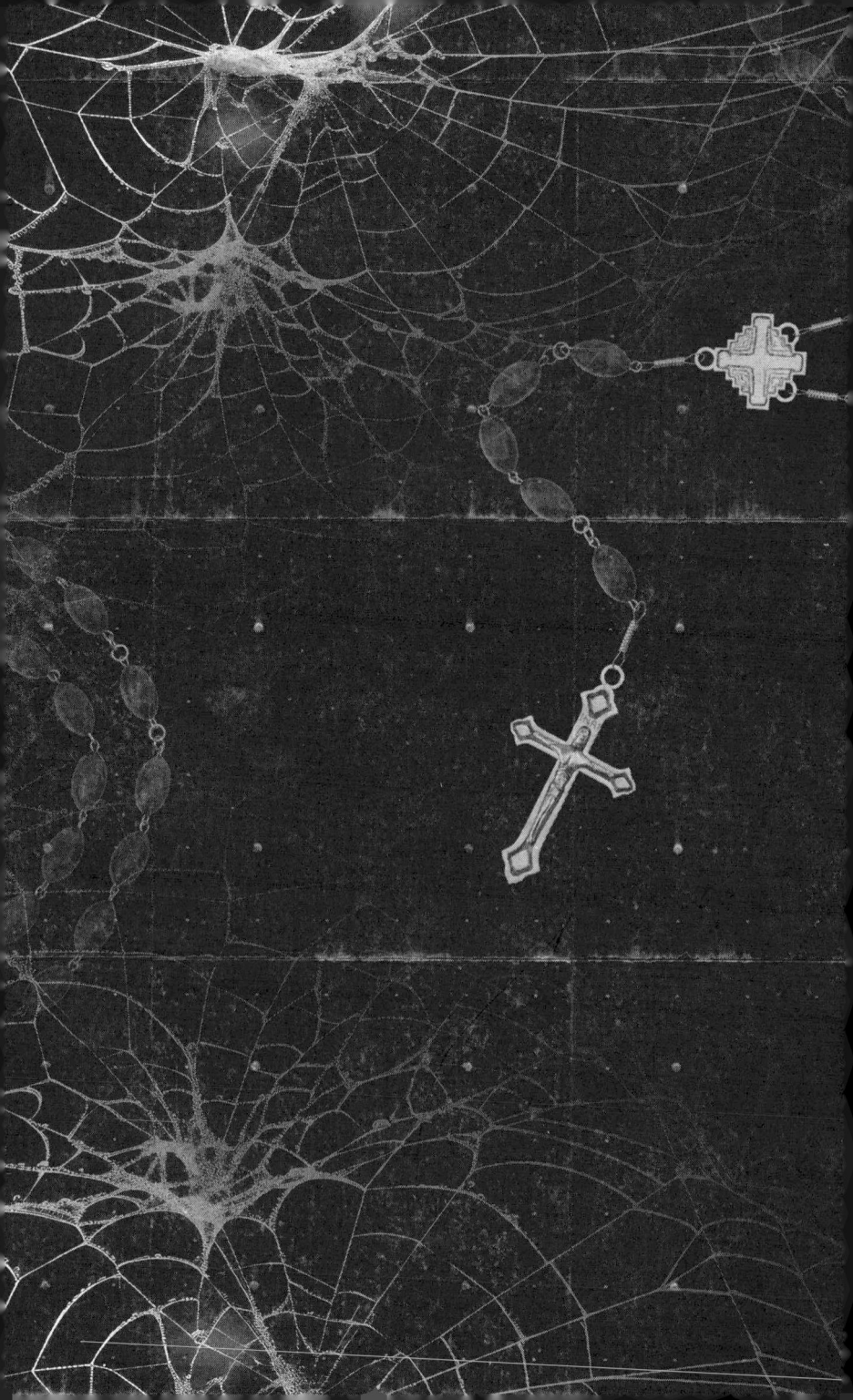

THREE

HILLY

I UNPACKED MY SUITCASE AND SORTED MY CLOTHES IN THE CLOSET. I set up a little spiritual station on the desk beside the bay windows. You could see the sky getting dark and the wind picking up all the leaves, making them fly over the ground. My spiritual bag was an item I took with me everywhere; a small ensemble of essential oils, crystals, and other miscellaneous items that had found their way to being a part of my life. I got into my spirituality after cleaning up my act. Every item in the bag had a purpose, from the tiny bottle of lavender oil for relaxation to the rose quartz for love, and the tiger's eye for protection.

Suddenly, I heard the floorboards creak behind me, and the sound brought me out of my thoughts. I turned around quickly, expecting to see someone standing there, but nothing.

The silence was interrupted by a soft shout from downstairs. "Hilly," my mom's voice called out, "we're leaving for the pumpkin patch soon."

I wandered down the hallway, my mind straying to Damon. The way he looked me up and down made me feel like he was examining me. I wanted to know how he felt about our parents being together. They were getting pretty serious; the last thing I wanted in the world was tension or unease. Damon was clearly going to be in my life for some time.

He gave off a vibe, the kind that tells you there's more to a person than meets the eye.. I knew I couldn't look at him in a certain way because there was a chance he was going to be my stepbrother at some point. *Would my mom remarry? Surely not.*

I saw an open door to my right, and peeked inside. Damon stood there, shirtless, in jeans and boots. As my eyes landed on his torso, I couldn't help but let my eyes trail over the rest of his body. His jeans were undone, hanging loosely around his hips, with a chiseled V that led down and disappeared into his black underwear. His well-carved abs were covered in black tattoos. I couldn't help but stare. *Fuck! His body looks like it's been chiseled by the gods.*

He pulled a T-shirt over his head, catching my eye. We locked gazes.

My cheeks flushed, and I jerked my eyes away from him.

"Sorry, I was walking past and..." My voice trailed off.

"No need to apologize."

My voice turned a little shaky. "Uh, you coming to the pumpkin patch?" I looked to the floor, feeling his steps as he walked toward me.

He stopped a few feet from me, and I could feel his gaze on me. I felt the urge to look upward and meet his stare. His eyes were so fucking sharp, yet there was a tenderness about them.

"Yeah, I'm coming along, step-sis," he replied jokingly.

Ugh, is that my nickname now?

"It's way too early to be calling me that, and it's kinda weird."

Damon's eyes turned mischievous. "Unless you have another preferred pet name you would like me to call you..."

I rolled my eyes at him. "I'm not your stepsister yet," I shot back.

He held up both his hands in mock surrender, the smile never leaving his face. "Okay, okay... I'll back off for now."

For now?

I shook my head, turning and walking down the stairs, feeling Damon behind me. I looked down and saw Mom and Richard waiting by the front door. They stood close in deep conversation, with Richard's arm casually wrapped around my mom's waist. They both looked really happy. He stared into my mom's eyes as if no one else in the room existed but them. He clearly had strong feelings for her. I never saw my dad show her that amount of affection. It was nice to see.

I turned around to look at Damon; he caught my eye and nodded. At that moment, I knew we shared the same understanding. Behind the teasing, it was obvious that he wanted his dad to be happy just as much as I wanted my mom to be.

I WALKED ACROSS THE FIELD OF SOLID MUD NEXT TO DAMON, WITH OUR parents hand in hand ten feet ahead of us. Various pumpkins of different sizes laid on the ground, their bright orange colors standing out against the soil.

"It's a little sickening," Damon muttered, lighting a cigarette.

"What is?"

He took a slow drag, then exhaled a thin stream. "Them two. They're like teenagers."

I followed his gaze to Mom and Richard, laughing and

talking with their heads close together. Richard brushed a stray lock of hair from my mom's face.

I couldn't help but smile at them. "I know. But it's kind of sweet. I can't remember the last time I saw my mom this happy."

"Yeah, you're right. It's just weird seeing my dad like this. He's normally so serious and always working. He's not the 'having fun' kinda guy."

We kept walking, the mud becoming softer the farther we went. The pumpkin patch was full of children running around, couples, and families caught up in the festive atmosphere.

Damon interrupted the comfortable silence. "So... do you think our parents are moving too fast? I mean, they only met a few months ago."

I shrugged, mulling over his question. "I don't know. But they seem to be happy, and that's what counts, right? As long as they're good for each other, I really don't see a problem."

Damon nodded and held out his cigarette. Hesitating for a second, I took it from him before exhaling the smoke into the air. Damon watched me closely; his eyes studied my face.

"Smoker, huh?"

I chuckled, handing the cigarette back. "Ha. Yeah... Better than some of the shit I've done in the past."

Damon raised an eyebrow as he looked at me. "Sounds like there's a story there."

Oh, I have stories, all right. But I wasn't about to spill my past to Damon on the first day of meeting him, what, so he could judge or pity me? No, thank you. I'd had enough of that from everyone else in my life.

I had to change the subject. "So tell me a little bit about yourself."

"Not much to tell... I work for my father, helping him out with the Wickedy app. How about you?"

"Me? I live with my mother and help her with her arts and crafts company." I paused, trying to think of something else to say. I shrugged and looked over at Damon. "I live a boring life."

Damon's head tipped slightly. "I hardly doubt your life is boring. You seem interesting enough."

I expected him to dismiss my admission or even agree with it. But there was something in the way he said it, a hint of curiosity, that made me feel like he saw more in me than I did.

Before I could say anything, my head whipped around at the sound of my mom's scream and to my surprise, Richard was grinning from ear to ear, scooping her up in his arms and carrying her in that classic wedding-style hold.

"It's very muddy over here, guys!" my mom shouted over Richard's shoulder.

Damon looked at me. I could see the hint of mischief in his eyes, with one eyebrow raised and a smirk on his face. I knew exactly what he was thinking, and I wasn't going to let him have his fun. "No way."

He threw his head back and let out a long and deep laugh. "Aw, come on, step-sis." There he went with that name again.. "It would be like a rite of passage into the family at this point."

I crossed my arms and made my way along the muddy puddle. Damon was still chuckling to himself, and I could feel his gaze watching every step as if he were waiting for me to slip up.

"Careful," he called out mockingly. "Wouldn't want you to ruin those pretty shoes."

I gave him my middle finger as a response. Damon brushed his thumb across his chin as he smirked.

I turned to walk away but misjudged my step and slipped, landing into the mud on my ass with a *thud*. Before I had time to even register what had happened, Damon rushed over, his feet shooting out from under him. He crashed right next to me, his body sinking into the mud.

"Ahh, fuck!"

We busted out laughing, holding on to each other as we both stumbled to our feet. I could hear our parents laughing off to the side—no doubt they had seen the whole spectacle.

"Are you alright?" Richard called out.

"Just fine!" Damon yelled back, giving a muddy thumbs up.

Our eyes met, his teeth surprisingly white against the sludge smeared across his face. My chest did this weird flutter, and a warm feeling creeping low in my stomach. Shaking my head slightly, I looked away, focusing on trying to clean off my clothes..

Mom and Richard walked over, each carrying large pumpkins. Mom looked determined but overwhelmed by the weight, while Richard carried one with a broad grin on his face, seeming to enjoy the challenge.

"We found some beauties," Mom announced, her voice strained as she clutched the pumpkin against her chest.

Damon stepped forward with his arms out. "Here, let me take that, Ruth."

Richard's eyes flickered between me and Damon. I quickly looked away, feeling a bit flustered.

"Let's get these back to the house then," Richard finally offered, breaking the awkward silence.

MOM AND RICHARD WERE EAGER TO CARVE THE PUMPKINS, BUT I decided not to join in. The dried mud was starting to get itchy and I needed a shower. By the time I made it upstairs, Damon had already beat me to it. I could hear the water running in the bathroom, and he was humming some sort of tune. It was pleasant, and I found myself smiling. Eventually the water stopped, and I could hear Damon shuffling around in the bathroom. I figured he was drying off and getting dressed. I waited for a few minutes before cautiously walking down the hallway in just a towel. The house seemed so quiet, except for some very faint murmurs coming from downstairs. I stopped at the door, listening for Damon. Not hearing anything, I assumed it was safe to enter.

My breath hitched as soon as I opened the door to fully naked, completely unaware Damon. My eyes darted down before I could stop myself. *His cock is massive!*

"Fuck! I'm sorry!" I screamed, slamming the door shut.

My heart beat in my chest like a drum. I squeezed my eyes shut to get rid of the image, but it had seared itself into my mind.

Damon stepped out the door with a towel barely covering his lower half; his hair was wet, and his body glistened in the light. "Sorry! I thought the bathroom was fr—I couldn't hear anyone in there..." was all I could say as my face flushed with my embarrassment.

Damon let out a small chuckle. "You're making a habit of this, aren't you, step-sis? Walking into rooms when I'm naked... Anybody would think that you're doing it intentionally."

"Very funny. I didn't do it on purpose, Damon."

"Yeah, yeah..."

With a smirk, he stepped to the side and gestured to the door. As I entered the bathroom, I knew his eyes were on me. "Wait. How did you get these scars?" He ran his fingers gently over my back.

I had totally forgotten about the scars on my back. They were remnants of my past that I wasn't ready to share. I turned my head to the side and then jerked right back around, suddenly feeling really awkward. My mind started racing as I tried to come up with something to say to deflect the question.

"Uh..."

Damon seemed to sense my unease. "It's ok if you don't want to tell me right now, but you will tell me soon." He leaned on the doorframe, his expression softening but his body tense. I gave him an awkward smile. He returned a small nod before closing the bathroom door. I slumped against the tiles, taking a second to collect myself.

No matter how hard I tried, I could not rid my mind of Damon's tattooed, wet body. It kept playing over and over in my head, like a loop that would not stop. *Ugh, I wish he would get out of my head.*

There was a tightening in my stomach as Richard called me down for dinner. How could I face Damon after what happened?

I walked into the dining room, and there they were, Mom and Richard at the far end of the table, laughing. They were unaware of just how awkward this situation was for me. I turned my head to look around the room, and my eyes landed on the bar, where I noticed Damon. He poured himself a glass of bourbon. There was a part of me that wished I could have the same. He turned around, his eyes locking onto me as he took a slow sip. The corner of his lips were slightly raised as if he knew the effect he was having on me. I sat down at the table, trying to focus on anything other than him.

Damon walked around the table without taking his eyes off

me. The intensity of his stare made me feel hot and flustered. He sat down opposite me and never took his eyes off mine, not fucking once. I turned away, pretending to be interested in the conversation between Mom and Richard.

"How was your shower, Hilly?" Damon asked, his voice dripping with that same teasing tone from earlier. He then took a sip of his drink, waiting for me to reply.

I clenched my teeth, setting my jaw, determined not to let him get under my skin. "It was fine."

Why was Damon having this effect on me? I hardly knew him.

I was so caught up in my thoughts that I hadn't noticed that Richard got up from the table. His sudden presence beside me caused me to flinch.

"Dinner!" He set the plate in front of me. *Oh, damn.* The meal looked amazing—Zucchette pasta shaped like tiny pumpkins, perfectly laid out in a creamy sauce. The aroma wafted up and my mouth began to water.

"This looks delicious, Richard. Thank you." I picked up the fork. Richard smiled at me and then sat back down, looking at my mom and carrying on their conversation.

Damon pushed a glass toward me and went to pour some wine. I quickly put my hand over the glass. "No alcohol for me, but thanks."

He looked at me curiously but shrugged. "Your mom says you're going to the Wickedy Woods party tomorrow?"

Before I could reply, Richard chimed in. "I don't know if your mom has told you, but I created the Wickedy app. I normally show my face at these events, but not this year." He looks over at Mom. "This year, I'm spending it with your mom."

"Yeah, I'm going with my friend Nadine. This will be my first Wickedy party," I said, then took a bite of food, hoping that would end the conversation. I didn't want a million questions.

However, Richard wasn't finished. "Damon will take you."

"It's fine—" I began.

My mom broke in, firm but kind. "Hilly, that's a great idea. Thank you, Damon." She looked over at Damon, smiling.

"Sounds perfect," I said with a forced smile on my face. Damon just smiled, and his eyes showed a glint like he had expected this outcome all along.

"You'll enjoy the party. They tend to get wild..." Damon said before glancing at his father.

I caught an exchange between Richard and my mom—her hand squeezing him, his slight nod in response. There was something unspoken between them. I had a feeling she had told Richard about my past. *Fucking great.*

"I'm looking forward to it," I replied. His knowing grin didn't help my nerves, and I must admit that I didn't have the most positive feeling about the party now. I reminded myself that I had gone out to bars with Nadine many times before and that I was strong. I had overcome the temptations that used to rule my life. This party might be wild, but I wasnt that same person anymore. Nadine and I would have fun.

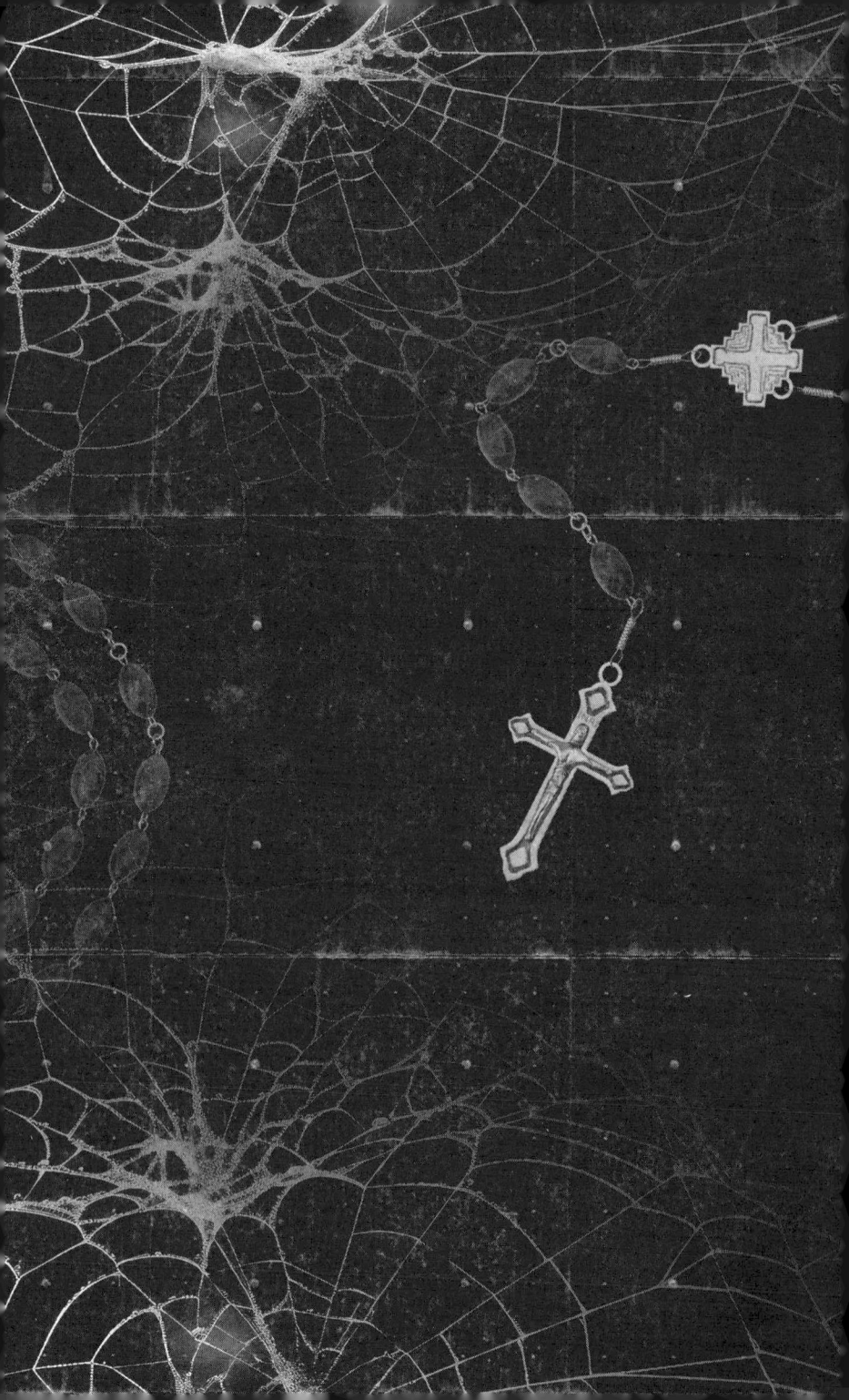

FOUR

DAMON

The moonlight cast shadows in the office as I sat at my desk with a glass of bourbon. I quickly minimized the window that was open as soon as I heard the door creak open—a habit developed over the years. I didn't need my father seeing what I was looking at. Not tonight.

Slowly, I stood, crossing my arms over my chest, and leaned back against the desk, watching him enter the office. "I need a favor." His voice was hushed and controlled.

Every time my father said he needed a favor, it was never something simple or easy. I kept a stern expression on my face, though inside, I braced myself. "What is it this time?"

He took a step closer to me, his eyes locking on mine. "It's about Hilly."

My muscles tensed at the mention of her name. Of course it had to do with Hilly. I arched an eyebrow, playing it cool.

"What about her?" I could feel the pulse in my neck quickening.

His eyes narrowed, and he glared as if to warn me. "I need you to keep an eye on her tomorrow night at the party. Make sure she stays out of trouble. No drinking and no drugs. Ruth told me about Hilly's past. If Ruth is happy, then I'm happy..."

He wanted me to babysit her to ensure she didn't mess up his plans with Ruth. I couldn't say no. I cared about Hilly more than I should.

"Fine." My voice was colder than I intended. "I'll keep an eye on her."

"Thanks, son." He patted my back with a warm smile before leaving.

I returned to the computer. Truthfully, I had spent hours investigating Hilly—something I never told my father.

Two months ago, when he told me he was dating Ruth, I wanted to make sure that Ruth wasn't a money-grabbing bitch after our fortune. That's when I stumbled upon Hilly. I knew I wanted to find out more about her. It was fucked up and wrong of me; I had full access to Hilly's Wickedy account, and at first, it was harmless, but then I couldn't stop. I stumbled upon messages between her and someone named Benny. The exchanges were casual at first, but soon became more intimate. I saw the nudes she sent to him. There I was for months, focusing on a woman I had never met. Every night, a new wave of jealousy washed over me. Each day, I waited for my father to finally introduce me to Ruth and her daughter. I knew Hilly better than she might have realized, and she was driving me wild. I was so fucking into her that it bordered on obsession.

I brought up Hilly's Wickedy account and realized that she hadn't messaged Benny for a couple of days. I wondered if she didn't feel the need to message him because of me.

I scrolled through her messages with Benny; the words and pictures fluttered by on the screen. Then, I stopped. It was Hilly, lying on a bed, with one leg bent at the knee and her other leg spread wide so that I could see her wet pussy. She had one hand cupping her round breast with her thumb and index finger pinching her hard nipple. My cock responded instinctively, throbbing against the fabric. I paused to steady my breath, trying to rein in the emotions the image had stirred up in me. I unzipped my pants and pulled them down past my hips. My erection sprung up, hitting my stomach. I wrapped my hand around my hard, aching cock, giving it a few strokes. A bead of cum glistened on the tip. I ran my thumb over it, releasing a growl. My body tensed with each movement as my grip tightened. My eyes remained fixed on the screen in front of me, and I took in every detail of her full breasts; her rosy nipples stood out. *Fuck, I want to taste them.* My breathing deepened as I moved my hand over my cock. The pressure and heat became intolerable as I pictured Hilly riding me, her body and boobs bouncing on top of me, screaming my name. I wanted to grab her throat, spit in her mouth, and claim her as mine. It was taboo and fucked up, but damn, it turned me on so much.

I felt ecstasy yet pain as I continued. In one final stroke, I moved my hand over the tip, and a small burst of cum squirted out into my hand. I let out a loud moan, the sound escaping before I could fully process it.

I slumped in the chair, my breaths were heavy and uneven. I remembered so many hours spent staring at the screen; the last two months, it seemed to have somehow turned into a daily occurance, jerking off to Hilly. She dominated my thoughts, making it difficult to focus on anything else.

I knew I had to keep an eye on her at the Halloween party, but the question loomed in my mind. *Am I strong enough to control my impulses?*

HILLY

THE NEXT DAY

Knowing Damon was taking me to this Halloween party, I was not looking forward to it. I was so confused about why I had these feelings for him; I found him hot, yet I didn't want to complicate things. I just wanted to spend the night with Nadine and have fun.

I walked down the hallway and kept my eyes straight ahead as I passed Damon's door. The last thing I wanted was to see him naked again. Thinking about it made me flustered, so I wasn't about to risk a repeat.

I made my way to the kitchen, and my mom was already at the counter with a cup of coffee in her hand. Her fingers tapped lightly at the side of her mug. I knew something was bothering her.

"Morning." I sat next to her.

"Morning," Mom greeted.

"Everything okay? You looked miles away there."

"Oh, I'm fine. Just tired." Taking a deep breath, she held it for a second before exhaling very slowly, as if to let go of whatever was bothering her.

She stood up, reached for a cup on the counter, and handed it to me. "Richard made some pumpkin spiced lattes."

Of course, he did. I was starting to get sick of the sight of pumpkins.

"Thanks." I wrapped my hands around the warm cup. I could smell the aroma of cinnamon and nutmeg. I glanced around the kitchen, half expecting to see Richard bustling about. "Where is Richard?"

"Oh, he's in his office. He had to make a quick call."

"He's obsessed with Halloween, isn't he?"

"Yeah," Mom replied, a slight smile crossing her lips. "He told me it was his daughter's favorite holiday last night."

"Oh." The word came out before I could catch myself. "That's nice..." I took another sip of my drink, hoping to ease the awkwardness.

"Hilly..." I could feel a question coming even before she finished her sentence. "How would you feel If I remarried?"

There it fucking was, the question I half expected but was dreading. I just stared down at my latte, and the steam curled up from the cup like it could somehow hide me from this conversation.

I felt like the adult in the conversation. Our roles were reversed, making me uneasy. Taking a deep breath, I looked up at her, trying to keep my voice steady. "Don't you think it's too soon?" I asked, hoping she'd understand where I was coming from.

She sighed, and her eyes seemed to grow tender as we looked at each other. "Well, I'm not getting any younger, and Richard makes me happy. I've been more happy with him than I ever was with your father, and I was with him for years."

My father flashed through my mind—how he had moved on after the divorce and started a new family. He found his happiness, so my mom had every right to find hers.

"Do whatever makes you happy, Mom," I replied with a smile that I allowed to seep through. I still felt it was a bit too early for marriage, but her happiness was important to me. She seemed relieved and relaxed as she placed her hand on mine.

"You like Richard and Damon, right?"

Oh, God. Damon. The thought of him being able to call me his stepsister sent a shiver through my body. He'd probably get a kick out of that, teasing me with that nickname until the end of time. I could already picture his smug grin, the way he'd find every opportunity to remind me of our new "family" connection. The thought of him being a permanent part of my life had me feeling excited... but scared because I don't know how to process or understand what I'm feeling.

I swallowed those feelings and forced a smile. "Yeah. They're nice and welcoming." It was true.

"Well, I'm not even sure if he's going to propose. But the signs are there."

"Signs?"

Her eyes sparkled as she leaned in a little closer. "His phone rang... with 'jewelers' on the caller ID. And yesterday, he was asking me all sorts of questions about marriage and settling down," she said in disbelief.

It did sound like Richard was planning something. "Don't look too much into it, Mom. I don't want you getting your hopes up."

She smiled, although, in her eyes, I could tell she understood. "I know, I know."

Before anything else could be said, Damon walked into the kitchen, his hair a mess that somehow managed to look effortlessly sexy. He had that just-rolled-out-of-bed look that, annoyingly, suited him perfectly.

"Good morning, Ruth." He nodded toward my mom. Then his eyes landed on me, and that same smug smirk spread across his face. "Hilly..."

I felt a small surge of irritation.

Damon didn't waste any time; he went straight to the coffee pot to pour himself a cup. *The thought of this guy being my stepbrother... I've seen him naked.*

"So, what's in store for today?" Damon asked, leaning casually against the counter as he sipped his coffee, his eyes flicking between the two of us.

"Your father and I are going into town to do a bit of shopping. He's going to show me around," my mom explained.

"Nice. Well, I would say I'd join, but shopping isn't really my thing." Damon laughed.

"I agree," I muttered under my breath.

Before I could say anything else, Damon turned to me. "Well, Hilly, why don't we take a little walk later?"

"That's a great idea. You can get to know each other better," my mom added as if she had been waiting forever for the suggestion to come up.

I glanced at my mom and found myself a little surprised at her enthusiasm for this entire thing being arranged for me. I was irritated by her tendency to try to make all the decisions for me without really thinking about what I wanted. I knew it all came from a good place. She just wanted me to get to know Damon.

I let out a sigh and reluctantly accepted. "Yeah, I suppose a walk sounds nice..."

MY HEAVY SWEATER AND SCARF ENVELOPED ME IN WARMTH, THE CRISP autumn air nipping at my cheeks. The sun glared through the trees, casting shadows across the stone path that wound its way through the forest near the mansion. Leaves fell from the trees, and acorns were scattered all over the path. Their brown shells were a dirty reddish-brown color, blending on the forest ground. I looked up, and I could see a group of crows sitting in the tree, their dark eyes fixed on me. They gazed right into my soul, judging in silence, enough to make goosebumps form on my skin. Damon and I walked side by side. Neither of us said much at first, but it was a comfortable silence. Though some kind of tension clung to us that I couldn't shake. Maybe it was just Damon—his presence, his confidence, the way he always seemed one step ahead of me.

After a few minutes, Damon pulled a pack of cigarettes from his coat pocket. With practiced ease, he flicked open the pack, holding it toward me to offer one. I pulled out a cigarette and Damon's eyes flicked to mine as he pulled out his lighter. He stepped closer, his hand brushing against my cheek, covering the flame from the wind. I tried focusing on the cigarette, but the way his eyes bored into mine was so intense, unyielding and almost... possessive. We both held still for a moment. It's like his touch had some kind of power over me. I took a drag, trying to settle the sudden rush of nerves, and the smoke invaded my lungs. Exhaling, I slowly let it all out again.

"Are you looking forward to the party tonight?" Damon asked, his voice cutting through the thick silence between us as he lit his own cigarette, its flame illuminating his strong features.

"Oh. Yeah... I love Halloween." I tried to sound more enthused than I felt.

"So do you have a costume in mind?"

"Just a corset and a witches hat."

His eyes shifted onto me again, his eyebrow arched up in interest. "A corset, huh?"

I shot him a death glare, my eyes narrowing at him in warning. "Don't get any ideas."

He sounded amused. "No ideas here." He held up his hands in a mock gesture of innocence. "Just curious, that's all."

We walked along the path for some time in complete silence, except for rustling leaves and the far-off chirping of birds somewhere deep in the trees. I was lost in this peaceful-ness when Damon broke the silence.

"You gonna be drinkin' tonight? It's just... you said no alcohol last night." His tone was different, like he already knew my response.

"I don't drink." I took a final drag of the cigarette before dropping it on the ground.

For the first time, I could see the concern in his eyes. "Why not?"

I hesitated as I wondered how to respond. "I just have a past, that's all." It wasn't easy to talk about, certainly not with someone I didn't know all that well. But there was something about Damon.

"Don't we all?" he murmured to himself. "Come on, tell me."

"I don't want you to judge or see me differently. It will make things awkward."

"Hilly, you've seen me naked. Trust me, I won't see you differently. Plus, I'm not one to judge."

"I was just an idiot in my past, that's all, but I'm pretty sure my mom has told your father. So... I guess I might as well tell you."

"I'm all ears."

I don't know why, but I really did want to tell him every-thing. Talking to Damon was easy. Maybe it was because we were out here, away from everything and everyone, with nothing but trees surrounding us. I barely knew this guy, yet I wanted him to understand me.

"I lost myself to alcohol and drugs at one point," I began. "It wasn't anything glamorous or rebellious. It just happened."

There was no judgment in his eyes, just pure attention that made me want to keep talking.

"I used to wake up next to random men." My voice was barely above a whisper. "Not knowing what I did with them, not even remembering how I got there. I was either drunk or drugged up. It was like living in a nightmare that I couldn't escape from. But I did it over and over."

Damon's face seemed to darken, and that usual smugness vanished. His voice was thick with a seriousness I hadn't heard from him before. "Hilly. If you were too drunk to say yes or no, that's not on you."

His words were like a gut punch, the harsh reality settling over me like a cold wave. Hearing it out loud from another person made it real. Damon reached forward, placing a hand on my shoulder. "It's fucked up. Those men—whoever they were—they took advantage of you, knowing you were too drunk or drugged up."

A lump began to form in my throat as his words settled in, my chest tightening. I had spent so long blaming myself, convincing myself that it was my fault that I'd put myself in those situations. But hearing Damon say it, acknowledge it for what it really was, made me realize just how wrong it was.

Tears welled up in my eyes and I turned away, the sudden vulnerability threatening to spill over.

Damon embraced me without warning, his arms firm around me. "I'm here," he whispered as his breath floated over my ear like a caress.

He just held me—no words, no expectations—only the quiet, steady presence of someone there when I needed it most. All those times feeling lost, alone, or overwhelmed by the weight of my past, I had never really had someone just hold me like this before—letting me know without words that I didn't have to carry it all by myself.

I drew back from him quickly, suddenly flushed with

embarrassment. "I'm so fucking sorry. I shouldn't have opened up like that." My cheeks reddened, and I took a step back from him. "Look, I'm going to be honest. I've..." I swallow hard. "I've never been held like that before. It scared me. I've only ever been intimate while drunk or drugged."

Those words hung in the air between us, raw and honest. I had never admitted it to anyone before, only barely admitting it to myself.

I was worried he would feel sorry for me, and I hated pity. Instead, he just nodded with a quiet understanding in his eyes. "You don't have to apologize, Hilly."

Suddenly, it began to rain. We looked up at the sky and then at each other and ran to a nearby drooping willow tree for cover. The long branches above sheltered us, but the cold rain was already starting to penetrate my clothing, and I couldn't help but shiver.

Damon noticed, immediately took off his coat, and draped it over my shoulders without hesitation. "Damon, you don't have to—" I started, feeling guilty for taking his coat when he'd be left cold.

"Shh. Just take it." He left no room for argument.

I shrugged my shoulders, pulling the coat tighter around me. Although it was oversized, the weight felt comforting.

We just stood there in the silence, watching the rain cascade all around us. The more I thought about it, the more I began to regret telling Damon about my past. My chest tightened, fearing that maybe I had said too much, too soon. That he would now see me differently.

Damon's voice cut through my thoughts. "Those scars on your back. Who did that to you?" His tone was insistent, as if he couldn't just let it go.

"I got in trouble with a dealer." The truth spilled out like word vomit. "Lashings were his punishment. I owed him more than I could ever pay back, and he wanted to make an example out of me. It's fucked up, I know."

His jaw tightened, fist clenching at his side as his eyes filled with blazing anger. The muscles in his neck were tense, and his whole body was taut. He took a deep breath, holding it for a moment before exhaling slowly.

"While you're part of this family," he started off, full of intensity, "you don't ever have to worry about your past coming to haunt you ever again. Do you understand?"

His tone was fierce, a promise wrapped in the unspoken threat. The anger in his eyes wasn't directed at me—it was for those who had wronged me, those who had taken advantage of me.

Why does Damon care about me? He hardly knows me.

I just nodded. Damon's gaze locked onto mine—I couldn't turn a blind eye to the possessive look that had suddenly filled his eyes. My heart almost skipped a beat at the intensity in his expression, and another pang of regret washed over me. "Everyone has a past, Hilly... I've done some fucked up things, too." He closed the gap between us.

I looked up into his eyes, their darkness revealing the depth of emotion that made me want more—more knowledge about the man behind the fierce protectiveness. "Tell me," I insisted.

Damon shook his head, his face showing his unease.

I just told him about my past. Surely, his couldn't be worse.

"I just told you about my past. Damon—" Before I could say any more, his hand rested against my waist. It was a tentative touch, but I flinched, moving away instinctively. Not because of him, but the sensation of any touch was daunting to me.

Damon's hand fell away, and I could see understanding in his eyes—silence, acknowledging my reaction. He didn't push, didn't insist, yet in his gaze, there was a sense of quiet support.

"Come on." He looked at his watch. "We've got a party to get to."

I nodded, catching my breath as my focus shifted. The party was looming ahead, and though I was still inside the emotions of our conversation, I already wanted to forget about it. I wish I had never opened up to Damon.

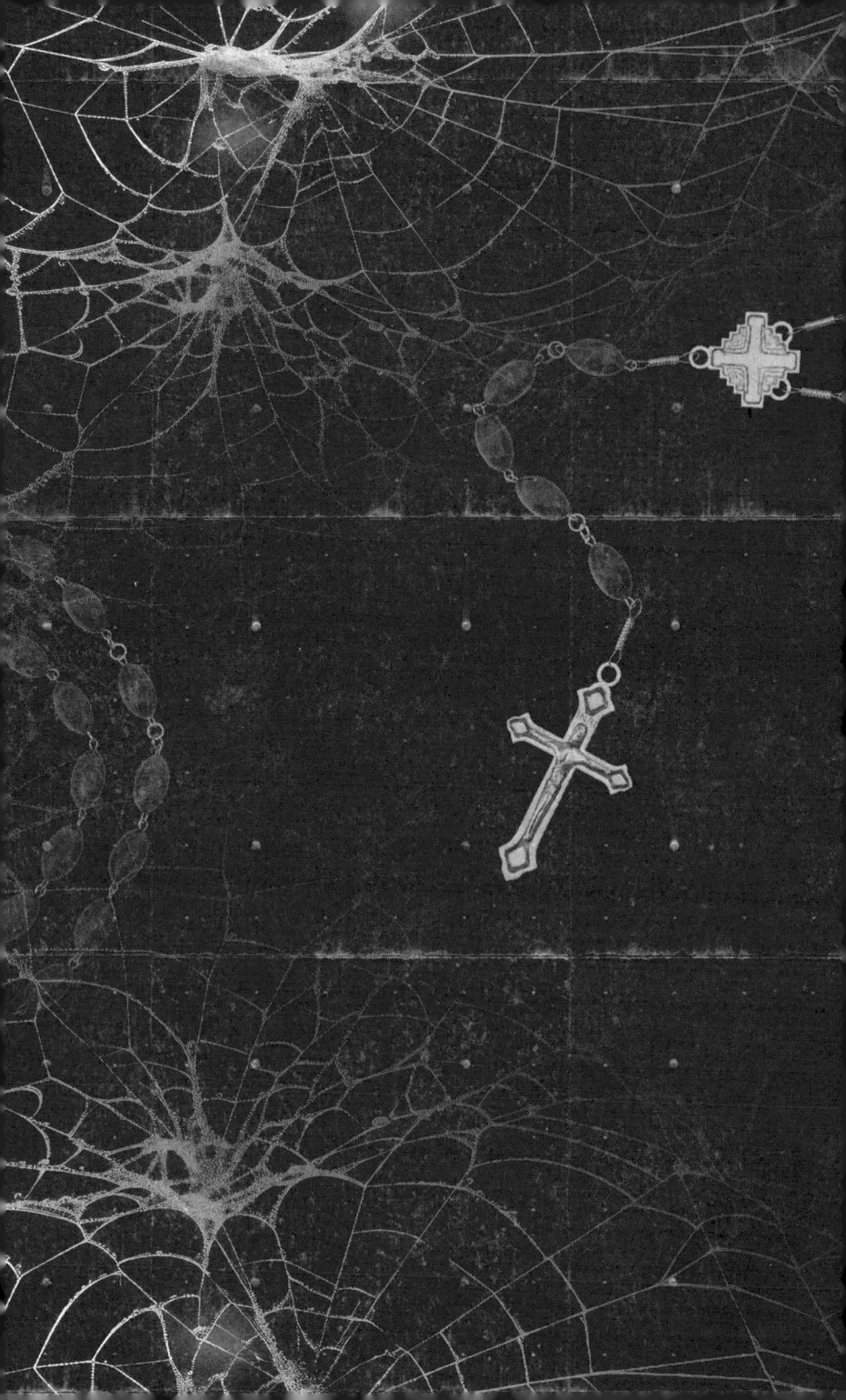

CHAPTER
FIVE
DAMON — TWO YEARS AGO

I sat in the car, my fingers tapping on the steering wheel as I watched the entrance of the bar. Never once did my eyes stray from the door as I waited, anticipating. Then I saw her—Sadie —stumbling out, reaching in her bag for her phone. She was probably calling for a cab. I hadn't seen her since my sister's funeral.

I flung the car door open, rushing toward her, trying to make my face look blank so that it wouldn't seem like I had been sitting there watching her the whole night. When I got closer, I called her name. "Sadie."

"Damon!" she called back, surprise written all over her face.

I gave her a lopsided smile. "I didn't expect to see you here... It's been ages." I tried to sound nonchalant.

"I know. Meeting some friends?"

I shrugged, dropping my hands into the pockets of my jeans. "Just wanted a drink. You know, to blow off some steam."

I gave her a smirk, one that I knew made women go weak. It did the same to Sadie—I'd caught the way she used to look at me whenever she and my sister hung out, the lingering glances, that slight flush in her cheeks when I walked into the room. She tried to play it cool, but I always knew. I looked her up and down, letting my eyes stay a little too long in every place. Meeting her eyes again, I made sure to give her more than just a "friendly" look.

"Actually... fuck the bar. What are you doing now?"

Sadie bit her bottom lip as she whispered, "Nothing..."

I inched closer. "Why don't we take a little ride and blow off some steam?"

I watched her swallow hard. Then, slowly, she nodded.

Without wasting any time, I took her hand, pulling her toward the car. It took everything I had to keep the disgust off my face, to maintain the charade if I wanted things to go my way.

I opened the passenger door for her, and I could just about see the last shreds of her will falling away. I closed the door and walked around to the driver's side, slipping in beside her and cranking up the engine. *This is way too easy.*

We drove in silence. Every few minutes, her eyes flickered to mine, and when I looked over, she was smirking at me. She would spread her legs just enough so that her skirt rode up. I wanted to tell her to stop and how stupid she looked, but I had to keep playing along, act like I enjoyed what she was doing.

My eyes never left the road as my knuckles turned white against the steering wheel.

"Damon, do you know how bad I've always wanted you?" Sadie purred.

I forced myself to smile convincingly. "Oh, I know."

She began to stroke her own leg. "You would come into your sister's room. The way you would look at me..." Her eyes locked onto me, searching for a reaction.

The way she touched herself in front of me—so fucking desperate. But I couldn't show that. I had to keep the act up. I quickly glanced at her hand on her leg, making sure she saw me looking.

"Sadie, you have no idea what I'm going to do to you," I confessed, my voice swimming in darkness.

She took the bait, a sly smile spreading across her face as she leaned in closer, misinterpreting my intent entirely. "Do what you want to me, Damon," she breathed, her hand sliding from her leg to mine, brushing her fingers against my thigh.

"Don't worry." My voice was falsely smooth as I covered her hand with mine, squeezing. "You'll get exactly what you deserve."

Her eyes were filled with excitement, and she was completely unconcerned about what I really meant. She settled back in her seat, satisfied, as though everything was falling into place for her.

Everything about her made my skin crawl. The way she touched me, the way she looked at me with those slut hungry eyes—like I was some kind of prize she had won. Her perfume, sickly sweet and overpowering, filled the car. I could barely breathe. *I hate everything about her.*

"You got anything that'd make this night extra fun?" I asked.

She reached into her purse, pulling out a little bag filled with white powder, holding it up between her fingers and grinning. "You're in luck. I made a stop at my dealer's before heading to the bar."

I already knew she had picked up the drugs. In fact, I'd followed her earlier and watched her every move as she made the exchange. That was all part of the plan. Every step she took led her closer to this moment.

"Perfect," I told her, though deep down inside, I felt nothing but revulsion.

"So... where are we heading?"

"Oh, I know a good spot."

We drove farther and farther out into the back roads. Trees grew dense on either side. I could see her eyes trying to make some sense of the darkness ahead, but she was too caught up in the thrill to question it.

"Damn. Who knew Damon Northwood had a mysterious side to him?" she mused to herself.

I scoffed. "You'd be surprised..."

As she laughed, I could tell she thought she was in on the secret, that she was about to experience me. Little did she know the danger she was really in.

We drove up to an abandoned warehouse deep into the forest, out of sight of prying eyes. Moss-covered stone walls seemed to blend into the surroundings, and boarded up windows should have sent warning signals into Sadie's mind. Instead, she leaned forward, her eyes filled with excitement. "This is different..."

I reached for her chin and turned her face back to mine. "Shh," I whispered. Her body relaxed in my hand as she leaned towards me. Her eyes fluttered shut, her face leaning in to kiss me. Her lips were barely on mine when I drew back sharply. "Let's head inside."

I opened the door and helped her out of the car. My hand closed tightly around hers as I led her toward the warehouse entrance.

"There could be crackheads inside," she said, her voice laced with nervousness.

"Don't worry. I've been here before. Plus, we're in the middle of nowhere." I sounded casual, leading her further into the warehouse.

The air was full of dust, and a faint odor clung to the walls. I led her through the main space, past rusted machinery and abandoned crates until we came to a small room off to one side. From the ceiling, one light bulb glowed unevenly.

There was an old couch covered with a dirty, faded cloth and a low table. I moved into the center of the room, turning to face her, trying to maintain a calm composure. "I thought we could just hang out here for a bit."

She seemed a bit confused but took a seat on the couch. She then pulled out the small bag from her purse and put it in front of her on the table. I sat beside her, watching closely as she fidgeted with the bag.

I placed one hand on the bag of drugs, and my other hand on her wrist. "Let me make you scream, Sadie."

I pulled her up from the couch and felt the weight of her body against mine as she casually went limp, her lips brushing my neck. Her kisses were eager and desperate. I couldn't help but pull back from her. "Damn, Damon. You're making me work for this."

This bitch was so fucking desperate it was pitful. She was willing to fuck me in a dirty warehouse without a care in the world.

"Come on." I held her hand so tightly I could feel her bones. I glanced up as we turned the corner, and her eyes followed. There, suspended from the ceiling with a chain around his throat, was her dealer. His body was bruised and bloodied, a grim testament to the retribution that had been dealt.

Sadie's body stiffened, her eyes fixed on the gruesome sight. I nudged her forward so she could get a clearer view of the body. A raw, ear-piercing scream escaped her lips.

She collapsed against me, her body shaking violently. I caught her in my arms and held her tight as she clung to me.

"I said I'd make you scream," I murmured in her ear, my tone cold.

I grabbed Sadie's face, turning it to view the ghastly body hanging from the chain. "Now, look at my handiwork..."

That was the vile creature that gave my sister a bad batch of drugs and took advantage of her while she was dying. I looked up at his body and felt nothing but satisfaction.

Sadie began to fight me, but her blows to my arms were ineffective

"You knew my sister was overdosing," I hissed into her ear through gritted teeth. "You watched him rape her as she died, and you did nothing!"

"I'm sorry!" Snot and tears streamed down her face as her cries echoed through the warehouse.

I pushed my face into the side of hers. "You were meant to be her friend, but you saved yourself and lied to the police about what happened."

I shoved her hard to the ground. Her body thudded against the concrete, and she winced, scrambling to her feet again. But the fear and shock made her clumsy.

"You know what's fucked up? You went back to him over and over."

Sadie fell back on the floor and crumpled into a trembling heap.

I spat at her as I bent down, gripping her collar and turning her to face the hanging body above. "That monster went around boasting about how he fucked a rich girl while she was overdosing!"

"Damon. Please... Please... I'll tell the police the truth. I will tell them what happened," she pleaded.

I looked down at her, my expression cold. "It's too late for that. You're gonna die just like she did." An evil smile curved on my lips.

Her eyes widened with a new kind of terror, her voice trembled as she tried to make sense of the situation. "You're gonna rape me?" She looked into my eyes, searching for compassion.

I couldn't help but scoff. "What the fuck? No! I wouldn't put my cock anywhere near your fucking diseased pussy!" I grabbed the back of her head, forcing her to look at me. "You're going to overdose on a concoction I got your dealer to make."

Sadie's eyes were red from all the crying, full of terror. A shriek emerged from her lips, and I cupped my hand across her mouth, silencing the cries. I yanked on her hair as a cruel laugh escaped my lips. "My sister didn't know she was going to overdose," I explained. "But you know what's coming, and it's not pretty." Her death was going to be so sweet, just like her perfume.

I let go and stepped back, looming over her. Sadie scrambled to her knees. Her hands grasped at my pants. "I'll do anything! Please!"

I gripped her tightly under her armpits, hauling her to her feet, and dragged her toward the couch.

"I guess you can do one thing for me."

I pushed her onto the couch, and she looked up at me. Her voice trembled with fear and hope. "Name it. I'll do anything."

"Die," I said with a chilling calmness.

She leaped up and tried to flee, but I caught her by the hair, jerking her head back. She howled as I dragged her across the cold, concrete floor. Her hands clawed at the ground. We returned to the couch and I reached under, pulling out a knife, its blade gleaming ominously in the dim light.

"Fucking sit down, you dumb bitch!" I demanded, with the knife in my hand, its blade pointing menacingly toward her.

Sadie froze, eyes wide and locked on the weapon. She nodded shakily and then collapsed onto the couch. There was no more room for negotiating or a chance for her to beg to a meaningless god.

I reached into my back pocket and pulled out a small bag filled with the very substance that had taken my sister's life. I poured out the contents onto the table in front of her without a word—the white dust formed a small mound.

"You die like my sister or like him. Now line it up." I flicked a card at her, which landed in her lap. She hesitated for a moment, her eyes darting from the powder to the knife.

With shaky hands, she swooped up the card and sat forward. Fear filled her as she slowly cut herself a neat line. She looked at me with pleading eyes, but I showed no mercy.

"You're the fucking Devil." She trembled.

I smirked as I dropped to her level, and I met her tear-filled eyes with a cold stare. "Well, I guess I'll see you in Hell." I threw a rolled-up dollar bill on the table. "You better hope and pray that you make it safe down there."

I inched closer and forced her head down, feeling her dry, bleached hair in my fingertips. "You know what to do next."

She picked up the dollar bill and hovered over the table as she hesitated. I watched her as she finally bent down, inching closer to the line, knowing this was her end.

Sadie inhaled the line of powder and raised her head back. A mad laugh burst from her. "Nothing—" she started to say, her voice relieved.

But her words were cut short as a stream of blood suddenly trickled over her lips. She wiped her finger under her nose, and as she drew her hand away, her breath caught at the sight of crimson staining her skin.

Her eyes went wide, then rolled back into her head. I calmly perched myself on the edge of the coffee table and watched as her limbs jerked uncontrollably. Her mouth opened in a silent scream.

Finally, with her body still, I put down the knife, leaned over, and pressed two fingers against her neck in search of a pulse. Nothing. "Safe travels to Hell, bitch," I mumbled to myself, pulling back my hand. All I could hear was the quiet dripping of blood from Sadie's nose hitting the floor.

I pulled out my burner phone and texted my father, and his response came almost instantly.

ME:

Done.

UNKNOWN:

Both of them?

I looked at Sadie's lifeless body on the couch. The image of the hanged dealer rattled my mind.

ME:

Both of them.

I tucked the phone into my pocket, feeling satisfied. I stood there for a while and then looked around. The corners of my mouth turned up in a smile as I looked at my handiwork. This was a twisted tribute to my sister.

This was for Ivy.

CHAPTER
SIX

HILLY

I MADE MYSELF VULNERABLE, OPENING UP TO DAMON. I DON'T KNOW what it is, but when I'm around him, I feel a sense of closeness that I've never experienced before. I don't know if I can allow myself to get close to him though. Not yet. The walls I had built to protect myself started to crumble, and I did not know how to rebuild them. I would have to keep him at arm's length to get a grip on what was happening to me.

I was lost in thought when my phone buzzed on the nightstand. I reached across the bed and flipped it over to see a notification from Benny. Hesitating for a second, deciding if I wanted to read his message, I opened the Wickedy app.

BENNY:

Hey, hope you're okay! Are you going to the Wickedy Woods party tonight?

ME:

I'm all good. Yeah. I'm going with my friend. You? (:

BENNY:

> Ahh, sweet. I'm going with some friends, too. I might see you there! Oh, just a heads up: there's a QR code on the app to get a free drink at the party.

ME:

> Thanks for letting me know! Hopefully, I'll see you there.

Benny and I had this sort of weird relationship. From what I'd seen of him on Wickedy, he seemed like a nice guy, easy to talk to and get along with. I didn't notice any red flags. We'd swapped the odd nude here and there—nothing too serious, just a little harmless fun. His invitation to go out on a date was tempting, especially now that I needed an escape from Damon. Benny was different. He didn't know anything about my past. With him, things could be simple, even normal. When I started talking to Benny, I had the notion in my head that it would just be an online thing—sexting, sending dirty pictures and videos. I could handle that because there wasn't anything physical, but the idea of meeting him made me feel anxious.

From outside the bedroom, I heard a faint shuffling. I tried to make out exactly what it was. It could have been the wind shaking the tree branches against the windows. Maybe something worse. The thought of having to deal with both a ghost and Damon this weekend already made me feel fucking drained.

Slowly, I stood up and tiptoed towards the door. My hand shook as I turned the doorknob. I flung it open, expecting to see something—or someone—standing there, but there wasn't. My heart raced with anticipation as my eyes cast over the empty hall in front of me. *Calm down... There are no ghosts. Stop being such a pussy.*

The door to the bathroom was ajar, but the light wasn't on. *Where is Damon? Am I here on my own?*

"Hello?" The echo of my voice rebounded down the hall. No response. I shook my head, feeling foolish. Just as I started to turn back, I felt strong arms wrap around my waist, and I was lifted off the ground.

"Boo!"

I let out a scream, more out of surprise than fear. I couldn't help but laugh when Damon put me back down. The adrenaline had my pulse racing.

I turned to face him. He wore a tight, crisp black shirt that seemed to cling to his muscular frame and black trousers that made him look so goddamn sexy, like he had just stepped out of some boardroom. But more stunning was the mask he had on. It was made of metal, smooth and polished. Everything around us was reflected off it. Including me, with my mouth dropped open. Everything but his eyes were covered.

I swatted at his shoulder. "Damon! You scared the crap out of me!"

He chuckled, his voice muffled behind the mask. "That was the point."

I crossed my arms, raising an eyebrow at him. "What are you even going as? You're just wearing a mask."

Damon stepped into the light, tilting his head.

"I scared you though, didn't I, stepsis?" he asked in that cocky voice of his. "If you'd like, I could get you to smear some fake blood on my chest..."

I rolled my eyes and walked away, tossing over my shoulder, "I'm going to get ready."

I returned to my room and closed the door behind me, perching at the edge of the bed while I checked my phone again. Benny had sent a photo of himself in his Halloween costume.

He was posing as a topless werewolf. It was ridiculous yet somewhat hot.

I had a little bit of time to kill, so I scrolled up to the previous messages, and my eyes locked on the nudes that we exchanged. Warmth started to spread through me. I felt a fluttering sensation between my legs.

My other hand wandered down to my stomach, fingers stroking the soft fabric. I bit my lip and reclined back onto the bed, letting my fingers trail lower, slipping beneath the waistband of my lace panties. Allowing the image of Benny's smile to wreak havoc within my mind, my fingers found their way onto my clit. The first touch was gentle, no more than a tease, but it had me moaning softly.

But just as my thoughts became wild, his image began to blur, replaced by Damon. His intense eyes, how he looked at me with desire. I faltered for a second, trying to focus back on Benny, but the pull was too strong. Damon would not get out of my head. I pictured him running his hands over every inch of my body, moving his lips up my neck to my ear, and moaning deeply, his voice low, saying things I'd never admit I wanted to hear.

The thought of Damon made my breath catch in my throat. *What if Benny wasn't the only one who could satisfy this craving? What if Damon... Fuck!*

I pictured his fingers moving in circles around my clit. Then I started mimicking how I pictured he would touch me. The thought of him in control and knowing exactly how to get me to come was almost too much to handle.

My thighs pinched together, my fingers working furiously against my clit. The image of Damon's dark eyes staring into mine, his lips curling into a smirk as he watched me touch myself, was too much to resist. I moaned again as my body arched off the bed and pleasure built even further.

Every stroke brought me closer to the edge. I was sensitive, lost in a haze of sensation. I struggled to keep my whimpers subdued.

I ran my fingers down and plunged them into my pussy. My back arched off the bed and my breathing was heavy. I pictured Damon's cock, filling my pussy and fucking me hard with every thrust.

"Fuck, Damon," I panted quietly to myself.

I continued to thrust my fingers faster, skillfully navigating my desires, but it's his face I saw, his body I craved. I moved my thumb side to side over my clit. My climax was building up as a wave threatened to crash over me. I kept my eyes shut tightly, trying to will him closer, to feel him real and solid beside me. "Come for me, Hilly," his voice moaned in my mind.

I desperately stroked my clit as my body was filled with a euphoric feeling that I hadn't felt in such a long time. "Damon!" I called out quietly as I fell over the edge, and pure bliss washed over my entire body like a tidal wave.

My stomach churned as I stood in front of the mirror. I needed to get Damon the fuck out of my head. I couldn't rid myself of thoughts of him and was desperate for a distraction. I spent time on my Halloween look, hoping it would help me forget. With my hair worn in loose waves, I put on a sleek black skirt and a mesh top with beautiful cobweb designs. I wrestled with the corset. The laces in the back had become tangled and I needed my mom to help me fasten it. Holding the corset in place, I stepped out into the hallway and called out for her in hopes that she would come and help me.

I clutched the corset to my chest when Damon suddenly emerged from his room. The mask was perched on the top of his head while he tugged on his cufflinks, too focused to look up.

"They went out to get food," he said.

I bit the inside of my cheek, attempting to ignore how awkward I felt. Damon flicked his gaze up, his eyes skimming over me. For a moment, it looked like he was admiring me.

"Uh—"

"You—you look really good," he stuttered. "Do you need help with your corset?"

I couldn't help but blush. Before I could even decline his offer, he strode toward me. I turned around, feeling nervous as he approached.

Damon swept my hair softly to the side, his fingers brushing against my skin. He started to pull on the laces of the corset.

"Let me know if it gets too tight," he murmured as he worked to make the corset fit just right.

With each tug on the laces, my whole body jolted slightly, and I kept one hand on the wall to steady myself. He was so close, I could feel his warm breath on my neck.

Damon broke the silence. "Is the top to cover your scars?"

I didn't trust myself to respond, so I just shook my head, hoping he wouldn't want to talk about my past. He finished lacing the corset up, his fingers brushing my neck slightly. "Ooh, stay here. I know what will go with your outfit."

He jogged into the room, and I was curious to see what he might bring back. When he returned, he slowly drew out his silver cross necklace in front of me, the light reflecting off the cold metal. He placed it around my neck, the pendant resting just above my heart. The necklace must have meant a lot to him; he was always wearing and fiddling with it.

I rolled it between my fingers, feeling honored. "Oh, Damon, you don't have to—"

"Shh," he interrupted, "I want you to wear it... You know, I'm glad you opened up to me earlier. I just want you to know you're stronger than you give yourself credit for, Hilly. I can tell you've fought away your demons."

The truth was I hadn't. They still wreaked havoc in my mind. But I've never been told I was strong before. Damon's words appeared to have had an effect on me, something that I couldn't quite put my finger on, but at the same time, it made me feel something other than fear and self-doubt. I turned my face toward him, searching his eyes for any traces of pity. His thumb gently moved across my jaw down to my chin. Goosebumps erupted all over my body.

"No one's ever gonna hurt you again, do you understand?" I could tell his promise was real, but it frightened me. Our eyes locked, and for a moment, it was as if the world had shrunk down to only us two. Just me and him.

His eyes bored right into mine, dark pools filled with an emotion I hadn't seen on him before, as if they wanted me to see, but just as quickly as the feeling washed over me, something in my brain snapped, and I shook my head, trying to regain control.

"Thank you, Damon, but I don't need protection, so you can leave your knight in shining armor act at home." I wanted to rebuild the walls that Damon had been chipping away at. I couldn't let him in anymore.

Damon's expression changed. He stepped back, and the softness in his expression vanished. In just a few seconds, that ease and warmth seemed to dissipate and be replaced by a more guarded version. *Did my words hurt him?*

The sound of the front door interrupted Damon before he

could say anything. Mom and Richard's voices carried up the stairs.

"You guys left yet?" Richard shouted.

Damon clenched his jaw. I could see the tension in his face. "Not yet..." His voice was a little harsher than usual.

"I'll meet you downstairs, Damon. I just need to do something."

Damon didn't say a word to me. He just shook his head, eyes flashing with an emotion that looked like frustration mixed with something else, and turned away.

I walked back into my room. The tension from the hallway made me feel uneasy so I reached for my small spiritual bag. I sat at the desk and pulled out a tiny bottle of lavender essential oil. The smell always comforted me during anxious moments. I set the bottle on the desk, unscrewed the cap, and brought it close to my nose, inhaling deeply. It's calming aroma began working almost instantaneously.

But before I could lean back in the chair, footsteps rushed into my room. A hand closed around my wrist, tugging my hand away from my face.

"You're doing coke?" Damon accused as he held my wrist in a vise-like grip.

I glared at him, insulted. "What the fuck, Damon? No!" I tried wrenching my wrist free from his grasp.

His eyes flashed to the desk. "What is that?"

"It's lavender oil! It calms my nerves, you asshole!"

I could see it in his eyes—the doubt, the judgment. Already, he was making assumptions, thinking I was someone who needed watching, someone who might slip back into bad habits.

My voice trembled with frustration. "I fucking knew it. I should never have told you about my past. Now you're judging me.." Damon's jaw clenched, and he placed his hands in his pockets.

"When we get to the party, stay away from me. I don't need you babysitting me."

"Hilly, I'm—" He tried to reach out. I didn't care what he had to say. Richard and my mom walked in, their timing impossibly perfect.

"Wow, look at them!" my mom said, beaming as she took in our costumes. "Let me get a picture!"

She whipped out her phone from her pocket, totally oblivious. Damon and I locked eyes for a second. We faked our cheesy grins and posed awkwardly as my mom captured us together in what felt like the complete opposite of how things really were.

"You better watch her tonight for me, Damon," my mom chirped.

"Of course I will, Ruth." His voice was level, but I caught the quick, pointed look he shot at his father.

I knew my mom didn't have any bad intentions, but they talked about me like I wasn't there, like I needed to be looked after like a child. Anger surged through me again, and my cheeks flared with a burning flush. My jaw clenched, too furious to talk without exploding. So instead, I reached for my purse while heading out of the room without saying another word. Their voices trailed after me, but I didn't care. I was so tired of being treated like someone who needed to be saved. I could take care of myself.

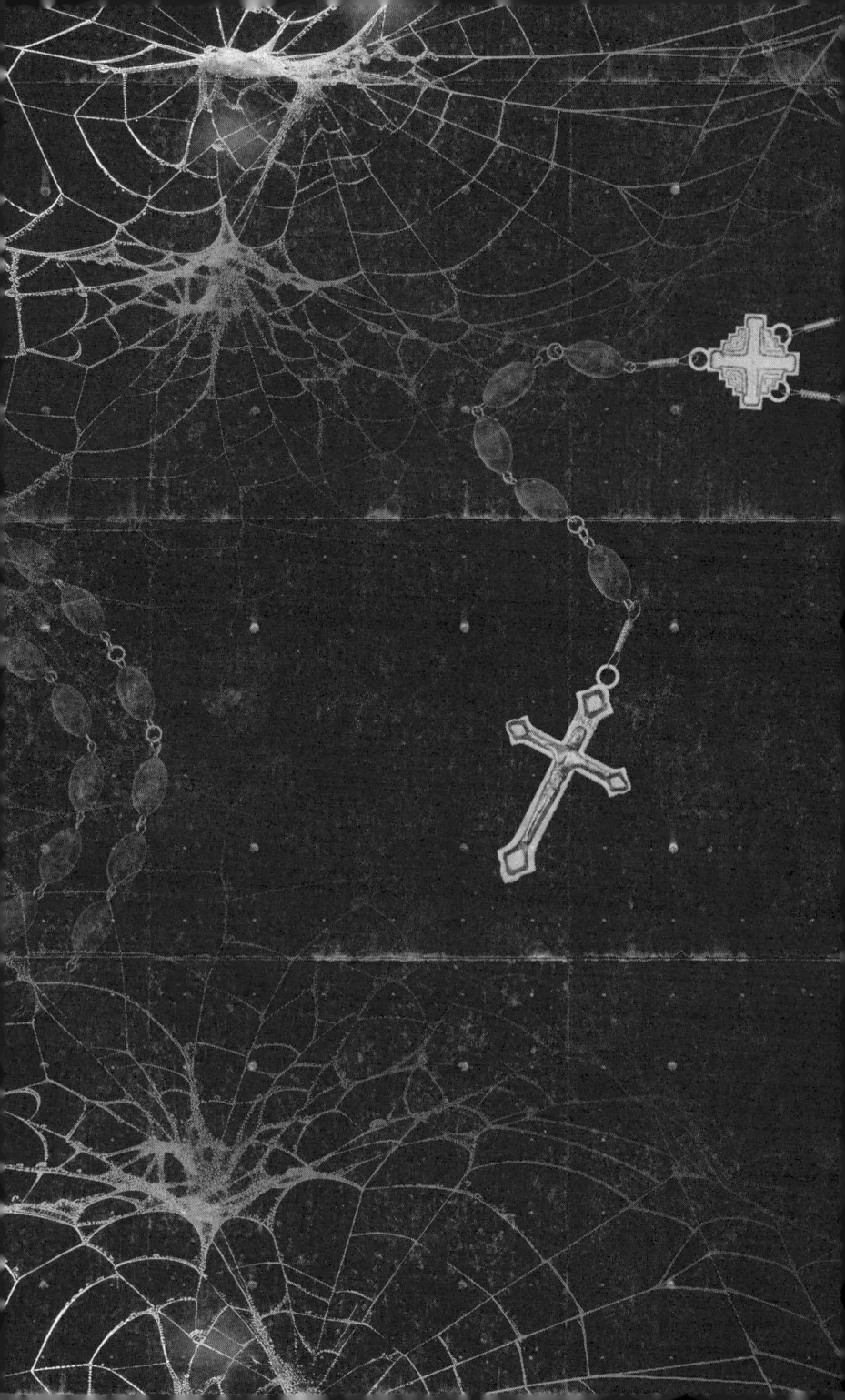

THE SUN WAS SETTING AS WE DROVE IN SILENCE, AND I COULD FEEL Hilly's anger radiating off her. Her arms were tightly crossed over her chest, and her eyes were looking out the window, refusing to glance my way. Fleeting shadows from streetlights carved across her face, showing me the hard set of her jaw and the distant look in her eyes. I knew she was still pissed off—rightfully so. I'd charged into her room and accused her without fucking thinking.

I cared more about Hilly than I thought I would and wanted to make her mine. I'd wanted her for weeks, and I had the feeling she wanted me too, even if she played it cool, which made it so goddamn complicated. I could never use her like the men in her past. The thought of her slipping back into those dark places she'd clawed her way out of scared the hell out of me. I'd seen what that kind of spiral could do. I'd lived through it with my sister as she lost herself, unable to do anything, to the very demons that now I feared might come for Hilly, too.

I didn't want to lose another person in my life.

I glanced at her again, but her expression was stone. The silence had become so thick I knew I had to find a way to repair this, to make her understand why I'd reacted the way I did. Yet every time I tried to form the words in my mind, they fell apart and left me with nothing but regret and a gnawing fear that I'd already screwed things up beyond repair.

I cracked the car window, thinking fresh air might cut the thick tension between us. The cold autumn breeze rushed in, chilling the car almost instantly. "Fuck. Better shut that," I mumbled as I rolled the window back up, feeling like an idiot. *Just say something, Damon.* I started to believe the silence would last forever.

"Is your father going to propose?" Hilly asked, very direct and stern.

Her question kind of caught me off guard, so I hesitated before answering. "Yeah, I think he is," I finally admitted. "He hasn't told me anything, but I know he's serious about your mom. He's been dropping hints."

I paused, waiting for her reaction, but she remained silent. The truth of the situation settled between us, adding another layer to the complicated dynamic we were already struggling with. "How do you feel about it?"

"If my mom's happy, that's all I care about." She shrugged as if trying to convince herself.

Her answer was simple. I nodded in silent agreement, keeping my eyes on the road. I knew I had to take this moment to apologize and try to set things right between us.

"Hilly, I'm sorry about earlier. I shouldn't have jumped to conclusions like that. I was out of line."

"You know what's fucked up? I trusted and opened up to you. You said you wouldn't see me differently."

"No. No... you got it wrong." I tightened my hold on the wheel. My knuckles turned white as I fought to keep myself in order. "I have my reasons." The words felt weak.

She turned her head, raising one eyebrow and extending a hand, gesturing for me to continue.

I took in a deep breath, searching for the right words. "Look, Hilly. It's not that I see you differently because of your past... The truth is my sister had a past with drugs, men, bad choices, the whole thing, and now she's dead." The memories washed over me as I swallowed hard. "When you told me about your past... Well, that hit close to home, and I am so sorry."

I looked over at her, praying she could understand where I was coming from—even though I messed up in showing it.

Her expression softened. "Damon, I'm so sorry about your sister. It must have been horrible."

"Yeah, it was. It messed with me for a long time. I shouldn't have acted the way I did with you."

"I understand why you reacted that way. But I don't want you to think I need to be watched and looked after. My past is my past for a reason."

"I know, I get it," I reassured her. She seemed to relax a bit, her defenses lowering at my words.

I lied to her, but there was no way I would stand by and not watch her tonight. I knew the Wickedy Woods party attracted some vile men. They would lurk behind their masks and costumes, finding anonymity, making them feel like they could get away with being predators. It was the perfect setup for the worst behavior. Thinking of Hilly in that environment made me feel sick, especially knowing her past.

I just could not rid myself of that protective instinct to look after her. Although I agreed with her, my mind was already made up. I looked down at the dashboard. "Damn it, I have to fill up."

"Perfect timing. I need to use a restroom anyway." Hilly shifted in her seat.

We drove a bit longer before pulling into a gas station that looked like it hadn't seen a fresh coat of paint in decades. It had a rundown vibe, like something straight out of a horror film. The hum of the overhead lights buzzed, and fog started to cover the ground, adding to the eeriness. We weren't far from the party now.

We both got out, and I began using the pump. Hilly adjusted her skirt and witch's hat and then made her way toward a dingy restroom. "You need me to grab you a snack or anything?" I called out.

"Just a bottle of water, please."

A car pulled up at the next pump. A clown stepped out, his bright, oversized makeup and shoes making him appear sinister instead of funny in the dim light. He never looked at me as he stumbled straight for the restroom like he was drunk.

I assumed he was heading to the same party, but something in how he held himself put me on edge. I stared at the door to the restroom, and a surge of protectiveness built up in me. I didn't like Hilly being in there with him all alone. The gas tank clicked, indicating it was full, but I didn't move. Something didn't feel right, and it was as if something inside me screamed to run to the restroom. I let my instincts take over and I sprinted across the parking lot, my heart pounding. I didn't hesitate as I slammed open the door.

Inside, I found Hilly standing face-to-face with the clown. His grin made my blood run cold. "I've got a magic wand I can show you, witchy," he sneered, grabbing his crotch in a foul gesture.

The cockiness in his drunken stance vanished when he laid eyes on me. He stepped back from Hilly, flipping his gaze between me and her. She ran to me with a face full of fear.

"I need to use the toilet. Go wait in the car, Hilly," I ordered, giving her a false sense of calm.

Hilly looked hesitant at first, but I gave her a warning look.

She shook her head, and without a word, exited the restroom. I stood my ground until she was clearly out of view, then I shifted all of my focus to the clown, my fists coiled tightly at my sides. He stumbled drunkenly toward the sink, his eyes meeting mine in the mirror as I stood behind him.

"When girls dress like that, they're asking for it, dude," he slurred, a sickening snicker slipping from his lips.

His words sparked a rage within me, churning my insides with pure disgust. My body was filled with ice-cold, seething rage, which built up, wanting to explode. I came to my decision. He needed to die.

Everything around me blurred into insignificance as the two of us remained there in that filthy restroom. His vulgar words kept echoing in my head, feeding my dark determination, and I threw myself toward him.

My hand lashed out like an iron grip on the back of his head. His face connected with the mirror. It shattered on impact, pieces falling into the sink below. As I pulled on his hair, blood flowed over his lips and his chin. He grunted in pain, dazed, not quite grasping what was happening to him. Smears of clown makeup and blood stained the shattered pieces.

His hand flailed limply in an attempt at self-defense. But I was quicker. Before he could even hit me, I pulled his head back, then brought his face down onto the sink edge, his nose crunching as he let out a muffled cry.

I dragged him across the disgusting tiles, his blood leaving behind a dramatic streak. He tried to speak, but pain had stolen his words. I pushed him into a stall, watching him slump onto the floor, desperately trying to hold himself up.

"Open your fucking mouth!" I growled, my voice low—a simmering torrent of anger.

He refused, so I grabbed his head and banged it against the cold, porcelain toilet. Finally, he opened his mouth to let out a pitiful cry. I held him down, positioning his open mouth at the edge of the toilet lip. His scream shot through the restroom.

"No one ever talks about her like that," I hissed.

In a fit of rage, I raised my leg high above my hip and slammed it down against the back of his skull. The horrific crack of his jawbone echoed around the stall as his face broke in half. Blood splattered across the surface, while his teeth cracked and scattered like explosive confetti. His body collapsed to the ground, lifeless and broken, like a discarded ragdoll.

I stood there, panting. My eyes were locked on the bloody, broken creation that lay at my feet. The adrenaline wore off, leaving me with a cold, empty feeling.

I should have dragged it out, made his death all the more painful, a slow-damned agony. Just the fact that he had once breathed the same air as Hilly was enough to fuel my anger again. *How could he?* How could he ever find himself worthy of being allowed near her? The wild monster of anger sat inside me, scratching at the very edges of my chest, wanting to be unleashed once again.

I adjusted my collar, making sure it was straight, then stepped out of the stall and pulled the door slightly ajar behind me. As my heartbeat calmed, I walked out of the restroom with a steady, composed stride, slowly pulling myself together.

Inside the gas station, the little old lady behind the register never looked up from her magazine to say hello. I searched the coolers, picked a bottle of water for Hilly, and put it on the counter. I paid for the gas, traded some pleasantries with the clerk, and stepped back outside. As I got to my car, my eyes went straight to Hilly, sitting in the passenger seat, eyes unfocused and deep in thought. I handed her the water as I slid behind the wheel.

She took the bottle and twisted off its cap, narrowing her

eyes slightly as she turned toward me. "You didn't do anything to him, right?" Her voice sounded suspicious.

I looked her square in the face and let out a dry chuckle. "Oh, yeah, Hilly. I killed the man," I admitted, dripping with sarcasm as I rolled my eyes dramatically.

Shaking her head, the curl of a smile played around her lips. "Hilarious, Damon."

I turned and grinned at her.

EIGHT

THE FULL MOON HUNG HIGH IN THE SKY, CASTING SILVERY LIGHT ON THE roads. It was like a piece of visual poetry—full moon, Halloween night, and yet the mood was eerie. Damon's story about his sister got me thinking. Now I understood why he acted the way he did.

Damon said nothing was ever going to hurt me again. I know I said I didn't need protection, but maybe he was right. Maybe I did, even if it was from my own thoughts. My past was a constant storm, wreaking havoc in the darkest corners of my mind.

My phone buzzed in my lap, bringing me back to the present moment, and I glanced at the screen. A message from Nadine lit up.

Nadine: Waiting at the entrance. You won't be able to miss me. Hehe.

I was extremely glad to be reunited with her. She may have been the only person who was capable of wiping out the nervous feelings inside of me.

We pulled into the parking lot and it was chaotic in the best way. People were everywhere—walking, laughing, stumbling—

each dressed in a wild array of Halloween costumes. Some outfits were creative, some terrifying, others downright ridiculous.

Damon turned toward me with concern etched all over his face. "What's up? You look a little nervous."

My eyes zeroed in on the crowd, all in costumes and laughing. I could feel the atmosphere humming around me. "Yeah. I didn't know it was going to be this busy."

He pulled the car into this space labeled *Northwood - VIP*. I turned sideways and snorted. "Really? VIP?"

He shrugged, cocky grin in place. "What? We are VIPs."

I quickly checked myself in the mirror, smoothing down my hair and making sure my makeup still looked okay. The energy outside the car was buzzing while a strange tension lingered between us. Damon stepped out and walked around to open my door. He extended his hand to me, just like a gentleman would. As I took his hand, for a split second, it felt like we were a couple.

I pushed the feeling aside, reminding myself that Damon and I were anything but a couple, no matter how the moment might have seemed.

As we approached the entrance, Damon had the mask perched on top of his head. Even though there was a large crowd, Nadine stood out. Rocking a lively bumblebee suit and striped black and yellow tights. Her antennas swayed slightly from side to side in the breeze. It was so funny that I couldn't control my laughter. What was she fucking thinking? A bee, of all things?

The second Nadine spotted me, she started jumping up and down and flailing her arms, like a child who had spotted their parent from across a crowded room. I waved back, still chuckling beneath my breath at how ridiculous she appeared. Damon raised an eyebrow. "Is that your friend? She does know it's a Halloween party, right?"

It hit me—the motivation behind her costume. Nadine had always had a deep-seated fear of bees and wasps, so she was dressing up as something that scared her. "She has a fear of bees... She's petrified of them."

Damon shrugged, his stare indicating respect. "Well, I guess that makes sense, in a twisted sort of way."

As we proceeded, I took in everything around me, amazed by the attention to detail in the decorations. The woods had turned into a type of Halloween paradise. The animatronics were concealed, their faint motions startling anybody who went by. The pathway was decorated with jack-o'-lanterns of all shapes and sizes, their carved faces emitting a tremulous glow. The air was heavy with the aroma of fake fog.

A vast arch of twisted branches stretched over the entrance, and the dark wood blended in almost perfectly with the night sky. The eerie green glow of a sign displaying *Wickedy Woods* intensified the fear as we approached the entrance.

Nadine came over and gave me a big hug. "Hilly, you look fabulous!"

"Thanks, Nadine. I see you chose to embody your greatest fear—the bumblebee."

She shuddered melodramatically. "How can you not find them scary? With their tiny wings, huge bodies... stingers!"

I grinned and shook my head at her. I nearly forgot Damon was standing right behind us. He cleared his throat, refocusing my attention back on him.

"Nadine, this is Damon Northwood," I motioned to him. Damon held out his hand, and Nadine took it, her eyes raking over him from head to toe, taking in his appearance. "So, your father is seeing Ruth, right?" Nadine asked, not missing a beat.

"Yup," Damon replied with a nod and a neutral expression.

Before the conversation could progress further, a group nearby began calling Damon's name. Their loud, energetic voices cut through the conversation, prompting us all to turn toward the sound. The group of men dressed in various costumes urged him over, apparently thrilled to see him. Damon gave me a short glance as if to see whether I was all right.

"Friends of yours?" I asked, one eyebrow rising.

"Yeah, one second, I'll be right back." Damon walked over. They greeted him with enthusiastic pats on the back and embraced him like one of their own. I found myself imagining Damon's life encircled by his friends who clearly respected him.

I turned to Nadine and explained that Damon was the son of Richard Northwood. Nadine's eyes grew wide, shocked by that little piece of information. "Wow. Your mom really bagged a rich guy."

Damon appeared next to me before I had time to react, along with one of his friends. The guy had dazzling blond locks that seemed almost too flawless to be authentic, and he was dressed in a toga costume.

"This is my cousin, Chase." Damon nodded in the blond's direction.

Chase greeted me, then did a double take when he saw Nadine. His eyes were full of admiration.

"And who is this beautiful lady?" he asked as he reached for Nadine's hand.

"This is Nadine. Hilly's friend," Damon replied.

Chase took Nadine's hand and pressed it to his lips.

Nadine giggled and blushed, her face tinged with a soft pink. Chase was a charmer. There was something about him, an air of confidence and cockiness, that reminded me of Damon. The confidence obviously ran in their family, and Chase had no problem whatsoever making an impression, especially with Nadine.

Nadine was taken aback. I had never witnessed her speechless before. Actually, I had never seen Nadine act like this around anyone before. It was as if she and Chase were two old souls reuniting. It was as if I was witnessing love at first sight right there before my very eyes.

I shuffled awkwardly, feeling like the third wheel in their blossoming romance. Damon stood alongside me, and he seemed to notice as well. Whatever was going on between Nadine and Chase was obviously unexpected, even for them.

"Right." I tried to cut through the atmosphere between Chase and Nadine, hoping to bring them back down to earth.

Just as all of us began to make our way toward the entrance, Nadine suddenly huffed in frustration. "Look at that line... It's gonna take ages to get in."

There was a notice beside the entrance. *All tickets must have been purchased online.*

"Nadine, you bought the tickets, right?"

Nadine's face fell and she bit her lip. "Crap. I thought you could buy tickets at the gate."

Before panic could set in, Damon stated with confidence, "I got this." He reached for my hand and Chase followed suit, taking Nadine's. Damon took the lead, and his group of friends fell into a line behind us. We made our way to the entrance. There was a slight parting of the crowd as he neared them, his demeanor an immediate indication that he wasn't someone to be questioned or messed with.

"Mr. Northwood." A lady at the gate looked him up and down, smirking. She opened the gate without hesitation. "Please, come right in."

The way she looked at him, like she wanted him. *Fuck, am I getting jealous?*

We passed by, and I couldn't help but be impressed. He didn't give the lady at the gate a second thought. He rubbed his thumb over my hand like he was reassuring me. *Okay. Kinda cute.*

Nadine gave me a wide-eyed look. Chase smirked, not letting go of Nadine's hand.

I scanned the scene around me. The edges were lined with wooden canopies. In the middle of everything was a huge open tent inside, lit with flashing strobe lights that cast erratic shadows on the makeshift dance floor. The bass of the music pounded throughout the ground. Weaving our way through the sea of people, my hand seemed to be holding onto Damon's a bit too tightly. I looked up at him and let go of his hand, feeling a little self-conscious, but he didn't seem to mind. We reached the bar finally. Damon smiled reassuringly before turning to the bartender and ordering our drinks.

"Oh! I have a QR code for a free drink," I told him.

Damon snorted, shaking his head. "Don't sweat it. Drinks are on the house."

"Of course they are…"

Nadine and Chase became engrossed in their own conversation. It was as though they were within their own little world, with nothing else around them.

The bartender gave me a green cup, whereas he handed everybody else a red one.

Great! Like I fucking need everyone to know I'm sober.

I didn't even have a chance to try it. Damon snatched the cup out of my hand and took a quick sip. "Just making sure it's non-alcoholic." He handed it back to me with a satisfied nod.

I reached out, took the cup from him, and rolled my eyes. I knew he meant well, especially after what he'd shared about his sister, but he was still very protective. I wanted to experience the party the way I had planned with Nadine.

"Hey, Nadine, how about you and I take a look around?" I yelled over the music.

Nadine hesitated, looking back at Chase. "Can't we stick with the guys?"

I cast her a glance. "Come on, Nadine."

Chase didn't seem fazed with the tension at all, leaning down and kissing Nadine on the cheek. Before we were able to walk away, Damon grabbed my purse and fished out my cell phone.

"What are you doing?"

"I'm putting in my number," he stated, not looking up from my phone. "You text me if you need me."

As Damon tapped away on my phone, I couldn't help but notice the attention he was drawing.

Girls walked by in groups, their eyes catching on him. There was nothing subtle about it; Every one of them wanted him. But there he was, focused on me. A part of me felt honored, almost smug.

He held out my phone with a serious expression. "I mean it, Hilly." I went to grab it, but he didn't let go and added, "What are you going to do?"

From the corner of my eye, I could see the other girls getting jealous. I felt fuzzy in my stomach, and my cheeks flushed. "I will text you if I need you," I reassured him as I slipped it into my purse and gave him a brief nod before turning to leave with Nadine.

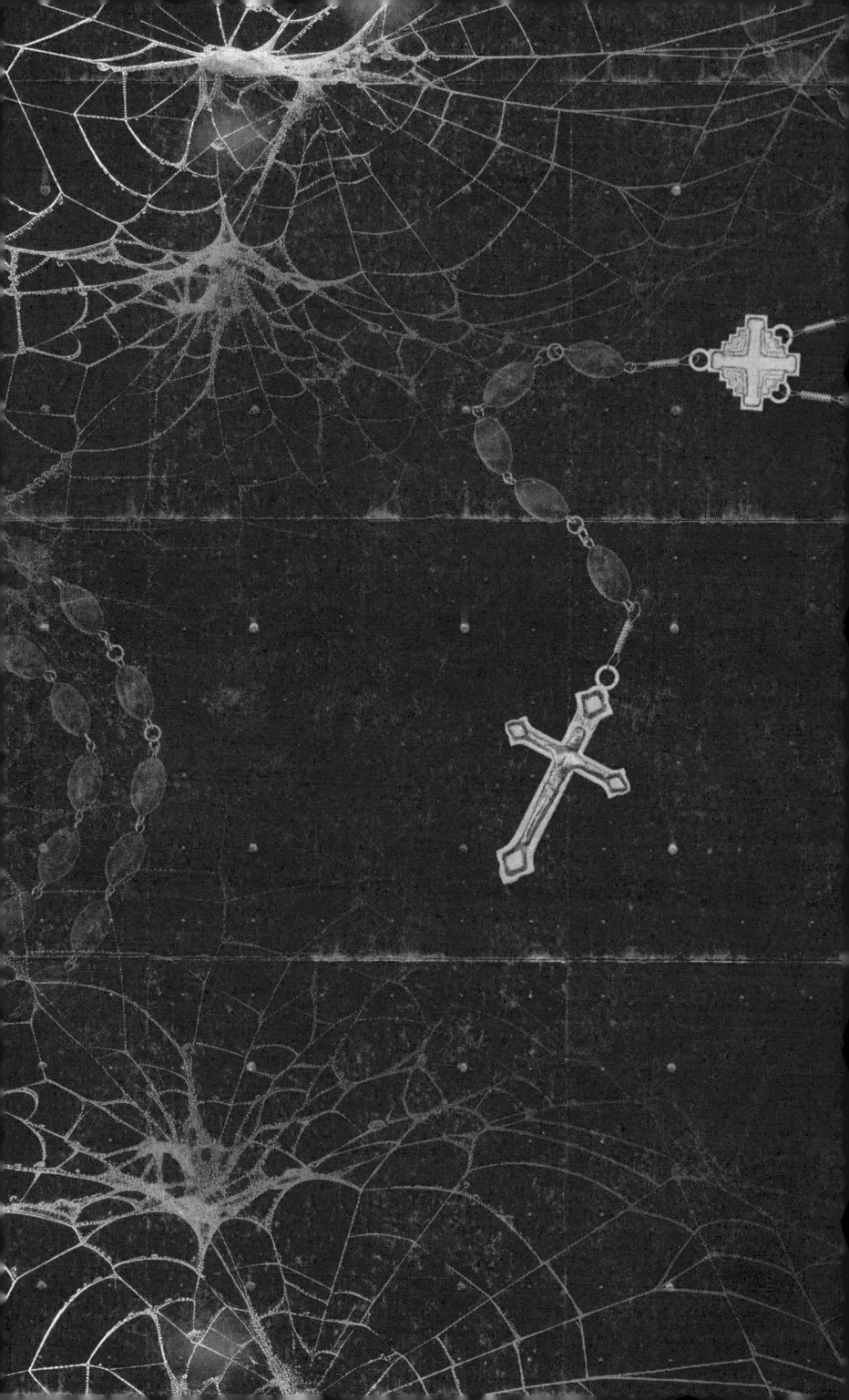

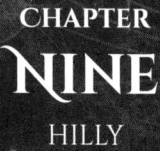

NINE

HILLY

NADINE AND I HEADED INTO THE WOODLAND, GLANCING AT EACH other with smirks on our faces, I could see the excitement in her eyes. The atmosphere was fun and frightening, from unique beverages and appetizers to face painting that varied from charming to spooky.

As we walked, I began to tell Nadine how I had opened up to Damon about my past and how protective he had become since then. Of course, she found it adorable.

"Sounds like he's really into you." She nudged me with her elbow. I rolled my eyes and brushed aside the statement.

"No... No. Plus it would be awkward. I'm pretty sure he's gonna be my stepbrother soon."

"Ooh, that makes it even more naughty."

Before I could react, Nadine's focus returned to Chase. She exhaled, leaning toward me as if she were in awe. "I think I'm in love, Hilly."

"Love's a state of mind. You've only just met him." I knew Nadine could get caught up in the moment, but this was rapid even for her. She pouted but didn't appear discouraged.

Suddenly, our eyes were drawn to the large flashing red

lights ahead, which spelled the words *Scare Maze!* Nadine and I exchanged glances, excitement building between us.

"You wanna go in there later?" Nadine's eyes shined with eagerness.

"Fuck, yeah!"

Nadine and I made our way back toward the dance floor, and the beat of the music began to grow louder with each step. Through the dancing bodies, I saw Damon's eyes darting to me, as if he could sense I was there. He was watching; he was being protective, even from a distance.

When we got onto the dance floor, Nadine drew me into the whirling group. The heavy, musty air from the fog generators surrounded us, adding to the crazy ambiance. Strobe lights illuminated all around us.

Nadine grabbed my hands and we began to sway our hips to the beat of the music. Everything else—the noise, masses, even Damon's watchful gaze—faded away for a minute, leaving only the two of us dancing to the music in our little universe.

All of a sudden, I felt a tap on my shoulder. I turn around to see Benny standing behind me, topless, with a broad smile. Instinctively, I shot my arms out and gave him a friendly hug. "Hey, you!" I yelled over the blaring music.

"Hi! Are you having a good night?" His eyes gleamed. I nodded my head enthusiastically as we began to dance together, going with the flow. "It's nice to finally meet you in person!" he yelled into my ear.

"I know, right? We've been talking for what feels like forever. It's good to finally meet you," I replied, smiling up at him. It seemed odd to see him in person after all the messages we shared.

Damon caught my eye as he cut through the sea of bodies on the dance floor like he owned the place. A girl in a tight, glittering dress slid right up to him, her arms snaking around his waist in a bid to pull him into the sway of the music. Damon pushed her away, his gaze never wavering, and continued through the crowd. She stumbled back, clearly caught off guard, but he didn't give her a second thought.

Benny broke my attention away from Damon. He leaned down and whispered in my ear, "I still have to take you on that date."

Suddenly, his friends came into view, dragging him away.

He waved at me, a promise in his eyes. I returned it.

I felt torn. Which was weird because Benny was nice. He seemed sweet and caring, but I didn't know if that was what I wanted. Damon was in the picture now and somehow, it just felt wrong to carry on with Benny. Damon was growing on me. I couldn't quite put my finger on why. He was going to be my stepbrother, and that fact alone made any other thoughts of us impossible. But I couldn't get past the way he made me feel. The way his presence stirred something in me that I didn't understand.

Nadine and I lost ourselves to the pulsating beats and fog. Then something crushed against my back. My immediate instinct made me think it was Damon, but I turned my head to see a man dressed as a vampire, complete with fangs and a cape, grinding up against me. His intentions were clear, and his crotch rubbing against my ass just made my skin crawl. "Back off!" I shouted over the music.

He didn't listen. The grinding continued, and I felt the pressure build as anger poured through me.

His arms wrapped around my waist. I fought and squirmed to try to get free from the vampire's clutches. He pulled me backward into his body, his hot, disgusting breath against my ear as he said, "Keep pushing your ass into me, sugar."

As I managed to create some space between us, the vampire's smirk contorted into a sneer. But before I could do anything, Damon was already there with his mask on—it was as if he appeared out of nowhere. Without hesitation, he launched himself at the vampire, delivering a fist to his face.

"You ever touch her again... watch what I fucking do to you. Now fuck off before you're never found!" Damon hissed, his voice threatening.

The vampire fell into the crowd and landed on his ass, knocking the air out of his lungs. Blood oozed from his nose, slithering down toward his lips and chin. Damon loomed above him, his face cold, hard, and unyielding—like a predator as it would gaze upon its prey. His hands were clenched into fists, his knuckles streaked with blood—the same blood splashed now across the vampire's face. There were no signs of remorse —just a darkness in his eyes, which I found calming. His unrelenting attention on me sends a shiver down my spine.

The vampire's friends were quick to notice the ruckus and started yelling. "Hey! Hey!"

Damon's friends fought with the other group, causing chaos. The atmosphere changed from festive to frenetic. "Get the girls out of here!" a deep, authoritative voice shouted, cutting through the sounds of the brawl.

Without wasting a second, Chase grabbed Nadine's hand and they began forcing their way through the mob.

Damon grabbed my hand firmly and drew me quickly through the crowd. We lost Chase and Nadine as he led me behind a wooden cabin, out of the chaos. I leaned against the rough exterior to catch my breath. All sounds of fighting and music seemed far away. Damon paced back and forth in a straight line, running his hand through his hair in frustration. His eyes were aflame with anger.

That look in Damon's eyes was enough to send a shiver of fear through me but I decided to break the silence. "I could handle myself back there..."

Damon halted his pacing and walked over, his presence filling the tiny space between us. He lifted one hand above my head and leaned against the cabin wall, practically enclosing me. I gazed up at him, and my breath caught as our eyes connected. He put his mask on top of his head. It was impossible to look away. For a second, neither of us spoke. The air between us was dense with silent thoughts and unresolved tension.

"No one ever gets to fucking touch you. Do you understand me?" His finger sat beneath my chin as he added, "Men like that are not what you need."

I felt the weight of his words and scoffed. "Oh, and what type of man is it that I need? Someone like you?"

His jaw tightened, and he tilted his head. "Maybe."

What does he mean by that? Is he just trying to get under my skin?

"Ugh. Damon, move out of my way." I whacked my hand on his arm, trying to show my dominance.

He let out a cruel laugh. "Look at you trying to act tough. Don't make me fix your attitude, Hilly."

His little remark definitely got under my skin. I shoved him again, but he didn't flinch. He grabbed and pulled me in, his face close to my ear, his breath warm across my skin. "I heard you whimper my name. You were touching yourself and thinking of me, weren't you, Hilly? You thought you were quiet..."

Oh, fuck.

I gulped loudly, my heart beating in my chest as I tried to pull away. I was speechless, my mind a whirlpool of feelings—the closeness of his body and how his words wrapped around me like a vise had me reeling.

For a moment, I was paralyzed, torn between the desire to

deny everything and the crushing reality of what he had just said.

I finally found my voice, however it was shaky and uncertain. "Damon, I—"

"You pictured me touching you," he breathed.

It was like Damon was inside my fucking mind, reading my thoughts from an open book. He made me feel so weak.

His lips traced a path up my neck, so intimate that I nearly lost my balance, wanting to melt into him.

Before I knew it, my body was leaning into him as if it was drawn to him, silently hungering for more of his touch. My eyes fluttered closed as Damon's warm lips rested against my neck. Everything around had fallen into oblivion.

"Damon, we really shouldn't be doing this."

His lips left my body, and he leaned back far enough to look at me. "Do you want me to stop?"

I felt longing and confusion colliding in my chest. I shook my head, refusing to say the words that would destroy this moment. I bit my bottom lip. It was so fucking wrong, but something inside me was wanting him, and knowing he wanted me too made me feel weak.

"Good," Damon stated, "because do you know how much it took not to bust into the room and fuck you? I wanted you to come on my cock instead of your fingers."

I couldn't help but let out a little whimper.

Our lips met and Damon's hands automatically dropped to my waist, drawing me closer, like he wanted our bodies to melt into one another. We eagerly explored each other's mouths as if long-simmering desires had finally been met. I buried my fingers into his hair, deepening the kiss. Damon made full use of my parted lips and plunged deeper, his tongue flirting with mine in a sensual dance.

Suddenly, I felt his hands leave my waist. His fingers

continued downward, tracing the contour of my hips before sliding to the hem of my skirt. Our lips rested against each other as I pulled my face back.

"Keep your eyes on me," Damon purred against my mouth.

My eyes locked with his, and my arms wrapped securely around his neck, keeping him close while his fingers worked their way up my skirt. He pushed aside my thin lace panties. I let out a quiet gasp as he began feeling my slit. His fingers parted my folds and started tracing slow circles on my throbbing clit.

Damon observed my response intently, and he must have caught a glimpse of my satisfaction. "That's my girl." His fingers delved deeper, exploring my wetness as I responded to his touch. The sensation was getting too much for me to handle, and I tried to hold back each moan. I couldn't help it, but my eyes fluttered.

"Keep your fucking eyes on me, Hilly," he demanded as his fingers moved at a faster pace.

My legs began to shake slightly, my body arching toward his hand. I was fighting with all my strength to keep my eyes open. My hips began to move on their own, gently pressing into his palm, wanting more. "Damon!"

He brushed his lips against mine affectionately before continuing. "Scream my name. I want everyone to hear you belong to me," he cooed, and his fingers continued to accelerate as they rubbed my clit, the intensity pushing me closer to the edge. "Do you like it when I touch you like this?"

My voice broke. "Don't stop."

"Beg me. Beg me to make you fucking come."

Damon was owning me, claiming me. I could see it in his eyes—the need, the want. *He wants all of me.*

It was as if a switch had been flicked, and he drew me in.

"P-please, Damon."

I clutched my hands against his shoulders and dug my nails in. I was so close. His fingers changed their pattern and moved side to side, driving me wild. My pussy was throbbing with pure pleasure and I could feel my whole body flush with heat.

"Tell me what you want."

"I want..."

"Use your words."

"I want your fingers inside of me. I want to come on them."

Damon let out a moan like he'd been holding it inside for much too long. It was as if my words had given him the permission to let go of any restraint he'd been holding onto.

Before he got the chance, our names rang out. "Damon! Hilly!" Chase called.

Damon pulled his hand away and sucked on his fingers.. "You taste so fucking good, Hilly."

Before I could say anything, Chase rounded the corner with a deep look of concern etched on his face. His eyes glanced back and forth between us. He knew something had gone on. He wasn't stupid. "Everything okay?" he asked.

I could tell Damon was frustrated, but he straightened up and returned to his usual controlled demeanor, his eyes still fixed on mine. "Yeah, we're fine."

"Uh... I'll wait for you around the corner," Chase stated as he walked away, his voice drifting off.

I stared up at Damon, my emotions in turmoil. The way he looked at me with hunger. I wanted more of him, wanted him to make me come. My heart pounded, and I felt a mix of desire and disbelief.

"We screwed up, Damon. We—" My voice was unsteady.

"No, we fucking didn't." He shifted closer. "Don't you dare say that. I want you to understand. You're *mine*. No one else is fucking touching you. You're mine to play with and mine to control."

His declaration rendered me speechless. The severity of what had just occurred hit me hard, and I struggled to make sense of it all. Damon's gaze was intense, displaying a combination of protectiveness and primal desire. I'd never experienced anything like this before.

He grabbed my hand and started leading me back to the party, but before we reached the corner, he fell to his knees in front of me, his hands sliding up my skirt with urgency. I gasped, half expecting him to finish what he started. Instead, he hitched his fingers in the waistband of my panties and tugged them down slowly over my thighs, then my knees, and finally over my boots. His eyes never once left mine. A small smile played on his lips as he licked them, tasting my arousal before tucking them into his pocket. "You won't be needing these."

The cool breeze hit my pussy, making me more sensitive. Damon adjusted my skirt, rose to his feet, and closed his hand around mine. I was out of breath, feeling confused yet at his mercy. *Maybe after all these years, I do need someone to have this kind of control over me.*

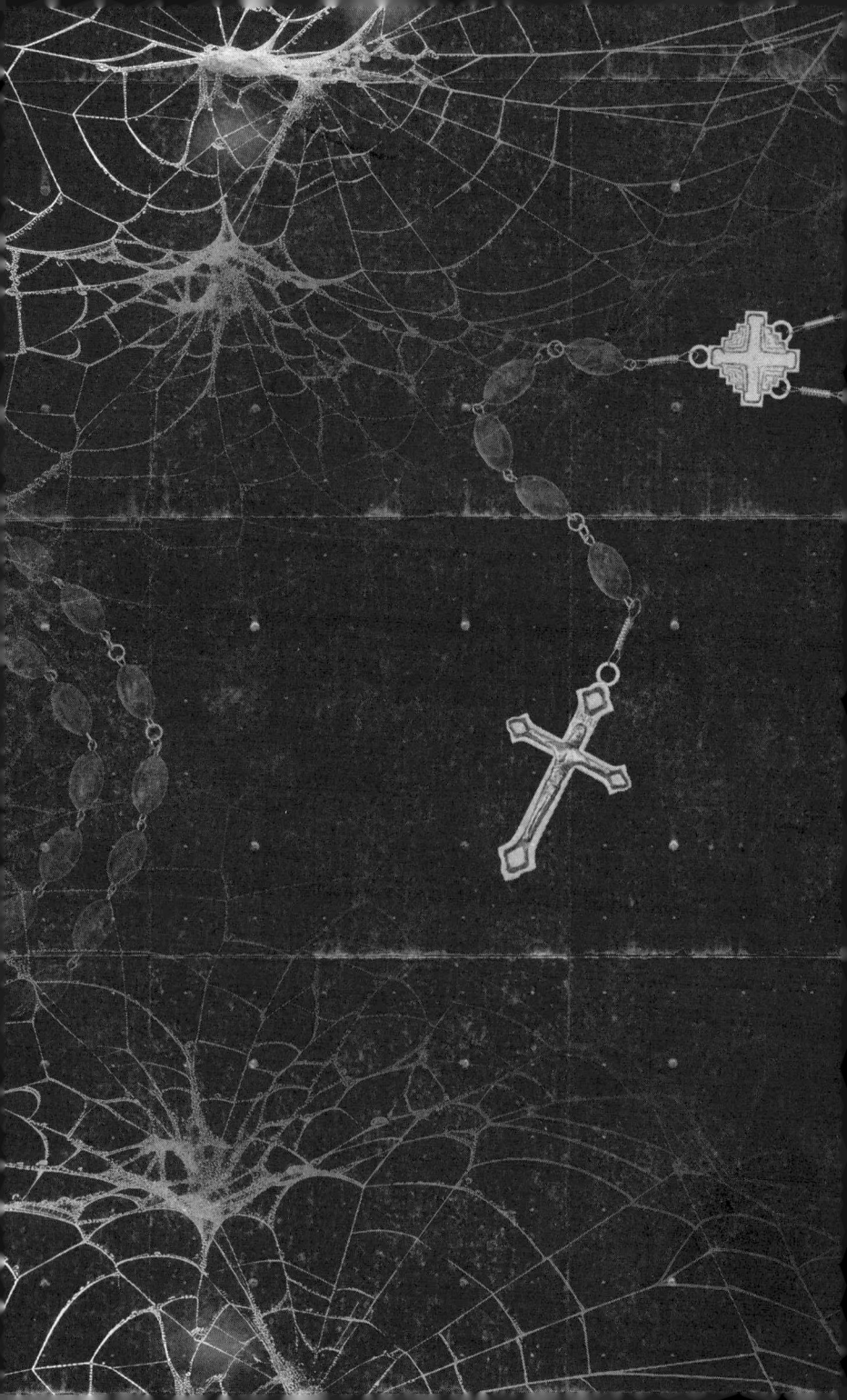

TEN

DAMON

Goddamn, I'd do anything to see Hilly come. She felt and tasted amazing. Those little whimpers she let out when I touched her were fuel for the beast inside me. I'd waited so long for this moment, and she was everything I'd hoped she would be. The urge to tell Chase to fuck off and take Hilly right there was almost too much to handle. But I wanted our first time to be special, not some quickie behind a wooden cabin. She deserved more than that after everything she'd gone through. I would make sure it was unforgettable for her. I'm gonna fuck my girl the way she's always deserved. She didn't realize just how long I've wanted her. How much I wanted to rip her away from all her hurt and shield her.

Every step was a reminder of how close we'd just been. It was driving me crazy as I walked around with the taste of her still on my tongue. Holding Hilly's hand felt like it should have been there all along. As we approached Chase and Nadine, I could feel his smirk before I saw it. The look on his face told me that he knew exactly what had just gone down, but I didn't care. Honestly, he probably did. Chase had a knack for reading situations. A quick look over at Nadine, with her smeared rosy pink lipstick and disheveled hair, told me that she and Chase also had their own little moment.

It was all so twisted, the secrets and half-truths. I watched as Nadine's eyes darted between Hilly and me, and somehow, we were all wrapped up in this strange, unspoken agreement.

I watched the girls walk ahead of us, linking arms and giggling like they were back in high school. It was nice seeing Hilly more relaxed. I couldn't help but glance over at Chase. He shook his head at me with that damn knowing smirk.

"Oh, shut up. What, like you didn't just do the same with Nadine?" I muttered.

Chase's grin widened. "What? I didn't say anything, dude!"

I stopped walking and shot him a look. "You don't have to. I can see it written all over your face."

Chase chuckled and refocused his eyes back on Nadine. "Dude, you're too easy to read."

"So the guys handled everything?" I cast a surreptitious glance at the passing people.

"Yeah. The vampire and his friends have been dealt with," Chase replied casually.

I nodded, feeling relieved. One less creep to fucking worry about.

Chase and I looked over to see Hilly and Nadine in a heated discussion with an old woman who looked like she had stepped from another century. Tall and stately in her long, dark green velvet dress, brittle gray hair cascaded down past her shoulders like a cape. In her hand, she clutched a glass ball that was almost mystical. It dawned on me then. She was a fortune teller.

We walked over, and as soon as the woman saw me, her face went white. She pointed at me directly, her eyes wide with fear. "Si, Si! El diablo disfrazado!" she exclaimed, shaking Hilly.

I didn't like how she had her hands on Hilly, but this was an old lady and I respected the elderly. "What the fuck is her problem?"

Hilly looked just as confused at me, her gaze darting between me and the woman.

The old women was crazy. She looked straight through me like I was a ghost.

Her voice became louder and frantic. "Diablo disfrazado!"

People around us started turning to stare. *What is she seeing? Who the fuck hired her?*

Is she just an actor who is really into the role?

Nadine tried to make out the meaning of the woman's words. "I think she's saying something about a devil in disguise.... or disgust. I don't know."

Hilly tried comforting the old woman, but her eyes looked distant. She reached down and grabbed Hilly's arm, trying to pull her. "Not safe!" she hollered.

Hilly struggled to understand. "What do you mean I'm not safe?"

The woman's grip grew tighter; her fingers dug into Hilly's skin. "El diablo!" she muttered in a coarse-sounding tone. "Looks just like a man, but deep down, he's pure darkness."

Hilly eyes searched mine for reassurance. However, I'd had enough of the old woman's drama. "Get the fuck outta here, grandma!" I yanked Hilly's hand and pulled her away from the crazy old woman. I put my arm around her shoulder, holding her close as we pushed through the crowd. Chase and Nadine trailed after us.

Hilly looked a little skittish. "I wonder what that was about?"

"Oh, don't worry about her. She's just some paid actress for tonight."

"Hm." Hilly pursed her lips.

I looked over her shoulder, expecting the old woman to be there still, glaring at me or hexing me, but she was gone.

I blinked hard a couple of times.

There was no need to freak Hilly out any more than she already was. Instead, I just pulled her a little closer and continued walking, trying to shake off the weird moment.

Nadine and Chase had spotted an apple bobbing station, and they acted like two kids on Christmas morning. They ran to that barrel like there was no tomorrow, laughing and shoving each other playfully. Hilly and I watched from a distance, feeling like their babysitters.

Hilly shifted, biting her nails. I guessed she was still nervous about the fortune teller. I looked down at her boots. "Your lace is all untied."

I was on my knees in front of her before she even had a chance to bend down. I didn't give a damn about the dirt. "Put your foot on my knee," I told her while tying the lace.

She stood above me and coughed. I caught a glimpse of her pussy. I froze, mid-breath, looking at her, and swallowed.

Man, the idea of putting my tongue between her legs was almost too much to bear. The thoughts were nearly sending me over the edge, but I shook it off and stood up, trying to change my line of thought. Nadine and Chase were in the background, enjoying their apple bobbing. It was a contrast with what was building between Hilly and me. When I looked over at her, it was clear she was nervous. "What's up, Hilly?"

"Damon," she began, switching from her nails to the inside of her cheek. "I feel like the lines have been blurred..."

By the look in her eyes, I knew that she had some regrets—it was written all over her face—but I could tell she had a craving too. She was scared of what we meant and maybe even scared of herself.

She was so fucking confusing. I knew she'd been getting off while thinking about me. I heard her. The way she looked at me? Reacted to my touch? You couldn't just ignore that. I'd been waiting for weeks, fighting every urge, holding back for the right moment until I finally met her. Learning about her past only made that craving stronger. It made me want to protect and keep her safe even more.

But before I could speak or even try to argue, a gaggle of girls ran up, asking Hilly if she'd jump up on stage for some charity thing. She looked baffled. "Uh—"

"It's all good. You just gotta stand there for two minutes," one girl chimed.

Hilly's eyes were wide with uncertainty as if silently screaming for help. But before she could say no, the girls surrounded her, holding tight, practically dragging her away. I sprang forward. "Hey! Wait!"

But as I reached out, a crowd surged between us, blocking my path. Chase and Nadine caught on, following behind me. The girls took Hilly onto the stage, and just as soon as she was under all those bright lights, it was plain as day how nervous she was, even though she was trying to play it cool. I had already caused a scene tonight; I didn't want to cause another one.

I met her eyes and mouthed, *Are you okay?* She nodded, but from where I stood, it was pretty evident she was as nervous as hell. *What the hell is going on?* Something felt off.

A man in a top hat and black suit went right up to Hilly on stage and jammed a mic in her face. "What's your name, pretty lady?"

She was clearly uncomfortable. "Uh, Hilly."

The instant she fidgeted, a wave of anger hit me. If that dude did anything else to make her feel uncomfortable, I didn't care who was around. I was so ready to tear him apart right there on that fucking stage.

"Welcome, Hilly!" He gave a stupid smile to the audience. "All the money we make tonight goes to local charities!"

I stood there with clenched fists at my sides, unable to pry my eyes away from Hilly. Every part of me wanted just to run right up there and drag her off that stage, but I hung back, keeping an eye on every move that jerk made.

The crowd grew thicker, and the fog came in again, blurring everything. At that moment, men began to whistle and catcall Hilly from the crowd. I felt myself flare up, but Chase grabbed my shoulder before I could do anything, trying to keep me calm. "It'll be fine."

The man did some stupid shuffle dance and then shouted into the mic, "So tonight, ladies and gentlemen, the bidding for this pretty lady starts at one hundred dollars!"

What the fuck! I saw red and was about to storm onto the stage, but Chase caught me again. "Dude! Just outbid everyone... You have the money!"

He was right, of course. But just the thought of someone else even thinking of bidding on her made me physically ill. My jaw clamped shut, and I fisted my wallet, determined to ensure nobody else got a chance.

Guys were mumbling to each other and staring at Hilly like she was some kind of prize. Some idiot in the back yelled out, "Come on, Pretty. Give us a twirl!" A woman up on stage spun Hilly in a full circle with her.

Someone shouted out the first bid, and I wasted no time, the words fell out of my mouth. "Five hundred bucks!" The crowd was quiet for a moment, totally and utterly stunned by how quickly things had escalated.

Before I could even think of it, the same idiot out in the crowd shouted again. "One thousand dollars!"

I scanned across all the faces for the ass that dared to outbid me. My brain was on overdrive, and thoughts just came running in. Maybe it was Benny.

Hilly looked out into the crowd, shielding her eyes with her hand against the super bright stage lights. She looked nervous, scanning the crowd for someone she knew. I caught her eye and gave her a little nod, hopefully conveying that all was taken care of.

"Two thousand dollars!" I made it clear I wasn't messing around.

"Ten thousand dollars!" was shouted by the anonymous man. The crowd actually gasped. Even Chase and Nadine turned around, wide-eyed. But I didn't back down. "Twenty thousand dollars! And no fees to Wickedy for three months!" The crowd exploded into cheers and a round of applause.

The man in the top hat sealed the deal. "Sold!"

Hearing the word was a relief, but the anxiety of what could have happened still lingered. I didn't even want to picture something of mine being sold.

Chase shook his head. "Dude, your father is going to be so pissed."

"I don't give a damn," I shot back. My eyes landed on Hilly as she leaped off the stage, running in my direction. "Nobody is getting their hands on Hilly unless it's me."

I took long strides towards her, meeting her halfway. I reached out and yanked her in close, my eyes darting around for the other bidder. A tall man in a dark purple velvet suit, his face hidden in the shadows, started winding his way through the crowd and disappearing into the fog. I could see it wasn't Benny, but whoever he was looked over his shoulder and glared at us. He wasn't done. Funny that... because neither was I.

"Thanks, Damon. I don't know who the fuck the other

bidder was..." Hilly mumbled so softly that I could feel her heart race from inside her chest, which was pressed to mine.

"Hey," I lifted her chin. "I had control. Just like always. I promised I'd always keep you safe."

Hilly tried to look away, her eyes moving to escape the moment. Oh, dear Lord, her attempt at concealment had left her so fucking exposed. I would never break my promise, even if my father and her mom didn't work out.

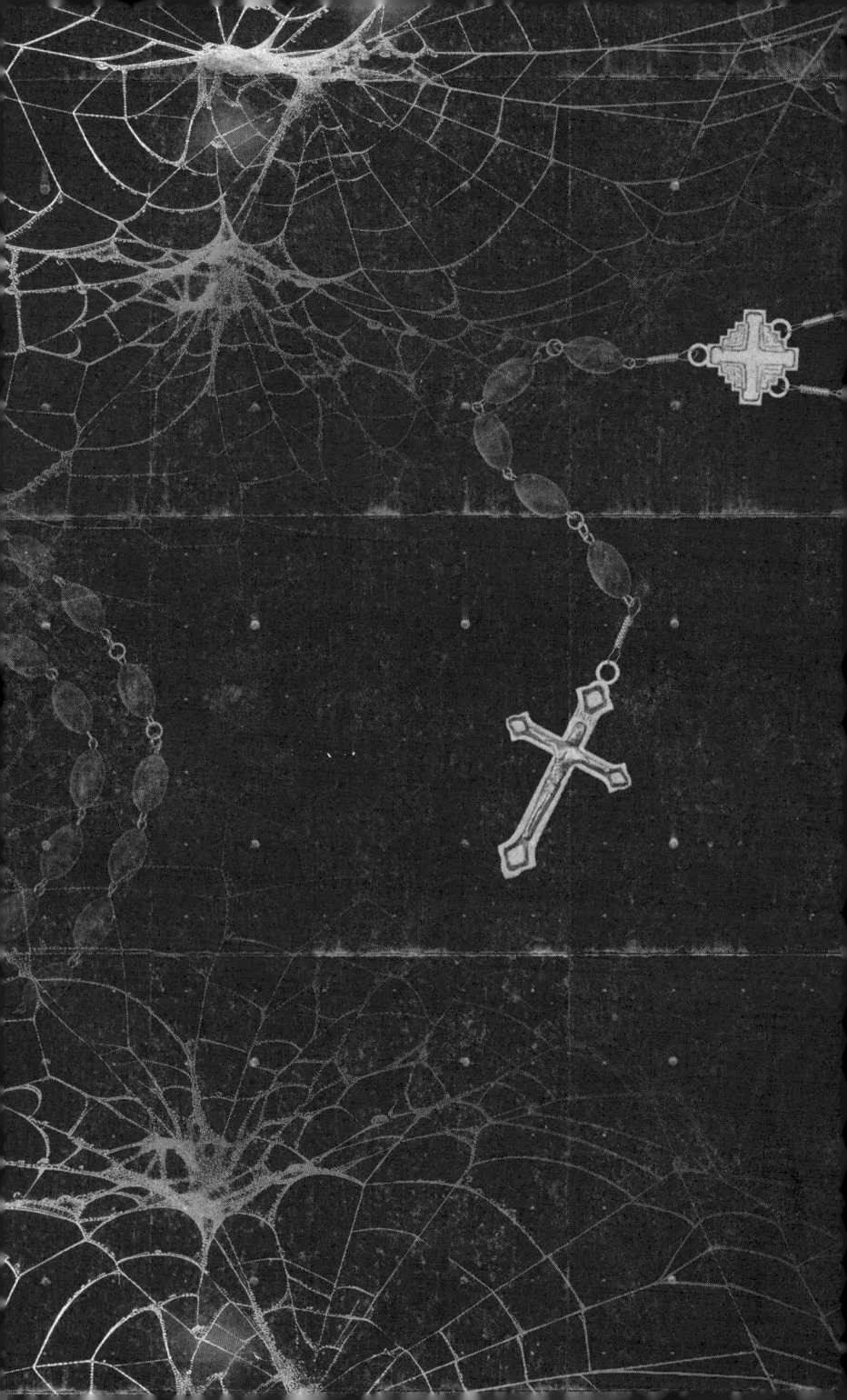

ELEVEN

When I was up on that stage, a hundred eyes were on me, and there was no way out or any possibility of escaping the suffocating feeling of my past. Every moment on that stage felt like the past seeping back into the present, poisoning everything I had tried to forget.

Someone out there was trying to pay for me.

But Damon's face stood out, cutting through the chaos. He made me feel safe. At that moment, when he stepped in to protect me from another bidder, it wasn't just about looking out for me anymore—it felt like so much more.

He had this way of drawing me in. I just couldn't resist. There was something in his eyes when he cornered me behind the cabin. The tension had been there for so long, like a storm waiting to break, and in that instant, it did.

When he said I was his, it wasn't a question. The words shook me hard and echoed inside of me like they'd been waiting to be spoken my whole life. Maybe that's all I'd ever craved—to be wanted and claimed like that, without hesitation, without doubt. Damon gave me the attention I had longed for, and I didn't understand why he wanted me. Knowing my past, a normal person would recoil in disgust.

Fuck. I tried to pull away, put up some barriers, create space, but he'd pull me right back in with just one look or a single word. He had control over me, and no matter how hard I tried, I couldn't keep my defenses up. I was stuck in that hazardous push and pull. The truth was, I'd never been that vulnerable, to anyone. Intimacy—sober—was foreign to me. And then, of course, there was the other side of it—our parents. They were serious when they spoke about the future. It felt careless, even dangerous, to let myself like him when I knew how sticky it could get. But the lines were so hazy between us. At first, his need to look after me felt overwhelming, like I was being smothered. But as much as I resisted, something about him pulled me in like a magnet.

Chase and Nadine had gone off on their own, leaving Damon and I alone in the wildly thick forest. I could hear bats flying above as we walked farther. After a while, we saw a little wooden cabin. The outside was weathered, but red lights glowed from inside. As we got closer, the sounds hit us. Moaning. Groaning. But not the kind that creeped you out. It was heavy, and unmistakably sexual.

I turned to Damon, my breath catching. "What the fuck is going on in there?"

He didn't answer immediately. He tried peering through one of the fogged up windows, wiping at it, but the condensation was on the inside too, obscuring everything inside.

We walked around a corner of the cabin, and a guy in a ghost costume and a girl dressed as a pirate leaned indolently against the side of the cabin, smoking.

Damon didn't hesitate to walk right up to them. "Yo, what's going on in there?"

The girl didn't look at him directly. Her eyes slid toward the ghost beside her, an amused smirk tugging one side of her lips. "The Wickedy that people don't see..." she said with a casual shrug, exhaling a slow plume of smoke.

I exchanged a glance with Damon. What kind of place was this?

I reached out, grabbed Damon's hand without thinking, and tugged him toward the cabin. "Let's check it out." A strange mix of curiosity and darker urges pulled me forward.

Damon hesitated, his hand tight around mine. "Wait, are you sure about this?"

I shook my head. "I don't know why I really want to check it out."

Before we even reached the first step of the weathered stairs, the pirate girl clutched a small wicker basket overflowing with lollipops. Without hesitation, I picked out one from the pile—it was a deep red color. My fingers peeled away the wrapper, its plastic edges crackling between my hands. I popped it into my mouth with a smirk, the hard candy pressing against my tongue. The familiar taste flooded my senses. "Mm... Cherry." The sweetness danced across my taste buds.

We stepped onto the creaking stairs together. We walked to the door, and the moment we went beyond it, the world seemed to shift. A hallway opened to us, bathed with that same eerie glow we had seen from the outside. Everything took on this surreal hue, almost dreamlike, which blurred the edges of reality. I turned right; an open door drew my attention. My heart racing, I peered inside.

Two women were lying on the couch. One was eating the other out, savoring the taste of the woman's pussy while her legs were spread open for everyone to see. The rawness of it hit me like a shockwave—the soft moans and heavy breathing. I watched while sucking on the lollipop, unable to tear my eyes away. All I could focus on was the energy filling the room as if something primal inside me had recognized it and craved it.

Damon's hand tightened in mine, anchoring me, and I snapped out of my trance just enough to look at him. His face was a mirror image of mine. We knew we stepped into something far more intense than we'd imagined. And now there was no going back.

I led Damon down the hall, and the sounds around us grew louder and more explicit, echoing off the walls as we neared another door. Damon reached out and yanked me close, holding me in place with firm arms. "Don't think for one second that anyone else in here gets to touch you. Do you understand?" All I wanted was him. But I didn't answer, as my mind was going crazy. I stared at his lips, awaiting his kiss. He let out a harsh breath. "You're so fucking confusing. I hope you know that." His lips crashed against mine.

The kiss was fierce, filled with everything we weren't saying. But then reality snapped back. I pulled away, breathless. Damon's eyes were dark with heat, but before he could say anything, we both turned toward the next room. We froze in the doorway, observing one man, his body drenched in sweat, with a woman beneath him. The room was filled with the smell of sweat and sex.

"Fuck." My heart raced as I watched, and my body filled with heat.

I felt Damon push up against my back—towering, intoxicating. He leaned in close, his lips brushing my neck.

The man had stopped thrusting into the woman, drawing

back, only to bury his face between her legs. The woman's body arched, her moans more insistent, her fingers digging into the sheets beneath her. It was so raw my breath caught in my throat.

Damon's mouth moved to my ear, and he seemed to pull me into some sort of shared fantasy. His hand slid up my head, his fingers tangling into my hair. "Look at him," he whispered. "Look at the way he's devouring her... the way he's worshiping her."

I leaned back, feeling the heat of him press into me. His hand in my hair tightened, and I bit my lip, teetering on the edge of my mind, spinning out of control. The night had gone from strange to something else,something I wasn't ready to understand but couldn't resist.

"Let me worship you, Hilly."

I turned around with the lollipop still in my hand, and cupped his face. He pulled me in for a kiss—our bodies molding against each other. The more I pushed, the more he stumbled into the hallway, and that's when his back hit a gothic-looking mirror.

Instantly, he spun me around to face the mirror. He stood behind me, his eyes locking onto mine. The only illumination was from the red glow, casting its crimson hue over us.

I stood there feeling weak. My heart was beating fast in my chest, my breathing shallow and rapid. Damon's body heat through the fabric of my clothing was both comforting and frightening.

He whispered into my ear, "I wanna taste your lollipop." His words made me shiver. He pushed his body against mine, his hands settling lightly upon my hips.

I brought the lollipop up to Damon's lips. My heart was racing in anticipation, and he didn't hold back. He didn't care that it had just been in my mouth a second before. His eyes fixed on mine as he leaned in, his lips opened a little, and his tongue traced over the top.

The movement of his tongue sent shivers down my spine. Every stroke against the candy was a tease, a promise of what his tongue could do to me. My legs felt weak, a subtle ache spreading through me. His eyes darkened, knowing full well what he was doing to me as his tongue swirled around the lollipop.

I could barely focus on anything else. *I've never wanted to be a lollipop so bad.*

"I want you to spread your legs for me," he ordered.

My cheeks flushed, and I felt my arousal spike as I obeyed, my thighs parting slowly. The cool air against my skin made me flinch, but it wasn't the temperature that set me on edge.

"That's it, now lift your skirt." His voice was a faint growl. I hesitated for a moment. My fingers shook before reaching out toward the hem of my skirt. I took another deep breath as I lifted it. My bare pussy was on display.

In the red glow of the mirror, everything seemed surreal, like this might somehow be a dream or a nightmare.

"Good girl..." he breathed as his lips moved up my neck. "Such a good fucking girl."

His words made me so fucking wet. I could feel it between my legs as I looked at my reflection in the mirror. The sight of myself, so exposed and vulnerable, turned me on even more.

The walls closed in around us, the distant sounds of muffled moans from other rooms. Damon's hands moved to the back of my head, his fingers tangling in my hair as he yanked me closer, his lips grazing my ear. His breath was hot against my skin. "Show me your pretty little clit."

I parted my lips, showing him my clit. I couldn't look away

from the intensity of his stare in the mirror. He had full control over me, and I craved it.

"Fuck, look at that beautiful pussy... and it's already soaking for me," he whispered into my ear.

The look of hunger flickered within Damon's eyes and he reached out, plucking the lollipop from my hand. "I want you to get it wet for me."

I didn't say a word as he brought it back toward my mouth, swishing my tongue around it slowly, coating it in my saliva.

He watched me lick the lollipop without breaking eye contact. His breathing grew heavier with each passing second and then he lowered the slick lolly down between my legs. The cool sticky surface brushed my sensitive skin.

"Now you're gonna play with yourself," he demanded, his eyes never leaving mine.

My fingers trembled as I took the lollipop from him. Slowly, I began to rub, watching his reaction in the mirror. His eyes darkened with desire, and his breathing grew heavier. I could feel the slickness of the saliva on the lollipop coating my clit, and my body moved at his command like some kind of puppet on a string.

"That's it," he growled, his voice full of need. "Keep going..."

I increased the pressure, my hips bucking slightly with each stroke. The pleasure built quickly, my clit throbbing from the movements.

"You like this, don't you? Me controlling you. You don't get to come until I say. Do you understand?"

I nodded, unable to form words, my head and body consumed by sensation. I could feel my clit swelling as I moved the lollipop quicker, my breathing quickening into short, ragged gasps. Damon's other hand shifted onto my breast, squeezing roughly. "We're fucking perfect together. Just look at us in the mirror," he said through gritted teeth.

My mind reeled as my body shook with arousal. He tugged my hair, and my head jerked. "Look at us!"

"Damon," I breathed, barely audible above a whisper.

He was amazing, his shirt open at the top with tattoos peering out. His dark hair was tousled, giving him an unruly look that sent my heartbeat soaring. He leaned forward, and our lips met. I could taste the cherry on his tongue. I let out moans into his mouth as I continued moving the lollipop all over my pussy.

His hard cock pushed up against me. It felt like it wanted to bust at the seams. I pushed up against him as he started to sway back and forth. Fuck, I wanted him inside me so bad.

"Now, I want you to coat it in your juices," Damon ordered.

I swallowed hard, my body already quivering. The hand inched down, the lollipop dripping with both our saliva. I reached my entrance and teased myself first, rubbing it against the sensitive folds of my pussy.

I felt Damon's eyes upon me, watching my every move. With a slight gasp, I slowly pushed the lollipop inside. My pussy clenched around it while easing it in. I began to twist it in small circular motions, letting it get coated in my slick juices. Every turn sent waves of pleasure through me.

I felt myself getting wetter, the lollipop moist as I continued to move it. Each twisted motion made my hips buck slightly. Damon's eyes didn't flicker; there was a small smirk dancing on his lips as he watched me pleasure myself for him. He was in complete control of my every move.

Slowly, I pulled the lollipop out of my pussy. It glistened in the red light with my juices. I lifted it up for Damon to see. He didn't need an invitation as his big hand wrapped around my wrist, tugging the lollipop toward him. With slow, deliberate strokes, he licked the mix of cherry and me. The view of him running his tongue over that candy weakened me. "Fuck, that tastes amazing, Hilly."

He pressed the lollipop against my mouth. I didn't hesitate; I opened my mouth eagerly and licked. Sweet cherry mixed with my arousal overpowered me. It was wrong, so wrong, but fuck, it felt so great.

My hand moved lower again, eager to rub the lolly back on my clit, but before I could, he caught me and clutched my wrist. "Uh, no," he teased as his breath tickled my ear.

I let out a loud whimper, my body trembling with frustration. His grip tightened, not enough to hurt, but enough to make me aware of his control.

I swallowed hard. "Please, Damon," I whispered, shaking with need. "Please, I need to come."

He let in a sharp breath, hips bucking against me. A dry chuckle twisted Damon's lips as his dark eyes danced with amusement. He was enjoying the sight of me begging. It turned him on, and I knew it. I could tell from the way his fingers tightened around my wrist, holding me in place, the pleasure so obvious.

"You always beg so sweetly. But you know the rules, don't you?"

I nodded, biting my lip to keep from trembling. The rules were plain and simple: I wasn't allowed to come until he said so. And right now, he had no intention of letting me. Not yet.

Before I could plead, the cabin door creaked open, and without hesitation, Damon pulled down my skirt, covering my exposed skin.

Damon's eyes were dark with unspoken promise, and in the aftermath of all that intensity, neither of us was ready to let go of the tension between us.

He squeezed my hand. "Come on, let's get out of here."

We didn't look back. The cool night air slapped against my

skin, bringing me back to reality, and tension slowly unraveled with every step. My body longed for his in ways I couldn't control, in ways that left me short of breath and trembling. Every time his hands grazed over my pussy, every time his lips lingered just a second too long, my body was set on fire. Twice now, he'd almost driven me over the edge.

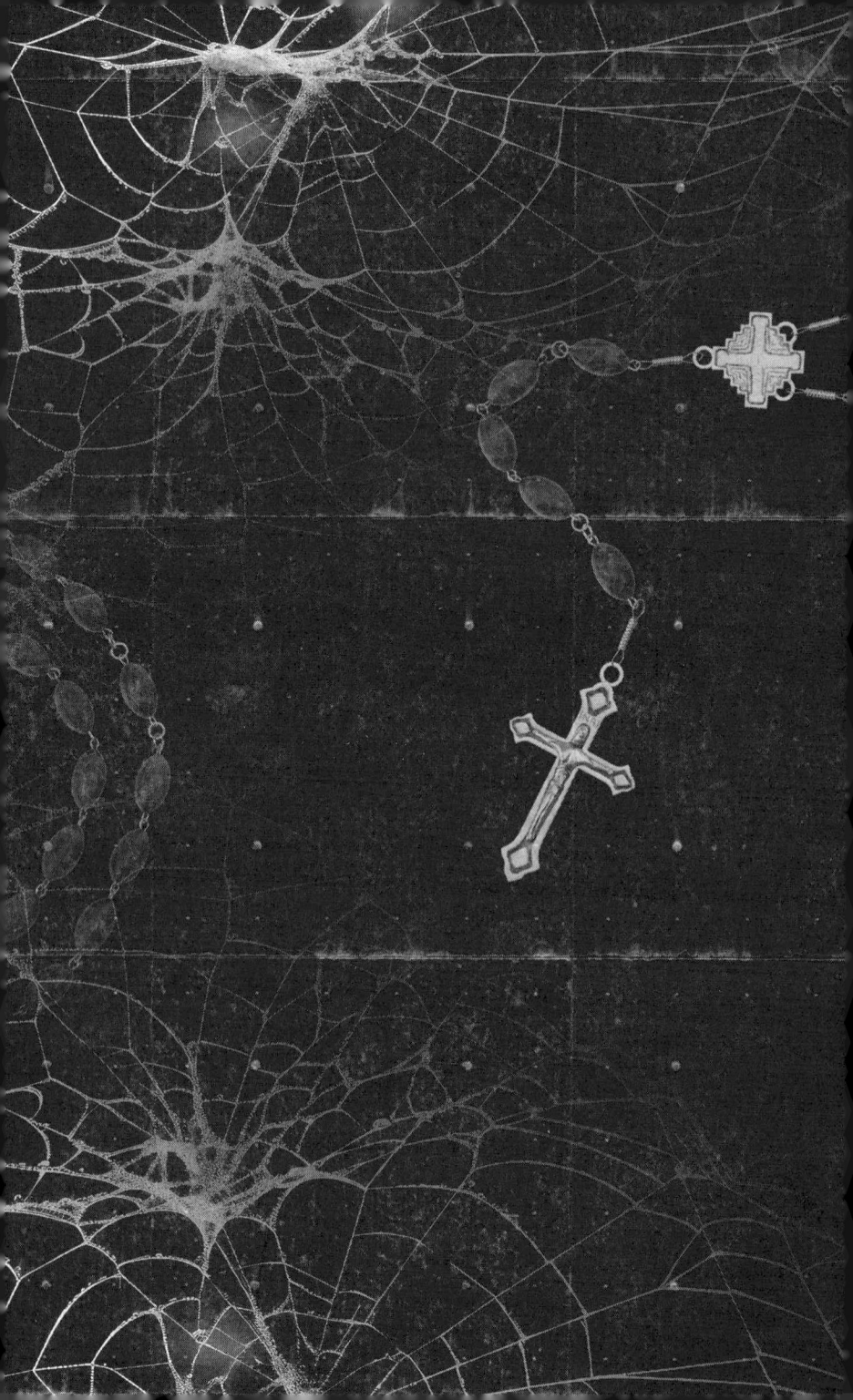

TWELVE

DAMON AND I WERE STANDING OUTSIDE THE PHOTO BOOTH NEXT TO the scare maze when we heard an excited scream behind us. We spun around to see Chase and Nadine running toward us, faces lit with pure joy.

"There you guys are!" Nadine yelled, waving.

"What's got you smiling?" I asked, turning to Chase and then back to her.

"No reason..."

"Fuck, yeah! A photo booth," Chase said, reaching out and snatching Nadine, pulling her toward it and yanking the deep plum-colored velvet curtain open.

The bench was only big enough for two people, so Nadine climbed right onto Chase's lap. Her costume got caught at the entrance so Damon had to push her through.

Damon sat down beside Chase, then patted his leg for me to take a seat. I rolled my eyes, knowing I wasn't wearing panties, and he'd definitely get a kick out of it.

Nadine's costume more or less filled the entire stall, so we were wedged in, heads sticking out around her. She handed around accessories—crumpled paper masks to make us look silly. Damon refused, pulling his metal mask lower instead.

Chase and Nadine started kissing so passionately even before the booth had started taking pictures that neither one of them noticed how Damon's hand crawled up my skirt. I did some adjusting, hoping to nudge his hand away, but he was insistent.

Damon murmured under the mask, "I'm just gonna put my hand right here."

"Jeepers Creepers" by Slayloverboy played within the booth from a set of tiny speakers, drowning out the sounds coming from Nadine and Chase, who were lost in their own little world.

Damon's hand was pinned between my thighs, his fingertip brushing against my pussy. Every subtle move caused my heart to race, and I shuffled on his lap, trying to act normally.

Finally, Chase and Nadine separated, laughing, each making ridiculous faces at the camera. "Cheese!" Nadine said, wide-eyed, grinning like the Cheshire cat.

I playfully stuck my tongue out as the camera as the flash went off over and over again. The booth finally shuddered to a stop, signaling that our photo session was done. Nadine sprang to her feet; her bumblebee wings brushed all of us in the confined space. We laughed as we tried to extricate her with one playful shove after another from each of us to get her moving out of the booth. Chase trailed behind her and we could hear their excitement as they waited for the photos to print.

Damon growled under his mask, oozing with frustration as he drew his hand from between my thighs reluctantly. I instinctively tried to stand, but his grip just got tightened around my wrist.

"Guys! Hilly and I are just going to go snap a few ourselves. We'll catch you guys at the scare maze!" Damon shouted.

Nadine and Chase didn't pay much attention as they looked at the prints. "Alright, dude!" Chase shot back over his shoulder as they walked away.

The booth's curtain dropped back into place, trapping us again in a small, secluded space.

Damon pushed me to my feet, his grasp firm. I stood, and he adjusted himself. "Sit back down, beautiful."

His words made me blush and I obeyed without thinking. My hands grasped at his shoulders for balance as I straddled his lap. Before I could react, he lifted his mask just enough for his lips to meet mine. He then broke the kiss, his lips moving down my jaw, nipping at the sensitive skin there before moving lower, toward my throat.

I arched my head back, giving him better access. My fingers threaded through his hair. As I sat on his lap, I could hear the camera taking photos.

My nipples hardened against the fabric of my mesh top. As my bare pussy rubbed up against his pants, I could feel the dampness pool between my thighs. The hardness of his bulge pressed against me, and I found myself grinding into it, seeking friction. He groaned, the sound low and deep in the back of his throat as his hands slipped down to squeeze my ass.

"Fuck, Hilly," he panted. "You're driving me crazy."

I looked down at him with half-lidded eyes. "Oh, yeah?" I teased, my hips rolling against his, feeling the pressure of his erection rubbing against my clit through our clothes.

"Yeah." His hand gripped my ass tighter.

My poor fucking clit. If I were a guy, I'd have blue balls.

Damon's hands returned to my hips, my movements becoming more desperate. "Show the camera how much you want me."

I obeyed, my hips grinding against him, every motion

bringing me closer and closer to the brink. Damon's breathing stuttered as he watched me, his eyes dark with arousal.

He let in a sharp breath, hips bucking against mine. I could feel my lips tremble as his hand slid up under my skirt, fingers brushing my skin. "Damon. I want you," I whimpered with a broken voice.

Suddenly, he pulled his fingers away. "God, you don't know how bad I want to fuck you. But not in here... You deserve better."

I fought the urge to scream as I ached for more. Panting, I tried to steady my breathing as my body thrummed with need.

Damon gripped my chin and tipped it up so that I met his eyes. "It's gonna be perfect when we do," he said like he was so sure of it, in a deep and purposeful whisper, with promise.

I bit my bottom lip and nodded, words escaping me, tension running all through my body. The whole night blurred—a hazy skew of teasing touches and thrown glances, stolen moments. It left me teetering on the edge of desire.

I want him—no, I need him.

Each look, every frolicsome touch, was like spreading an insatiable craving in me until I was ready to go mad.

I stood, smoothing down my skirt, trying to pull myself together before leaving the booth. Damon cracking his knuckles had me looking over my shoulder. He didn't say a word, tight-faced as if fighting with himself. He suddenly reached out, grabbed me around the waist from behind, and pulled me into the warm strength of his body.

I felt the rise and fall of his chest against my back as I reached for the photos that had just finished printing and flipped through them. They were beautiful but also shockingly intimate. Our eyes locked with an unmistakable hunger in every shot. My lips were slightly parted, my eyes filled with desire, while the mask partially obscured Damon's face. We didn't just look like a couple posing for fun, we looked like two models from some dirty magazine. I swallowed hard. They were sensual and raw, rife with the unspoken energy that had built throughout the night. Damon's breath danced across my neck as he peered over my shoulder, looking at the photos with a satisfied groan.

THIRTEEN

WE GATHERED IN THE FRONT OF THE SCARE MAZE, MY NERVES ALREADY frayed. The fog began to curl and wrap around our feet and up our legs like a supernatural serpent. Dimmed and flickering purple lights cast their ghostly glow along the narrow path, giving only a peek to the gnarled branches framing the forbidding door. Overhead, threatening from the darkness, indistinctive shapes hung. Rusted chains swayed alongside butcher knives that moved back and forth with soft clanging by the cold breeze. This only made the unnatural silence more eerie, a fact that seemed strengthened by groaning from some invisible, shifting shadow within the distance.

Damon nudged Chase's shoulder, and the four of us dropped silently into the low-lit entrance of the maze.

Suddenly, Nadine lit up. "I say the girls go off separately. The first group to complete the maze wins."

I turned to Damon, and my eyes instantly locked onto the flicker of hesitation crossing his face. I could tell he wasn't too psyched about the idea of splitting up.

"Yeah, that sounds good," Chase added giddily, leaning in to kiss Nadine's cheek.

Nadine giggled, but Damon kept his eyes on me, seeming to wrestle with his decision to let me off on my own in some maze. *I'll be okay*, I mouthed to him.

The guys turned, going the other way as Nadine and I went on deeper into the maze. The labyrinth paths were narrow, enclosed with false wooden walls in a tangle of cobwebs. It seemed like somebody was around every bend and we realized all too well that something was waiting for an opportunity to pounce upon us at every turn.

We were at the bend in a sharp corner, and the scarecrow unexpectedly jumped out from the shadows, his ragged form looming over us.

"Fuck!" Nadine screamed, stumbling backward as her hands flew to her face. My heart pounded my chest, and I couldn't help but burst out in laughter.

"That scared the shit outta me," I panted, still trying to catch my breath as we pressed forward, knowing the worst was yet to come.

The deeper Nadine and I pressed into the maze, the more it wrapped us in thick fog— sticking to the earth as it pumped from hidden machines. We could hardly see but a few feet in front of our faces; the effect was both creepy and disorienting. Then, from the mist, coalescing like some sort of specter, stood a figure in disguise—a girl dressed up as Little Red Riding Hood. Her eyes were wild with some unrestrained energy, and her mouth twisted in a horrible grin that promised horrors. In her hands, she held a mock-wolf's head, dripping in mock-blood in a style far too dramatic.

"Holy shit!" I yelled, fear skating down my back.

"Why is Little Red so scary?" Nadine shrieked, clinging to my arm.

We went backwards for a second before pressing ahead.

Behind us, the actor's hilarious laughter echoed deeper into the maze.

We were doing great, making our way through the maze without one dead end. I just knew it. The guys would get creamed... Until we reached a fork in the path. A left or right decision was what we faced. Nadine pulled on my arm. "Come on, let's go right!"

But before I could follow her, a figure in a creepy plague doctor costume stepped out from behind a stack of wooden boxes. His black mask was ominous. Nadine reacted in a split second, freaking out and taking off into the fog. "Nadine!" I screamed, spinning around, but she was gone. A wave of panic washed over me. "Nadine!" I shouted again, but my words felt like they were getting consumed by the fog.

Suddenly, I was on my own. I began to walk, trying to catch up with her, scanning the path ahead for any movement. Ahead of me, a figure came into view. I felt relieved as I called out, "Nadine!"

The figure turned, but it wasn't Nadine; it was the old fortune teller from earlier. Her dark, unsettling eyes latched onto mine, and I froze, cold shivers running down my spine.

She leaped at me and before I could react, her gnarled hands latched onto my arm like a vise. Her fingernails, sharp and jagged, dug into my skin. "Do not go around that corner, child," she hissed. "El diablo awaits you!"

A cold dread seeped into my bones, which quickly turned to anger. I yanked my arm back against her grip. "Get off me!" But her nails sank deeper—sharp enough to break the skin. Blood welled where her claws dug in. "You're hurting me!"

Desperation was etched across the old lady's twisted features. Her wild, terror-filled eyes locked with mine as she pleaded.

In the surge of adrenaline, I shoved her off me harder than

I'd meant to. She hit the wall behind her with a thud and let out a whimper as she crumpled against it. Guilt flashed through me until I looked down at my arm, bleeding from the deep scratches she'd left behind.

My vision was blurred with tears as I stumbled forward, hitting something solid. I looked up to see him, Mitch, my ex-drug dealer, sheathed in a dark purple velvet. His face was a ghastly canvas, distorted with a skull tattoo.

The old lady's voice trembled behind me. "El diablo. He's been lurking in your shadows all night. I warned you." Her words hit me as I heard her back away, her whimpers getting distant. It made sense. She wasn't saying it about Damon. The whole time she looked straight through him like he was a ghost.

My feet were frozen in place as I locked eyes with his cold, soulless gaze. Every word Mitch spoke dripped with malice. "Hilary... Hilary... Hilary."

No one ever used my real name, apart from him. I tried to turn away, but he gripped my bleeding arm, and I went to let out a scream for help, but before I could, Mitch dropped his mouth to my ear and whispered, "I wouldn't do that if I were you." His breath was cold and foul against my ear. His grip on my upper arm tightened as he lifted it, and then he dragged his tongue across my blood, savoring every drop. "You always tasted amazing when you were frightened..."

A shiver of disgust rippled through me, and I started shaking uncontrollably. The sight and the feel of his vile touch made me feel sick.

I was utterly speechless, immobilized. I wanted to call out for Damon, but all that came from my throat were heavy breaths as tears blurred everything. *What the fuck is he doing here?*

"I've been trailing you all night," Mitch said. "Almost won you at the auction."

"Wha—what do you want, Mitch?" I tried to sound tough, but my voice shook.

A slow, sly grin spread across his face. "You fucking owe me, little one."

I tried to tear my arm out of his grasp, pulling it backward, but his fingers went deeper, resisting like metal.

"No!" I spit, the pound of my heartbeat loud in my ears. "No! You took what you wanted from me, and then left these ugly scars on my back!"

Mitch's fingers clamped tight onto my arm. He exhaled an icy laugh, low and creepy, as he brushed a strand of hair from my face with this creepy tenderness.

"What, did you forget about the dead body you woke up next to?"

The words hit me.

Dead body.

Dead... body.

Dead. Body.

I buried the memory deep in my mind, trying to erase it. I remembered that terrible morning—waking up beside a corpse. I remember his eyes were wide open, absolutely motionless—hard as stone. That vacant, frozen gaze sliced deep into me.

I knew he had been inside me as the tacky reminder stuck to my underwear.

Maybe I snapped. But there wasn't any blood, no sign of violence. How could I have done such a thing?

Mitch had been there. He said I must have killed him during a twisted, drug-fueled trip. I believed him. Blood was on my fucking hands.

But something felt off when I questioned Mitch about the body. I was too scared to question him to his face, so I just left it and accepted what Mitch told me. It was like there was a piece of the puzzle missing, something just didn't add up. Had he put the body there? I was high, after all, and Mitch was good at manipulating.

I don't have it in me to kill someone. I couldn't. *Could I?*

Mitch grabbed my cheeks, snapping me back to reality. His eyes feasted on my uncertainty. "I got rid of your little problem, didn't I?" There was malice in his tone. "You'll never be free from your debt."

The words choked me. I could feel the rising panic in my chest.

I let my legs buckle under me, with the weight of it like an avalanche swallowing me. All I really wanted to do at that moment was be taken away from it all. Mitch clung hard to my body, lifting me up like a rag doll.

My feet were no longer touching the ground. Panic set in. I wasn't walking, he was carrying me.

"Get the fuck off me!" I cried out loudly, wrestling in his grip, my body going crazy trying to tear itself free, but it was no use.

Mitch slammed me to the ground with brutal force, pinning my weight as he straddled my chest. His eyes burned with rage as he raised his hand. It came down hard and fast across the side of my face; the loud slap rang in my ears. A blast of sharp pain shot suddenly down my cheek, and for a moment, everything hazed around me. White spots flickered across my vision. The sharp, piercing ringing in my head was so loud that it covered up the world and made it impossible to pay attention to anything else. The shock of his slap stunned me, leaving me wordless.

The ringing wouldn't stop, deafening in the silence between us. My body shook, frozen by fear, as the taste of blood filled and dripped out of my mouth where I'd bitten my lip.

This was no nightmare I could run from. This was very much real. This was my past coming back to haunt me.

"Bitch. I told you not to fucking scream!" Mitch seethed as he picked me up, "Now we're gonna go on a little drive."

I was drifting into unconsciousness; the darkness was creeping in and there was nothing I could do. All my desperate, muffled cries vanished into the roughness of his palm as I tried to call out for Damon.

I need you, Damon.

Damon. I need you!

Everything became consumed by the screaming chaos of the scare maze, which engulfed us. The laughing from a distance and the horrified screams of strangers merged into some kind of nightmarish chaos.

My tears blurred my sight, but I saw the fire exit. He'd found it and he carried me through with terrifying ease into the blackness.

My face streamed with tears combined with blood, dripping profusely from my wounded face. He grunted as he carried my limp and helpless body through the forest.

We finally reached his car. With one hand, he fumbled to open the trunk. The latch clicked as it popped open, while his other arm kept me tightly pinned against him.

"Please, Mitch. Please don't do this!" I kicked out my legs, and my arms flailed about, but he was too strong—too insistent. He threw me into the trunk, and my back hit the metal. All the air in my lungs escaped at once.

Before I could plead with him, he whipped a gun out from the back of his waistband and thrust the cold barrel right at my face.

"Shut the fuck up!" he spat, his eyes filled with fury. "Don't make me shoot you right here!"

I froze, catching my breath. The way he looked at me, I knew he wasn't lying. The truth was something that I had seen before. He shot a man in the leg for taking his drugs. I knew he wouldn't think twice.

Fear seized me as the awful truth settled that if I didn't listen, I could be next.

He let the trunk drop with a vicious bang and the dark swept over me. After years of burying my guilt and fear, it all came flooding back, and I was drawing in it now. I tried to focus. My mind was chaos—full of questions. *What does Mitch want from me? Why, after all these years, am I being dragged back into this nightmare?*

The thick and choking fumes of oil and rubber filled my lungs. There was a relentless thud of the tires hitting the tarmac, each impact rattling through me like some kind of warning that I couldn't get away from. A cold chunk of metal that bored into my chest reminded me where I was. I fumbled with a shaking hand over the necklace against my breast. The cross—Damon's cross—was my tether to my life.

I squeezed until the tips of the cross dug into my hand and pierced the skin of my palm, confirming that I was still alive. Each teardrop that fell was a testament to the fear and help-lessness.

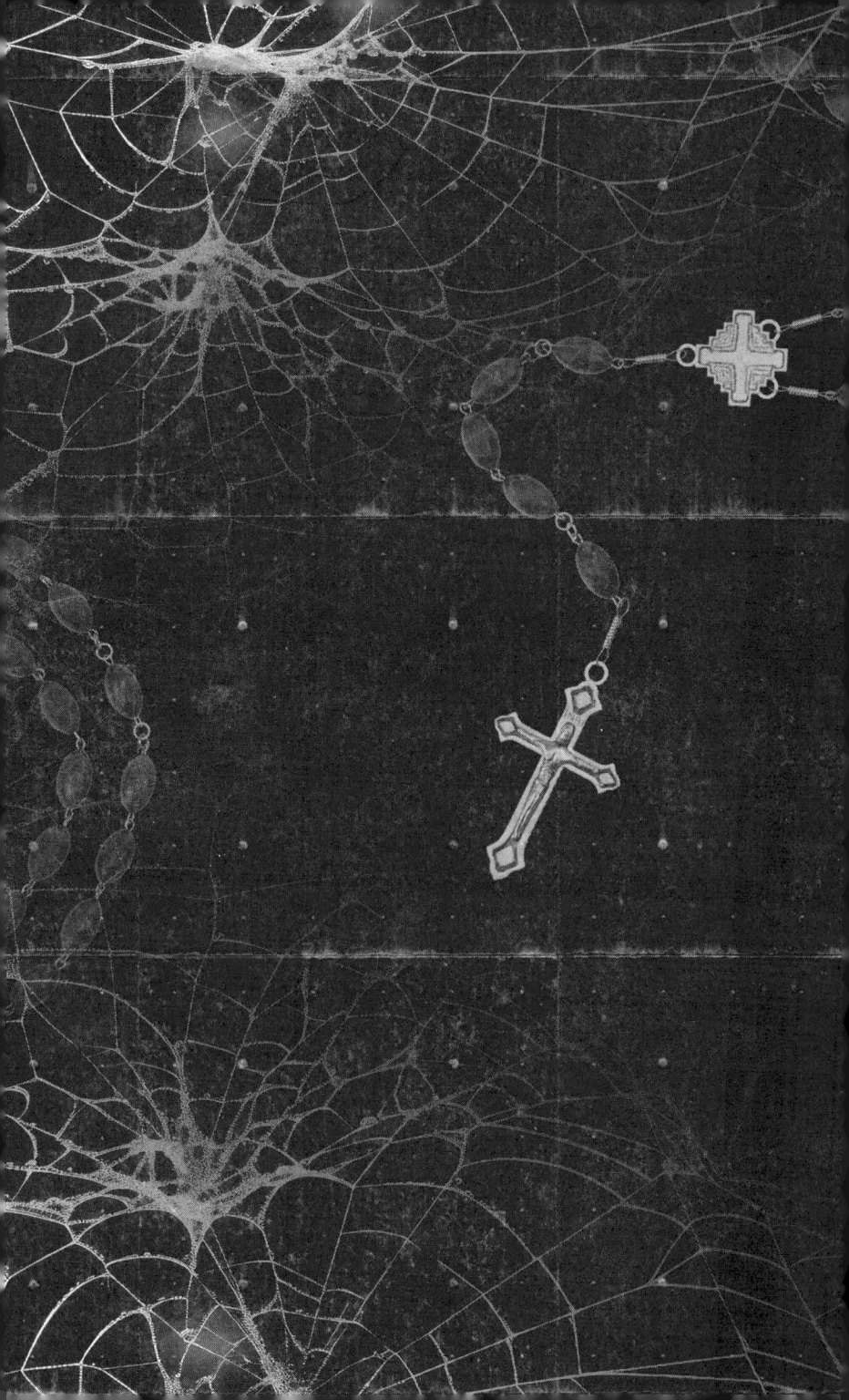

FOURTEEN

DAMON

I LEANED AGAINST THE FENCE, FEELING RATHER PROUD OF MYSELF FOR having outwitted Hilly. I could imagine her helplessly making her way through the maze, freaking out at every little scare.

Chase and I were near the exit, taking it easy while we puffed on our cigarettes. He sucked hard on his, dropping the ash to the floor. "You think they're at the halfway point by now?" He smiled.

"They're probably stuck or something."

Another few minutes later, I realized we were waiting much longer than expected. I threw the cigarette down, crushing it with my boot, and looked around. I noticed a small stall nearby and saw the flickering light of a hanging lantern shine upon trinkets and oddities displayed on a wooden table. The vendor —an elderly man arranging roses on display that were black as midnight, their petals velvety and rich. I walked over, leaving Chase to finish his cigarette. I only intended just to look while we waited for the girls, but there was something almost weirdly appealing about the roses. I dug into my pocket and fished out my cash. The stem was slick, almost artificially perfect. I twirled it between my fingers, thinking of how surprised Hilly would be when she emerged from the maze. I could clearly imagine her face—half annoyed, half amused—as I held out the flower.

Chase blew out a cloud of smoke as I walked back, grinning with raised eyebrows. "How romantic, dude..."

I shrugged, smirking. "I figured she'd need something to cheer her up after losing."

Chase chuckled and took another drag. "She's gonna like it."

With the rose in my hand, I stood by the exit, waiting for Hilly.

Suddenly, a girl in an angel outfit passed by. Her white wings shone under the moonlight. She cast a glance at the black rose and gave me a flirtatious smile.

"Ooh, is that for a beautiful lady?" she teased, obviously hoping for me to flirt back.

I barely acknowledged her. "Yup. She's currently walking around the maze. So you better move on." My voice was sharp but calm.

Her smirk faltered as surprise flickered in her eyes. She hesitated, then turned on her heel and continued to walk.

Chase snorted, shaking his head. "You really know how to shut 'em down, huh?" He chuckled darkly.

I shrugged, the stem turning beneath my fingers. I wasn't here for anyone but Hilly.

As the minutes ticked by and the girls still hadn't appeared from the maze, I started to get this feeling that something wasn't right. The more I stood there, the more unease chewed at my gut. I turned to Chase, who seemed more than happy to stand there puffing away on his cigarette.

Nadine suddenly appeared, out of breath as she rounded the corner, gasping. "Dammit!" she said, panting and doubling over. "You guys beat us."

Chase walked over to her and gave her a casual hug, but I barely even noticed. My eyes followed the dark exit to the maze, waiting for Hilly to come out, but she never did.

"Nadine. Where's Hilly?" I asked tightly.

Nadine straightened up and wiped the sweat off her forehead. "Oh, I lost her in there." She shrugged, trying to make it sound like nothing.

The words hit me in the pit of my stomach. My heart started racing; a coldness ran through me. "What do you mean you lost her in there?" I took a step forward, my voice dropping, sharpening like a blade. Rage simmered within me, coiled and ready to strike. Nadine raised one eyebrow, confused. "I don't know..." she whispered. "I just turned around, and she wasn't there anymore."

My patience snapped and I strode right up to her, grasping her shoulders. "Where did you see her last, Nadine?" I implored, shaking. Her eyes opened wide, and for a moment, she was absolutely stunned, just staring at me.

"Dude! What the fuck!" Chase yanked me from her. "She's probably lost! It's a maze!" His voice was loud yet sounded far away. My heart was like a drum inside my chest, and my mind wouldn't stop racing.

The rose fell from my fingers, its black petals coming loose as it hit the ground. I didn't say another word as I sprinted inside the maze. The world around me started shrinking until all that mattered was finding Hilly.

I fucking knew I shouldn't have let her wander off. Even if I found her safe, a part of me wanted to punish her for making me worry.

If anything bad had happened to her, I'd never forgive myself. She belonged to me—every thought, every breath, every inch of her. She was mine in ways no one else could understand.

The idea of losing her clawed at me, twisting my mind with rage. I'd drain blood from anyone who dared to come between us. No one could take her from me. Fucking *no one.*

I RAN THROUGH THE MAZE, YELLING HILLY'S NAME INTO THE DARK. Actors jumped out at me from behind various props. I didn't flinch once. The fog machines hissed as I ran past, puffing great clouds into the air. *This fucking maze should be scared of me.*

I rounded the corner and stumbled right into that old woman from earlier. She was terrified. Her eyes were wide with fear, but I didn't care. I grasped her face and made her look at me. The fear added fuel to the fire, as I tightened my grip on her chin. "Where is she?" I snarled.

"El... El diablo has her."

The words cut me like a knife, twisting me inside. "Who? Who is he?" I yelled, clutching tighter as she fell limp and fragile in my hand. I pulled her into a corner obscured by fog; it seemed to swirl around us like a living thing.

"A... A... devil man. In the purple suit," she panted, her eyes popping with fright. "He's been her shadow all night, lurking, watching and waiting."

Some fucker has Hilly. My girl.

Nobody had any right even to touch her, much less to look at her. She was mine in all respects. And now, someone had dared to take her away from me.

A wave of pure anger washed over me, blotting out everything else. All that mattered was that I got back what I'd lost. My fingers fell onto the old woman's throat, shaking violently from the rage. I pinned her against the wall with my grip, tightening instantly as I looked into her wide, terrified eyes.

Her life wasn't important. This old woman was just another hurdle, another worthless thing in my path. She'd lived long enough. If anything, I was doing her a favor and ending her misery.

My fingers pressed deeper into her throat, squeezing harder, feeling the life drain from her bit by bit.

I didn't care that she was begging for mercy with her eyes. All that mattered was that Hilly was gone. Nobody was going to get in the way of me getting her back. Not even this old woman hanging on to her last breaths.

She didn't even struggle. It was as if she knew her time had come. Her eyes rolled into the back of their sockets, and her mouth hung open as I heard her final raspy breath leave her old, frail lungs. I tightened my grip one final time and then released her. She crumbled into a heap on the floor, no more than old rags and gray hair.

I stood over her, watching for a moment as the anger still seethed in my veins. "Happy Halloween," I spat.

The darkness swallowed her whole as if the shadows were waiting to claim her.

Suddenly, the cross that I had given Hilly flashed into my mind. It was more than just a symbol. I wasn't prepared to take any chances when it came to my Hilly. Of course I wouldn't let her go to a Halloween party without knowing where she was one hundred percent of the time.

I pulled out my phone and opened the app. The map blipped her location, speeding north.

I ran to the first fire exit; the metallic door was open already. *I bet this is the way the fucker bought her out!*

I sprinted to my car, yanking open the glove box and grabbing for my gun. Its cold steel was a grim reminder of the stakes. Without hesitation, the tires screeched out of the parking lot, leaving behind a dust cloud. The road in front of me was an abyss where every shadow seemed to be a lurking threat. *I'm coming for you, Hilly. And I swear nothing will stop me. I'll kill anyone that stands in my way.*

FIFTEEN

HILLY — TWO YEARS AGO

I FELT THE PILL MITCH HAD GIVEN ME START TO TAKE HOLD, LIKE A FOG seeping into my head. My head was light, detached like it was floating above my body. The hallway swayed in all directions, shapes twisted in the dull light. Mitch's hand led me upstairs as my vision blurred, the edges softening. It felt like a nightmare coming into focus. I blinked hard, trying to focus on Mitch's face. The skull tattoo on his face stood out, but everything else seemed smeared and out of reach. He turned toward me—his grin slow, cruel.

"You're my best girl, aren't you?" The words echoed and I could only nod weakly, as if my body no longer belonged to me.

A figure waited at the top of the stairs. I squinted, but my eyes wouldn't allow me to focus on their face. I rubbed the heels of my palms over my eyes, but it made no difference. My chest clenched with a spike of panic, but my limbs felt too heavy. I tried to fight, but before I even registered it, Mitch pushed me forward.

The door swung open with a creak that seemed to pierce through the haze. My legs buckled and I fell onto the bed as the room closed over me.

"Mi—Mit—" I tried to call out. My fingers grasped for Mitch but wrapped around nothing but cold air.

"She'll be out cold in a second." Mitch's voice echoed as if he were standing far away, observing. "Then you can do whatever you want to her."

My eyelids fluttered, fighting to stay open. It was all going in slow motion, like an old film playing before me. I could just about make out the ceiling above me, cracked paint blurring. The dark shadow moved closer. I could smell him before I could see his face. Some foul, sour stench turned my stomach.

I heard footsteps go into the darkness, echoing through the room. It had to be Mitch, leaving me behind in this twisted nightmare.

I forced some words out, weak and broken. "I don't... want... this anymore."

The room fell silent, and for one second, I hoped he hadn't heard me. But then, thundering footsteps approached the bed.

A hand shot out from the dark and clamped around my throat. The pressure was suffocating as I gasped.

"You'll do whatever I want you to do," Mitch's voice hissed, venomous and cruel. He leaned in closer, reeking of alcohol. "I will do what I want with you, do you understand?"

The world slipped away, plunging me into darkness.

WHEN I FINALLY OPENED MY EYES, THE DARK OF THE ROOM swallowed me in. A ray of sun managed to creep through a crack in the curtains, dust particles floating within the beam.

I tried to sit up, but my body felt battered and bruised. A dull throbbing pulsed between my legs. I was shaking as I reached down, my fingers brushing against the wetness coating me. A sickening feeling churned in my gut as I brought my hand up slowly, and the stench hit me instantly. The smell was unmistakable, and I knew what happened. My body had been used.

I clutched the covers, tugging them tight against my naked body, shaking uncontrollably. I turned my head, eyes dropping to the other side of the bed. I was shocked to see a man lying beside me. They normally disappeared before I woke up. His eyes were cloudy, wide open, staring at the ceiling.

I couldn't help but reach out and touch his arm; something felt wrong. He was freezing and stiff. I tried to move him to get his attention, but he didn't even flinch.

Oh, shit.

As I swung my legs off the side of the bed, the room started to spin around me, my body shaking with anxiety and fear. My head was pounding as a scream tore from my throat, and then I tumbled out of bed, slamming down onto the hardwood floor. My knees cracked against the wood, but I barely felt it. Desperate, I crawled, hitting the wall as I backed myself into the corner.

Mitch stormed into the room. He eyed the bed, then back to me. "What have you fucking done, Hilary?"

My heart raced as confusion and terror rose through me. I brought my knees to my chest and hugged them as tightly as my arms would allow me, clenching the sheets tighter against my shaking body.

Mitch strode over to the bed, reaching down to press his fingers against the pale, clammy skin of the man's neck. He spoke again; his voice was flat, almost cold. "He's dead."

Denial tumbled out of my mouth. "No... no."

This can't be happening!

His face took on a serious tone as he squatted in front of me and narrowed his eyes. "You must've had a bad trip and lashed out. You stupid girl!"

"No... it wasn't me. I didn't... I don't remember..."

This doesn't feel real.

Something dark, something evil, lurked in Mitch's eyes as he grabbed my chin, his fingers digging into my skin. "I'll sort this out," he said calmly.

I swallowed hard. "But... But won't people know he's missing?"

Mitch didn't bat an eye. "I'll sort everything out. You do as I say." There was no room for discussion. "Now, get dressed."

His hand fell from my face, and I sank back onto the floor. My body seemed to go into slow motion, shaking as I crawled towards the scattered clothes. I fumbled for them, my hands clumsy, my heart pounding in my chest. Mitch's voice slithered through the silence behind me, creeping in like a snake. "Oh, Hilary," he said with perverted amusement. "From this day forward, you'll always owe me."

The words just seemed to hang there. It was as if the room had closed in upon me, choking and constricting, an ever-tightening noose pulling at my throat. I wanted to scream and run, yet I didn't know what to do.

HILLY

PRESENT DAY

I had been fighting my past for ages, just trying to keep my demons from taking over inside my head. Some memories just find their way back in, no matter how deep you bury them down. Some nights, I'd let myself think back to waking up next to random guys. I couldn't even picture their faces. They were just shadows lying next to me. I wanted those memories to rot in the dark corners of my brain.

There was no place left to run or hide as I was cuffed to a chair. My hands were bound tightly as the cold steel bit into my wrists, leaving angry red marks. I looked around the room, taking everything in.

I know this place.

I can never forget it.

The room was modern, with expensive furniture. The walls, once white, had streaks of neglect, and although expensive, the furniture was covered with dust. It was as though someone tried to create a perfect facade of luxury.

The fucking smell—it crawled into my lungs and dragged me back to where my demons were kept. It was the smell of fear, of helplessness, of every terrible thing that had happened between these walls.

I looked across and stared at the very embodiment of my greatest demon, Mitch. He sat there, his legs splayed in some sort of odd arrogance, as if he owned not just the room but even me in some perverted sort of way.

His presence was like a black hole, sucking everything in its vicinity into the darkness. First, his words were honey, dripping with sweetness, like coating on the bottom of a blade tipped with poison. He made me feel like somebody, the kind that can numb the void. And I was desperate. That desperation clouded my judgment.

He spoke to the fractured parts of my soul. He had a connection to them because he was the one who created them. It was all one big lie. I was just another notch on his belt, another broken thing for him to play with. He got me hooked on drugs before I could understand what the hell was going on. It was all pretty innocent at first—just to take the edge off. Pretty soon, I was chasing after that high, craving to feel anything other than the emptiness constantly clawing at me.

"You were always my best girl, little one," he stated, moving closer and touching my thigh. It was a phrase he tossed around casually. He made it sound like something to be proud of, like being his "best" was a badge of honor, except it wasn't. It was an ugly brand that I couldn't get rid of.

His voice sent shivers down my spine, but I willed myself to keep still, refusing to flinch beneath his penetrating gaze. I would not give him that satisfaction.

I'm not that girl anymore. I'm not his to break.

Being Mitch's "best girl" wasn't the glamorous title he made it out to be. He'd drug me, just enough to keep me numb. In those moments, the world would go into a haze. Everything was in slow motion. I'd slip into that nothingness, and that was his intention.

When I was high, he'd bring in his "friends." They treated me like a plaything, an object for their amusement—one after the other, hands roaming over my body as if I was just an empty vessel, hollowed out by drugs, a lifeless shell for them to use and discard. Mitch sometimes only looked on, leaning against the wall, a self-satisfied smile on his face.

I remembered at some point trying to scream, trying to push them away, but my body wouldn't listen. I wanted to disappear, but Mitch would make sure that didn't happen.

His finger trailed lightly down my thigh, dragging me back into the cold, suffocating weight of the room. The air felt thick and heavy as his touch anchored me into the nightmare I couldn't escape.

I gasped as my heart felt like it exploded against my ribs, but I tried to keep my face steady.

"Why now, Mitch?" I managed to ask. "It's been years..." Tears pricked the corners of my eyes.

He leaned in closer. "Seeing you tonight made me realize just how much I've missed that money-making pussy."

The word smacked me across my face. It tasted horrible in my throat.

I tried to shift in my seat, but the cuffs continued to dig into my skin. A shiver ran down my spine as Mitch's hand moved up, his fingers painfully wrapping around my thigh, pulling me closer to him.

His face hovered a few inches from mine, and his rancid breath was hot, grazing the side of my face. Every exhale smelled of cigarettes and something worse, sticking to my skin. A gravely sound escaped him as he drew a deep breath, filling his lungs with my scent, savoring it. "Is that fear I can smell?"

My limbs were immobilized, and I couldn't get my mind to catch up with what was happening. *I don't understand why now. After all this time!*

Mitch's laugh rumbled in the air. "Oh, yeah," he whispered, his lips brushing my ear. "I've missed this."

"I-I need to use the toilet," I stuttered.

Mitch's dark, predatory eyes were focused. At first, he didn't say anything,, letting the silence stretch long enough for me to regret speaking. Slowly, he rose from the chair, towering over me like a shadow. The gun caught my eye as he swung it at his side. My stomach twisted into a knot as he got closer. The floorboards under him creaked. He leaned down and started to uncuff me. "Don't fucking try anything stupid," he growled.

I gazed down at the raw red marks etched into my wrists. Mitch's hand shot out in a heartbeat, and his fingers fisted my hair. His grip was painfully tight as he dragged me out of the chair. My tears finally broke over my lashes and trailed down my cheeks.

Mitch gripped my arm like an unyielding vise, and almost pulled me out of my boots as we staggered along the suffocating dusty hallway. Once we reached the bathroom door, he gave me a hard push. Without thinking, my hands reached out to cushion the fall. I thudded into the door, and it flung open, casting me onto the cold tiles. Mitch's voice sliced through my whimpering. "The door stays open."

I wiped the tears from my swollen eyes, trying to steady my hands. The bathroom floor was too familiar; I'd cried here so many times before. Then something hit me—a thick, suffocating stench, a foul mix of piss and mildew clinging to the air.

I shook, tremors vibrating through me as I crumpled to my knees against the cold floor, bile rising in my throat. The world slowed while my mind raced, looking for a way out—any shred of hope. But there was nothing except Mitch with his gun.

"Go ahead." He flicked the gun toward the toilet. "I'm watching." His voice was laced with sadistic pleasure. The whole thing was a game to him. I crawled toward the toilet, my body feeling weak.

Slowly, I hiked my skirt up, my hands shaking as I sat down on the cold seat.

I heard him snigger. "No panties?" he chided with amusement. "You've always been such a filthy whore."

I felt so much shame. Every inch of me was exposed in ways I couldn't even comprehend. I hadn't felt like that in years, not since the last time I was in this very bathroom, trying to clean and scrub cum off myself. That memory hit me like a gut punch. Every second I spent here, the walls I'd worked so hard to build against the demons were crumbling, piece by little piece. Memories were clawing their way out of the darkness, flooding my mind like poison.

My fists clenched in my lap, and I dug my nails into my palms until they were marked. "What do you want from me?"

I heard the click of the gun cocking. His voice dropped down to a menacing whisper. "Once I've had my fun... you're going to make me some money."

No!

To him, my life was simply a transaction, a game from which he could play and profit.

"You can't do this to me!" I sobbed.

Mitch strode towards me, jamming his gun into my temple. My body squeezed tight in terror as the barrel was rammed deep into my skin.

He leaned in close, and I could feel the heat of his breath on my skin as he laughed. "I could dig up that fucking dead body and replace it with you," he hissed, his face mere inches from mine, feasting on the terror he saw reflected back. There was nothing—no empathy or humanity. Just a crazy hunger—an intense, twisted craving for control. I just knew, right then, he wouldn't back down. He never would.

A knock at the front door tore Mitch's attention away from me. His narrowed eyes still glowed with fury.

"If you move one inch off that toilet, you're gonna wish you were dead." He shoved the nozzle of the gun back into his waistband and stared at me for another minute. His weight shifted instantly, his body tensed. Then he walked toward the door.

My heart pounded hard against my chest.

Cops, maybe? Nadine? Damon?

That little spark of hope flared up in me, fragile and desperate. I hoped Damon would finally come and rescue me. I looked down at his cross and clung to it like a lifeline. It was my only connection to him.

If I make it out alive, maybe I can figure out my feelings.

My breath quickened, trying to catch the muffled sounds.

"Who is it?" Mitch's voice was loud.

For one second, it felt like the world held its breath with me.

"Trick or treat!" piped a little kid's voice, innocent and oblivious to the nightmare that was going on. Mitch grumbled in his sour way and I heard the creak of the door. "Here's three dollars. Now get outta here."

I could hear one of the kids, a bold little dude. "We're not interested in money, mister. We want candy."

I just envisioned Mitch looming over the trick-or-treaters. Their persistence had bought me precious seconds, and I didn't want to die in that bathroom on the piss-stained floor.

Using the toilet to hoist myself up with shaky legs, I could make out Mitch's voice well enough, and he was still trying to shoo the kids away.

There was a window to the left of me. It was my only chance of getting out. It was small, maybe too small, but I knew I had to try. Consciously, I took every step slowly. My fingers fumbled as I tried to jiggle it open, the frame itself screeching in protest—years of rust and grime trying to stop my efforts.

Come on, come on... I pleaded in my mind as my heartbeat resounded in my ears, second after second. I wiped my hands on my skirt, trying to get rid of the sweat, and then attempted to pry the window open in desperation.

Suddenly, a searing pain shot through my head as I was pulled backwards by my hair, jerking me away from the window. I was thrown onto the floor, my head hitting the toilet bowl, and blood started to trickle down my cheek. My scream came out raw and frantic, which seemed to fuel Mitch's rage more.

"I told you to stay fucking put! Why do you test my patience? You stupid bitch!" he hissed, standing over me, eyes afire, and the veins in his neck were pulsing.

"Mitch, please!" My chest was heaving as I struggled for breath. "Let me go!"

"Get on your knees..." he growled, like a predator ready to pounce on its prey.

I shook my head, my whole body shaking in my refusal—one final, small, desperate defense to keep the last shreds of my dignity, but Mitch wasn't going to have any of that.

"GET ON YOUR FUCKING KNEES!" he raged.

The words barely left his mouth before he clubbed the gun against the side of my head, splitting open my cut even more. Then, in one swift, quick motion, he took hold of my arm and pulled me off the floor, flinging me across it like a rag doll. The room spun around me; my sight was blinded by the pain and panic. He pushed me down again, landing on my knees.

"Open your mouth, you filthy little cum slut." I started to shake as I dropped my head and cried, trying to make sense of it all and how I'd gotten myself to this point, on my knees, in front of this monster. "Don't make me pry your mouth open."

I forced myself to look up. Tears blurred my eyes as I saw his smirk. Gradually, my lips parted. He said nothing but pushed the nuzzle of the gun into my mouth. Cold metal met my tongue.

All I wanted to do was back off, scream, and run. *How the fuck did I end up here? I want to be in Damon's arms. Safe.*

"Now... pretend it's my cock and suck," he ordered.

If it were his actual cock, I would have bitten off. But I was petrified and started sucking on the barrel as he loomed over me, his terrifying smile getting wider. He watched me, the hungry predator that he was, relishing every second. Then he slowly shut his eyes and lost himself in some sick daydream, throwing his head back with a loud, intentional crack of the neck. The sound was chilling—like a bone snapping. His smirk deepened as he exhaled very slowly, almost with satisfaction. "Those fucking lips. How I've missed them..."

I sobbed right onto the barrel, and my entire body was

shaking like crazy. The side of the gun caught the corner of my mouth and ripped my skin. Mitch didn't care that he was being too rough; he loved to inflict pain and see people bleed for him. The nasty taste of iron coated my tongue, mixing with the taste of blood.

I want it to end. Right here. Right in this filthy bathroom. I want him to pull the trigger.

If death is the way out, I'll welcome it.

Mitch pried his eyes open slowly, a sick smile curling his lips as he looked down at me. "That shit makes me wanna come." He pulled the gun from my mouth.

Before I could process the words, his hand shot out, clenching my hair by the root, and he pulled with so much strength. Pain shot across my scalp as he dragged me up the hall. I screamed, my voice echoing off the walls as I kicked and bucked, my legs flailing uselessly.

He began to whistle an eerie tune. The sound put a chill down my spine. He was mind-numbingly placid all of a sudden.

When we entered the kitchen, he let go of my hair and pushed me down. I curled up in the corner, bringing my knees up to my chest, and held tight.

I was terrified of him—how his fury could switch to icy calm in an instant. The raging, snarling beast had gone silent, but that quiet was far more dangerous. He continued whistling as his eyes stayed on mine while he pointed the gun at me, the barrel steady.

My body went rigid, racing in fear and looking for an out that didn't exist. He could end me right there if he wanted to, and part of me wished he would. Instead, he reached toward the counter with his free hand, fingers curling around a small pill bottle.

I knew what was in it. *Fentanyl.*

My heart sank, and nausea rolled through me. The pills

inside that bottle had stolen pieces of me before, leaving me hollow, and I knew exactly what would happen once he made me take them.

"You know what comes next." His eyes watched mine while one of his fingers removed the cap from the bottle with ease as if it were some sort of ritual he had perfected.

I screamed, my voice turning raw and full of terror, but he barely flinched. He laid the gun down on the kitchen counter and knelt next to me. "Shh... Shh."

Mitch placed a pill into my hand and then raised it, presenting it like some delicate gift. I flinched and tried to jerk back. "Once you take it," he murmured, "you'll be loose for me. Just like you always were."

I knew what the pill would do—how it would numb me and leave me helpless.

He picked up the pill from my palm and held it between his fingertips, then brought it to my mouth. "Open wide. You're good at that."

I shook my head. "N-o," I managed to choke out, the word trembling yet defiant.

His face twisted into a sudden rage. "FUCKING OPEN, YOU STUPID BITCH!" he shouted, his voice sounding like a thunder-clap. Without thinking, I spat at him. My saliva hit him directly in the eye, dripping down his cheek.

Oh, I'm dead.

I waited for him to slap me, but his jaw clenched, and he slowly wiped the spit away. He stood up and loomed over me as I desperately tried to predict his next action.

He scooped the gun off the counter and said nothing. Again, he wiped his face, then pointed the barrel at me, his finger flat against the trigger. "Get up," he said. It was eerie how calm he was as if nothing had happened. "Come here."

I stood up, my legs shaking beneath me, every step heavier

than the last, fear constricting my chest. I tightly held the cross necklace in my hand and inhaled deeply, trying to calm myself, drawing in what little strength I could from the tiny symbol of safety. *Damon Northwood.*

Mitch reached out, snatched the cross from around my neck, and flung it across the room. Then he grabbed the front of my corset, pulling me sharply toward him. I barely had time to gasp before his fury boiled over.

He threw my head hard down against the counter. I felt an ache inside my skull—my vision blurred. The cold surface pressed against my cheek as he bent me over. My skirt betrayed me and rose by itself. My body fought, straining hard against him, but it was impossible. His rage fed him even more strength as he pressed me down. "I'll show you how a whore gets fucked."

A stream of blood ran from the cut on my forehead, its heavy, metallic scent filling my mouth along with the tears streaming down my face as I sobbed. My chest rose and fell with each tortured breath. He pinned both my hands behind my back as he clamped onto them, his fingers digging in to hold me in place as if I were some object under his command.

He set the gun down on the counter, a few inches from my face. I heard his zipper slide open—one deliberate, slow move. I let out whimpers as I heard the rustling of fabric—his pants being pushed down.

I squeezed my eyes shut, still denying in my mind what was going to happen. My body shivered, buckling in anticipation. He was going to break me, make it so I could never be put back together again. *Death is better than this. Drugs were a luxury last time. I know what he is doing—making it so I remember everything, remember every feeling.*

I clenched my eyes shut, trying to prepare myself. I clung to the only thing that could possibly help me through my nightmare. I thought of Damon. I saw his arms around me, the reassurance and safety. I saw his power, the way that he seemed to make me believe that maybe I was salvageable. But that image shattered quickly when Mitch started wedging his knee between my legs to pry them apart. I tensed, beginning to feel sick as he adjusted himself. His cock pressed against me, his breath warm and disgusting as he rubbed on me.

I was angry with myself for not being able to fight back. *How could Damon even look at me after this? How could I look at myself?*

Tears streamed down my face, hitting the counter and mingling with blood sticking to my skin.

This is it. Prepare yourself, Hilly. Survive.

Then, without warning, an earsplitting bang sent a shockwave through the kitchen. Mitch's cock instantly went limp between my legs.

I forced my eyes open.

Standing in the doorway, framed by the moonlight, was Damon. "Trick or treat," he seethed. His eyes were burning with rage and fury. His nostrils flared and his chest heaved as he stood there, the gun aimed at Mitch. "Go for the gun, I dare you."

"What are you doing in my house? Get the fuck out!" Mitch yelled, letting my wrists go, pulling up his pants and taking a sudden step back. I stumbled a little, pulling my skirt down to try and maintain what dignity I had left, but I couldn't quite look at Damon. Shame weighed upon me like a physical burden, forcing my gaze to the floor.

"Hilly." Damon said my name with relief. "Come here."

How did he find me so quickly? How did he know where to look?

I hesitated for a moment, my body shaking as I willed my legs to move. I couldn't bring myself to look at him; I couldn't bear to see the disappointment in his eyes. So I looked at the blood-stained floor, my heart pounding as I moved toward him, feeling numb against everything.

Mitch yelled louder. "You're seriously saving this whore?! WHO EVEN ARE YOU?!"

Damon didn't even pay attention to Mitch's shouting; his hand tightened around the gun.

"Hey, Hilly," he said in a reassuring tone, despite the rage I could sense seeping from him. "Look at me... Look at me."

Looking up, into his eyes, and my chest painfully tightened as our gazes locked. "Did he rape you?" His tone was serious as his jaw tightened.

My head dropped, shaking from side to side. Damon exhaled loudly, his relief palpable. He wrapped his arm tightly around my shoulders, pulling me against his chest. I breathed him in, his scent flooding my nose. It made me feel safe in a way nothing else could. Tears slipped down my face, as he held me firm—his embrace protective, unyielding, like a shield I didn't know I needed.

In the silence, I heard shuffling from the other side of the kitchen.

I turned and saw Mitch going for his gun, his fingers stretching toward it. Without hesitation, Damon pulled the trigger.

It fired with a loud bang. The sound carried off the walls. Mitch let out a piercing scream as the bullet hit his hand, and blood sprayed everywhere. His scream echoed off the walls, full of pain and shock, but there was no mercy in Damon's eyes.

Mitch clutched his hand to his chest, then dropped to the floor, blood dripping onto the tiles under him.

How festive.

Damon aimed his gun at Mitch and kept his gaze locked on him. His voice emerged cold and detached. "Go wait in the car. I don't want you to see this."

But I wouldn't move. The fear that had paralyzed moments before morphed into something nearly unrecognizable— darker, stronger. I shook my head. "No, Damon. I wanna stay... I wanna see him die."

Damon turned to me, and in that brief moment, his anger was replaced with pride. A smirk danced across his lips slightly —a trace of satisfaction. Leaning in, he cupped the back of my head before softly kissing my forehead. "That's my strong girl."

There's no turning back.

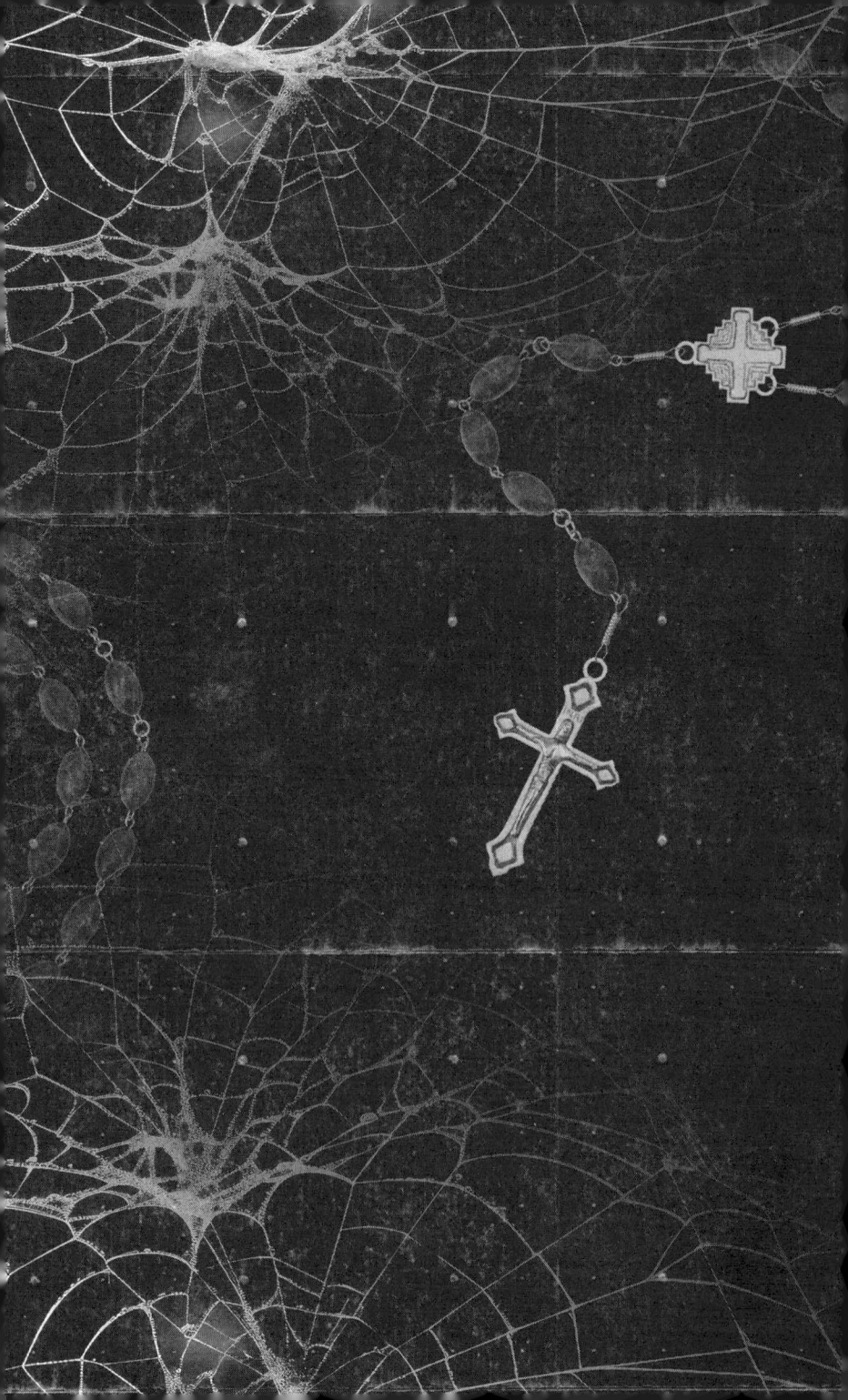

CHAPTER
SIXTEEN
DAMON

I DIDN'T WANT HILLY TO SEE THE MONSTER INSIDE OF ME THAT I buried deep. But when she told me she wanted him dead, it filled me with joy and excitement. She was facing her demons, and I couldn't have been prouder. *That's exactly what I'm going to do—make him pay, make him suffer, and watch as the life drains out of him.*

I could sense my own demons rearing their ugly heads. The way he was leaning her over that counter, trying to take and hurt what was mine. My anger became too much for me to control. My eyes were solely focused on the guy. *This motherfucker is gonna die today.*

I should have put a bullet in his skull and been done with it clean and fast. But my demons wanted more; they wanted to quench their thirst.

A quick death was too good for him. He didn't deserve mercy. I wanted him to feel every inch of the pain he'd inflicted on Hilly—his death slow, twisted and agonizing. I wanted him to beg, make him realize that he crossed far too many lines and that there was no way back for him. This motherfucker deserved everything that was coming his way.

"If I die, you're gonna have people coming after you. I hope you know that!" His yelling jerked me out of my thoughts and back into the room. He struggled pathetically in the corner of the kitchen, with his back against some cupboards. As I walked over to him, I couldn't help but chuckle at how he thought he could intimidate me with empty threats. "Let them come, and I will do the same to them." I didn't care about the words spilling from his lips. "This is the guy that scarred you, right?" I asked calmly, my head turned just enough to be able to glance at Hilly. A nod of hers told me what I needed. "What's his name?"

"Mitch," Hilly mumbled.

A flicker of panic darted in Mitch's eyes. "I supply drugs to powerful people. If you want money, I've got it."

This dumb cunt still didn't get it. He couldn't pay his way out of this. This was about Hilly. What he had done to her. The scars, the wounds that would never go away. How he'd become her demon, the ghost that haunted her.

I looked down at him, cowing under me. Tears welled up in his eyes as he looked up, broken and desperate. That was the first time I had ever seen a grown man cry like that. Tears and snot streamed down his face. It was fucking disgusting.

Fucking pathetic.

"This is for her," I seethed.

I pulled my arm back, fists clenched, sending my fist flying straight into his face. The sound of bones breaking was like music to my ears. His nose busted on impact, and blood splashed across the kitchen cupboards. His scream was muffled, but I didn't stop.

His screams were only feeding the darkness in me.

I hit him again, much harder; my knuckles found his teeth and I could feel them shatter. He lay in a heap of blood and tears, whimpering there like a wounded animal. Disgust began to build in me as I looked down at him, trembling in his own mess.

I kicked his chest. "Quit crying like a little bitch," I growled, wiping the spit off my lip and closing in on him.

"Sto—stop," he choked, his voice a broken whisper. His face was swollen, and his eyes were bulging as if terror were the only thing keeping him conscious.

I turned back to Hilly, seeking her approval. She smirked and stood there staring at me—cold and pitiless.

I turned back and grasped his collar. His body was limp in my grip, like a rag doll. "Stop?" I snarled, repeating the word back at him. He was drained, just barely hanging onto whatever thread of hope he'd left. I leaned in close, my breath brushing his ear as I whispered through clenched teeth, "You know, I bet she said that, too."

I let him go, and he crumpled to the floor, his body landing in a dull thud. He tried pleading again. *His voice is really pissing me off.*

My eyes scanned over the counters and landed on the knife block sitting next to the stove. An idea filtered through my brain, and my lips tugged upward into a dark smile.

I pulled a knife and ran my thumb across its edge. *Perfect.*

My pulse was racing. I could already imagine the knife slicing through him. With my free hand, I threw another hard punch at his face. His head snapped back and he went limp—out cold.

I hunched over him, reveling in the calm before the storm. I slipped my fingers through his bloody lips and forced his mouth open, clamping on his tongue. Without giving it a second thought, I slipped the knife under it and, with some pressure and a flick of my wrist, I sliced his tongue clean off.

Blood filled his mouth and trickled down the side of his face onto the floor. The severed tongue fell to the floor with a disgusting *slap.*

He came around, his body running riot with spasms, his eyes going wide with fear, letting out a muffled scream. It was music, and I feasted on his cries. His suffering was making me feel so good, and I couldn't help but enjoy every second of it.

Mitch laid on the ground, kicking weakly, but he was no more than a slug writhing in his blood. Incoherent gurgles came from his throat as crimson overflowed from his mouth, staining everything red. No pity came from me.

Hilly stepped close, her face glaring down at him with no remorse.

His screams finally diminished as his body grew limp again.

I dropped to my knees beside him, grabbed the waistband of his pants, and jerked them down in one vicious pull.

"What the fuck are you doing?" Hilly asked behind me.

I didn't even turn my head for her. "This rapist ain't going to hell with a cock."

He lay there so small, so pathetic. It was almost funny how little he seemed now, stripped of everything, irreparably broken.

As I raised his cock, vomit rose to the back of my throat. *I really should have worn gloves.*

The weight of it in my hand was repulsive, warm, slick, and limp like a sea cucumber. In one swift motion, I cut it clean off. It sliced through the flesh with ease, flopping in my hand, trickling blood. I couldn't help bursting into a fit of laughter. I waved it back and forth, sending droplets of blood flying onto the floor. I didn't stop there. Some kind of sick compulsion took over. Before I even had time to think, I simply leaned over and slapped the severed cock hard across Mitch's blood-soaked face. The wet smack seemed to echo. His limp body jerked involuntarily. I just stood there for a moment, staring at what I'd done, and something inside just snapped. Laughter erupted from deep inside.

Hilly stared at me, speechless.

"Sorry..." I mumbled, laughing under my breath as I chucked the severed cock across the room.

"Oh, my God! It went out the window!" Hilly exclaimed.

A shot in a million! Fuck yeah!

I turned to Hilly, but her eyes were empty—no fear, no anger, not even relief. Her face was a mask, blank and unreadable, and it gnawed at me. *What is she thinking? Is she judging me? Does she see something different in me now?*

I needed her to understand it was for her. Every drop of blood, every fracture, it was all because of her. I would kill anyone from her past, tear apart any demon that would try to crawl its way back into her life. I wanted her to feel safe, to understand that I'd burn the world down before I let anyone harm her again. But I stood there, soaked in his blood, waiting for something, anything, from her.

Glinting faintly in the light, I saw my cross lying on the bloodstained floor. Without a second thought, I walked over and picked it up. I went to place it around her neck, but she stopped me. Something dark flickered in her eyes. "Wait. I have an idea."

She dropped to her knees. Mitch must have gained consciousness because his bloodied hand feebly rose toward her—a pitiful request for mercy.

Without saying a word she raised the cross high above her head and, with a face twisted in rage, brought it down with all her strength into his eye. I could hear the sound of cracking bone and wet squelching of flesh as she dug the cross deeper, screaming at every thrust. "Asshole! Fucking asshole!"

Her voice was hoarse as she screamed at him, arms unmerciful, the cross pounding into his skull with a wildness beyond control. An eyeball flew across the room like some obscene missile. Mitch's body started to spasm, jerking violently as she continued her onslaught.

Blood sprayed across her hands and face. The scene was gory but also arousing. She didn't stop. "Atta girl!"

I'm so fucking impressed.

Mitch's eye was nothing but a black, bloody hole. The man who used to have power over her was dead.

Hilly stood next to me, panting, covered in blood. She drew a big quivering breath and shook her head like she was shaking off all of what just happened. I reached for her hand. My fingers slipped between hers, latching on tight, anchoring the both of us into this moment. "He's dead." I tried soothing her, placing my necklace back around her neck. "You don't have to worry now."

Her face was streaked with blood, tears streaming down her cheeks. Suddenly, she seemed to look broken and fragile. "I'll always have to worry. He was just one demon that taunted me. I have many more."

What does she mean? It made my blood boil, but most of all, it made my heart ache.

I brushed the tears off her face. My thumb swished streaks of blood clear. "Yeah? Well, I'll fight them all with you, Hilly. Every last one."

I guided her to the sink, snatching up a cloth and soaking it under running water. She didn't say a word, didn't move. I began to clean the blood from her hands and her face as tenderly as possible, as if it would wash not only the mess of the night but the years of scars underneath. "You will never be alone... Never. I will protect you from whatever demons, and I will end them all, just to make sure that you're safe, Hilly." My words were a promise. Of course, it couldn't be fixed overnight.

What I would do was stand next to her in the dark and fight with her until the last fucker vanished. Hilly meant the world to me. Her pain, her scars, her demons—they were mine to carry now, too. There was no way in the world I would ever let her face any of it alone again. She was mine, and I would protect her with everything I had. *It's for her. It's all for her.*

SEVENTEEN

HILLY

DAMON FUCKING SAVED ME—NO HESITATION, NO MERCY. HE unleashed his fury on Mitch, showing him no restraint. I loved every brutal sound of his bones cracking. Every bone that Damon broke had broken a link in the chain that Mitch had around me; every punch and slice of the blade freed more and more. Damon didn't stop until Mitch was utterly destroyed.

I was still scared that Damon might have seen things differently. He had watched me snap, lose control and free all my pent-up anger that I had been harboring for so many years. It felt good, freeing, and amazing.

I grabbed the necklace and plunged the cross pendant into Mitch's eye, spraying his blood everywhere. Damon didn't even flinch. I was so fucking consumed by rage, wanting Mitch to suffer every bit of pain I'd endured. *Payback's a bitch, huh, Mitch?*

My mind started going crazy.

I still didn't understand why Damon wanted me. How could he even stand to touch me after knowing what I'd been through, after seeing what I'd done?

My past was ugly and tainted. I just wanted to be an

unmarked woman. He should've walked away the moment he knew the truth. *But he didn't.*

We were miles away from Mitch's. The car jerked, and the bumps in the road pulled me out of my thoughts. Inside the car, the dark, silent space was heavy with what we had just done. Damon seemed unfazed, but I was still processing tonight's events.

Damon blew out a big breath. "Are you okay?" He glanced at me with wide eyes. "That's a stupid question. I'm sorry."

I was relieved yet still horrified by everything that had happened. I looked up at the full moon, its glow following along beside the car like a silent companion. Bats flew across in the distance. It was almost ironically appropriate. It was Halloween, and everything about the night was like a real-life horror story.

It weighed on me and with each passing second, I couldn't hold it inside anymore. Damon needed to know the truth. He deserved it, even if it changed everything. "I've killed before, Damon..."

I couldn't look at him. I wouldn't. I kept my gaze on the moon as though somehow that distant light could absolve me of the blood that I had on my hands.

He chuckled. "You say that like it's supposed to bother me," he said, turning to me with a grin. "I know you would've had your reasons. You're not a natural-born killer."

I searched his face for any trace of disgust, but instead, he merely shook his head, smiling, as if the weight of what I'd just told him was no more than an afterthought.

"So..." I take a deep breath before I continue. "Do you still see as Hilly? Or as something else?"

Damon scoffed, his eyes rolling. "You just watched me cut a man's tongue out of his mouth. Then his cock." He shrugged nonchalantly. "And you're worried I'm gonna see you differently? Everyone's got their sinful shadows."

"Sinful shadows?" I repeated.

He nodded as his eyes were fixed upon the road. "Something you have done in the past that is just so sinful, it clings on you and becomes a part of you. No matter how hard you try to shake it, it's always there, lurking behind you like a shadow."

His words seemed to hang there in the silence between us, digging deep into my chest. *Sinful shadows.* It sounded like the perfect description of everything I carried, all that had twisted me into what I'd become.

Damon's hand inched onto my thigh, his thumb tracing circles against my skin. My heart started to race in my chest. But he kept his gaze firmly on the road, utterly unaffected. He was calm. Too damn calm.

My mind started to spiral, the weight of everything I had done crashing over me all at once. I felt my breathing pick up, shallow gasps, the car walls closing on me. The air seemed thick and suffocating.

"Pull over."

"What?" Damon asked, confused.

Panic clawed at me. "Pull over!"

Saying nothing, Damon pulled over onto the shoulder, where gravel crunched beneath the tires. I didn't wait. The second the car stopped, I yanked open the door and took off, running into the dark trees.

"Hilly... HILLY!"

I ran, my chest burning as cobwebs and branches whipped against my face, twigs snapping beneath my feet. With each step, the cuts on my skin deepened, the forest clawing at me, tearing into my flesh. But I didn't care. All I knew was that I had to escape from everything. The cold night air ripped through my lungs and whipped at my cheeks as I continued to gain distance from Damon.

My mind unraveled, and it all became too much to bear. Mitch's dead eyes flashed in my head, the feel of the cross in my hand. When Damon sliced his tongue. Each image hit, drowning me in panic. I could taste blood in the back of my throat as each breath tore my insides to shreds.

The trees were closing in on me tighter and tighter, the forest growing darker, my legs burning, but I couldn't stop myself. I wouldn't. I wanted to run until nothing was left of me. Another shadow in the dark, lost to the night.

Suddenly, my foot caught something solid, and I fell onto cold ground. The wind was knocked out of me. Grunting, I leveraged myself up on some fallen stone wall. That's when I saw it. A graveyard a few yards in front of me.

The graves looked ancient, whittled down by time, leaning at odd angles. The fog wrapped the place in an eerie stillness. I stared, my chest heaving. The whole thing felt surreal, like a hallucination.

I ran, my feet pounding through crispy leaves and wet earth. I knew I had to get away. A gravestone loomed ahead of the others; it seemed darker and looked like it had been there the longest. A skull was etched deep into the stone, its hollow eyes staring back toward me.

I collapsed in front of it, letting myself slump to the ground, leaning back against the stone with its hard edges digging into my back. I buried my face into my hands and pressed hard against my skull to block out the flood of thoughts that threatened to consume me.

Fuck off!

Fuck off!

Just fuck off!

I ran my fingers over my scalp and tugged on my hair,

inflicting my own pain to see if this was actually real. This was all too much for me to handle. I wanted to scream, to tear myself apart. But the only thing I could do was sit there, pressed against the gravestone, as the fog grew thick around me, encasing me in its chill grasp.

Then I felt someone's fingers digging deep into my shoulders. Instinctively, my eyes screwed tightly shut, and I kicked and flailed with all remaining strength in my body.

"Goddamn it, Hilly, it's me!" Damon's voice cut through the chaos. But I didn't care. My mind was racing in circles, lost in that fear, smothered under the weight of all of it. I couldn't stop. My body fought on instinct, legs kicking wildly, arms flailing as if I could somehow push the nightmare away.

Damon straddled my hips, pulling both wrists into one hand and pinning them above my head. He used his free hand to grab my chin and force me to look at him. His full weight pinned me against the chill, damp earth below. Finally, my muscles gave up. A wave of fatigue washed over me and I had no fight left in me. I opened my eyes, and I saw Damon right on top of me, his face inches from mine. There was no sign of anger, just concern. "Shh... I've got you, beautiful. You're not that person anymore. You're safe." He moved my tangled hair away from my face. His touch was so soft that it was almost calming. As my sobs broke loose, I couldn't help as tears overflowed out the corner of my eyes and fell down my temples.

I know I'm safe. Yet somehow my body will never forget.

Damon didn't move. He just laid on top of me, holding me down, anchoring me into the ground. He was the only thing that kept me from slipping into a black hole. "Hilly, look at me."

He rested his forehead against mine and stared straight into my soul. His eyes were so dark, nearly black in the moonlight. They pinned me in place, keeping me from getting lost.

His hand cupped my cheek, his palm soft as his thumb

stroked the falling tears away. "Don't ever run away from me again," he whispered, his words full of emotion. "I almost lost you once... I'm not going to let that happen again. Do you understand?"

His words began to sink in, tightening my chest. I wanted to say something, but I slowly shook my head. My lips began to quiver, and my heart raced.

He didn't wait for words, which was good since I had none. He simply closed the space between us. His hand wrapped behind my neck and drew me in. His lips were warm, moving against mine in a gentle caress. Every stroke of his tongue felt as if he was telling me everything he wanted to say—how much he cared, how much he wanted to protect me, how much he was scared to lose me.

I melted into him, my hands reaching for his chest, clutching his shirt as if he were my only lifeline. The graveyard melted into the background. There was nothing that mattered more than me and Damon.

His breathing mingled with mine as we both worked to catch our breath. "You're safe with me."

I believe him.

Damon had stripped me bare, layer by layer. The barriers I built, the walls I constructed so carefully, came crashing down with every kiss, every touch, and every hot breath on my neck. Around him, I was weak. Just one look, one word, one touch, and I knew he would have me completely undone. Yet somehow, being with him kept me feeling alive and in control of myself more than ever.

When he touched me, he made me feel seen in a way nobody else had ever made me feel.

But that wasn't the plan. I wasn't supposed to want or need him like this. He was going to be my stepbrother.

Each time he kissed me, he drew me further into something

from which there was no escape. What was meant to be a bit of fun had turned into a want, a need, my everything. I was lost in Damon and didn't know if I wanted to find my way back.

Damon's lips left mine, leaving a warmth that begged me to reach out and pull him back. Instead, he stood with a smirk on his face and offered his hand. I took it, and with ease, he pulled me to my feet. There was something different in his expression, a flicker of focus as his eyes shifted past me. Curious, I turned to see what had caught his attention.

Behind us stood a small, stone church. The weathered and worn structure was almost mesmerizing. The lead-framed, stained glass windows glinted weakly in the silvery moonlight. The colors were not as bright but detailed, telling tales long forgotten. Ivy and light pink roses crawled up the stone sides, almost ingesting the ancient wood of the door. It had clearly been left for many years to disintegrate, but it was hauntingly beautiful. "Wow," I breathed.

Damon didn't hesitate. He placed an arm around my waist, hauling me off the ground. I squealed in surprise as he slung me over his shoulder. The world spun as hair fell over my face while he carried me toward the church.

With each step, the church loomed closer, it's dark silhouette against the night. Everything in the world seemed topsy-turvy.

Damon set me down as he took a step toward the door. The ivy, which had grown thick over the wood, clung to it like a second skin, but in one quick tug, he removed them. He turned the handle, and after a few moments, the door let out a groan and swung wide as if it had waited years for us.

He entered first, his eyes scanning the inside, and I followed close behind, stepping into the shadowy space.

Wow.

The church was a beautiful but forgotten masterpiece.

Along each side of the hall, wooden benches were dull and scratched from use over the years. A deep red, dusty carpet stretched down the center aisle. Moonlight streamed through the colored panes of the glass-stained windows, casting beautiful patches of blue, green, and red across stone floors.

Far down the opposite end of the church stood an altar of white marble unscarred by time. It was draped with a torn cloth drooping over the edge, frayed and forgotten.

There was a chill outside, but for some reason felt colder inside, as if time had frozen the air inside the church. A shiver wracked through my body, the icy chill seeping right into my bones. Though the church was in disrepair, the air inside wasn't heavy with the stench of decay. Instead, the faint fragrance of roses wafted in through the broken windows. The soft scent mingled with the dust and worn wood.

This church is truly breathtaking.

Damon must have seen me shudder as he went over to an old iron stand where a few dust-covered candles stood. He pulled out his lighter and gave it a flick. At first, the candle sputtered, refusing to light, then sprang to life. The warm glow spread through the church, casting flickering shadows across the walls. The flame caught tiny dust particles hanging in the air, making it fizzle and spark.

The church was lit only by the soft light of the candles and the pale, ethereal glow of the moon. It looked even more beautiful as if the space had come alive just for us.

"Come here, beautiful." Damon stepped closer, his hand sliding around my waist to pull me close. His lips found the soft part of my neck, and his kisses were slow. A sigh escaped me as his touch was intoxicating—a kind of drug that took me somewhere else, somewhere I didn't have to think.

His hands, his lips. They brought me to life as if nothing else mattered. I wanted to lose myself in it, in him, and forget all the things that haunted me.

But something in the back of my mind dug its claws deep and held tight to gnawing doubt. It refused to let go and give in to the power of the moment.

I stumbled backward, my heart pounding. I moved just out of Damon's grasp. His eyes showed a flash of concern, but he didn't say a word. He just stood there and waited. "Why do you want me? How can you even touch me?" I took a deep breath. "My past... My fucking past."

I scanned his face for anything that might explain why he wasn't disgusted. I couldn't understand how someone like him, who knew I was tainted, could want to hold, kiss, and touch me. Deep inside, I couldn't shake the fear that the closer he got, the more likely he'd realize and pull away for good.

"Right. Come with me." Damon took my hand, pulling me toward the far corner of the church to a small, antique, wooden confession box standing half-concealed in shadow. Aged and worn, the wood had darkened from years of neglect, yet still standing. He hauled the door open, the hinges loudly screeched in the empty church, and gestured for me to step inside.

I hesitated, not certain where this was going, but the gravity in his eyes seemed to swallow all my nerves. I took a seat on the small bench. The space felt small; the air was thick with the scent of musk and forgotten prayers. The mesh screen that divided the two enclosures allowed a little view of Damon as he sat opposite me.

I tried to lighten the mood and chuckle nervously. "Is this the part where I say, 'forgive me, Father, for I have sinned?'"

Damon didn't laugh. "Hilly... You keep talking about your past like it defines you. But I think it's about time you hear about mine."

My stomach coiled at his words. It wasn't what I had expected.

"Just promise me you won't run away," he said. His tone made me sit up straighter.

"I swear."

"I'm not the man you think I am. Mitch isn't the first person I've hurt," Damon began. He took a deep breath. "I've... I've killed before and done some terrible things."

My body immediately tightened.

"I killed my sister's drug dealer and her best friend, who betrayed her." He paused, his voice breaking. "I killed the clown at the gas station." In that instant, it clicked. "And... when I went looking for you in the maze... I killed that crazy old lady."

His voice fell flat, detached as if reading a checklist of sins. I sat there, frozen, and let the weight of his words sink in. I should've been scared, horrified, but I wasn't. There was a surreal calm, a sense that maybe I had always known Damon carried shadows like these. "The difference between me and you. You're a fighter, and I'm a killer. I would do anything for those I care about."

His words struck me deeply, not due to their shock value, but because of the way he delivered them—like a man who had accepted the truth about himself a long time ago, like a man beyond redemption. I didn't see the killer he thought he was, but a man who cared enough to kill for *me*.

"I'd torture anyone who ever hurt you, Hilly." Damon's voice took a more menacing tone as he cracked his knuckles. "I'd drain every last drop of blood from their body." He paused. "I'd sell my soul for you... if I had one. I know there's a place in Hell waiting for me."

Hell doesn't deserve him. There's nothing he could do to make me stop wanting him.

I shifted on the bench, making a loud creak echo across the

church, and it seemed like the world outside held its breath with me.

"Say something... anything."

"Why? Why would you kill for me?"

"I just told you I've killed multiple people, and you're asking why I would kill for you?"

"But... I'm nothing, Damon."

"Why do you do that? You put yourself down all the time! You're *everything*. I couldn't save my sister, but I can save you. From the moment I met you and saw those scars, I knew. All you've ever wanted was to feel safe."

He wasn't wrong. Every inch of me ached for safety, for a place that wasn't haunted by my past. Yet somehow, he saw right through me. *He saw me for who I was.*

I could hear the soft rustle of his feet as he came out of the confession box. The door swung open, and I lifted my head toward him. Standing at the threshold, bathed in the soft glow of candlelight, he looked like a god.

"And I want you all to myself, Hilly," he growled, so possessively. "No other man will ever touch you again."

He held out his hand, and without thinking, I reached out. We touched, and a burst of heat spread through me. He hauled me up off the bench and before I could catch my breath, his arms were around my waist, holding me against him. Strong, firm. It was as if he was afraid I might slip away. The world outside evaporated into nothingness. I felt nothing but him— the beat of his heart loud in his chest, his warm breath skimming over my skin.

Damon wet his lips with the tip of his tongue before they met mine. He was domineering as our tongues met urgently. His hands started moving over my back, his fingertips tracing the back of my corset as our bodies dissolved against each other.

I could feel the heat radiating off of him, tension running through the muscles of his arms.

He's strong. So fucking strong.

He took control, hands firm as he pushed me against the cold marble altar. The chill of the stone sent a shiver through me. I groaned into his mouth, my body arching as our breaths became one. He pressed his chest to mine and, with a rough, teasing bite, caught my bottom lip between his teeth. I couldn't help it, a moan escaped from my lips as my whole body went into sensory overload, reacting to his every move. His dominance over me was undeniable, and I found myself wanting more.

His mouth broke away from mine, his lips red and swollen from our kiss. "I want to see you... All of you."

The way he said it made me feel like I could melt right into the altar behind me. His fingers found the lace of my corset and began untying. He paused for a moment, his eyes flicking up to meet mine, seeking approval. Out of breath, I gave him a slow nod, smirking as I leaned back against the altar, offering myself up to him.

His eyes darkened as he undid the lace. Finally, the corset came loose and slithered from my body to the floor. My nipples were hard, pressed against the mesh of my top. Damon's hands ran down over my stomach and grasped the hem of my top, pulling the thin material over my head. The moment it was gone, my breasts spilled out.

He stepped back, his eyes devouring every inch of me, lingering on my nipples. "You're perfect," he breathed.

I could feel his hunger, the rising and falling of his chest as he struggled to restrain himself.

I reached for his belt, tugging him closer until our bodies were practically flush against each other. My fingers flew to the buttons on his shirt, desperate to run my hands all over him.

Our lips met again, and I started working his buttons, one after another. His shirt fell open, and my hand went down the hard lines of his chest, tracing the muscles flexing beneath my fingertips. My palm skimmed over the ridges of his chiseled abs, feeling the emanating heat of his skin.

I pulled his shirt off and flung it somewhere, not caring where it landed. The second it was off, his lips were on my neck, and my eyes fluttered as his scent filled my senses.

His hands went lower, sliding over my waist with purpose. When they reached my ass, he squeezed hard enough to make me jolt, before he continued down to the backs of my thighs. He pulled me up and placed me on the cold marble altar. My legs dropped over the edge. The chill of the stone immediately bit into my skin. All I could focus on was him. The church walls were amplifying every noise, moan, and breathless gasp.

He stepped between my legs, his body pressing close as I kicked off my boots. His hands were back at my waist already, tugging down my skirt.

The stained glass let moonlight filter in, casting fractured colors across his features. I sat up on the altar, naked, exposed, my heart racing in my chest. Smitten, yet utterly consumed by him.

"Fuck," he mumbled, his eyes eating up every inch of my body. His breath hitched as if he couldn't quite believe I was his for the taking. It felt like I was his entire world.

I trust him.

"Hilly, I plan on fucking you in all the ways you deserve."

His words sent a wave of weakness through me, making my body shake at the promise. The ache and wetness between my legs became unbearable. Not thinking, I parted my legs further and invited him closer.

Every nerve in my body was on fire, raging inside me, trying to find release. Damon was the only one that could do that. I needed him more than ever, and the hunger in his eyes told me he was about to claim what he wanted.

"You ready for this?" he asked.

I nodded, unable to even utter a word because my throat had dried up from the anticipation. His tongue quickly darted out and tasted my erect nipple. Then his fingers traced a path down my throat, leaving trails of goosebumps. They slid down, brushing against my stomach. "You'll never want any other man after this."

Damon wasted no time; his fingers delved between my thighs in search of the wetness there.

"You're so wet for me. Do you like it when I touch you here?" His thumb pressed against my clit, circling slowly, sending waves of pleasure through me. I bucked my hips against his hand, desperate for friction.

"Damon..." My voice broke as I pleaded. I was at his mercy, and he knew it.

He yanked his hand away from my pussy, and for a second, there was a flash of panic across my face. His mouth crashed onto mine, his tongue forcing its way into my mouth, hard and commanding.

His other hand cupped my face. "Look at me," he ordered, breaking the kiss. I met his gaze. "You're going to surrender to everything I offer right here on this altar."

My breath hitched, and I nodded. The thought of being claimed in such a sacred place sent another wave of arousal crashing through me.

Damon's hand moved back to my pussy, and his fingers easily glided into my wet folds. He pushed two fingers inside, and I gasped at the sudden fullness. He curled his fingers and hit a spot deep inside me. I couldn't help but grind against him.

"That's it," he growled. "Look at you, riding my fingers."

He thrust in and out of me; his strokes hit that sweet spot, a teasing pushed me further toward the edge. I could feel a ball of heat growing in my lower stomach. "Oh, fuck."

"Feels good, doesn't it?" Damon cupped my face, his thumb grazing over my mouth. "Tell me how much you're aching for it, Hilly."

I looked up at him through half-lidded eyes, his features almost demonic. "Yes," I moaned. "Fuck yes, Damon..."

"Look how your tight pussy stretches for me."

I arched my back and moaned softly as his fingers continued to stretch me in ways I'd never felt. I could feel my inner walls tighten. The cool air of the church heightened everything.

"You're so fucking hungry for my fingers." His other hand slid down my hip and pulled me closer against him.

I could hear the suctioning and slurping noises as he fucked me with his fingers.

He let out a chuckle, looming over me and quickly removing his fingers before falling to his knees between my legs, his hands holding onto my thighs. "I want to eat you out until I've memorized every single fold of your pussy."

The tip of his tongue darted out and his lips curled wickedly. My glistening pussy was at the ready and waiting for Damon to fuck me like he owned me. Without wasting any more time, his mouth descended upon me with need, his tongue thrusting deep into my folds, searching for every drop of wetness. "Fuck, you still taste like cherry."

"Don't stop... Don't stop, Damon." I squirmed.

His tongue returned to my clit and was relentless, sucking with precision. Every movement was more deliberate and intense than the last. I could feel an orgasm building. I gripped the back of his head, pulled him in closer, and ground myself against him, covering his face with my juices. He ate my pussy like it was his last meal.

His fingers found my entrance and began to probe and tease before thrusting into me. It was such a sharp intrusion. "Yes, yes, yes!" I chanted. *He's fucking incredible.*

"That's it, Hilly. Let go. Give me everything." His breath was hot as he started sucking my clit.

I let out one final, desperate cry as I came undone, bucking on his fingers as my climax tore through me. I could feel my come coating my inner thighs. My vision blurred and stars danced in the dark of my closed eyelids as the world spun away into blissful oblivion.

I finally managed to gain control of myself. I blinked hard a couple of times and saw Damon looking up at me, his gaze fixed firmly on my face. His eyes were dark with lust. "Do you realize how beautiful you are when you orgasm?"

Before I could say anything or move an inch, he pressed his face hard into my quivering pussy. "Oh. I'm not finished..."

Without warning, his tongue plunged deep into my entrance, his nose rubbing my swollen clit as he lapped up my juices, covering his face. It was too much, nearly whipping me into a frenzy. Another orgasm began to build—stronger, more insistent. He wrapped his arms under my legs, gripping my thighs.

I let out a piercing scream. "Ah, fuck!"

I want him to drown in me.

I couldn't think. I could only be consumed by the sensation of his tongue, mouth, and hands bringing me close to climax. Finally, with one final desperate thrust of his tongue, he tipped me over the edge. I screamed as my ass shot clear off the marble altar. My voice echoed off the rafters of the church. I shook and convulsed, every pulse stronger than the last.

I collapsed back onto the altar. My breathing was ragged, my body trembling with exhaustion.

Damon lifted his head from between my thighs, his lips wet

with my juices. His warm breath feathered my pussy. He finally released my legs, making me quiver as I sat up. He moved beside me without uttering a word, and instantly, his presence dominated the space. "Open your mouth, beautiful."

I did, my lips parting. He bent over me, and I watched, mesmerized, as a thin ribbon of saliva fell from his mouth to mine. "Taste yourself," he rasped.

I closed my mouth, savoring us. Then his lips crushed against mine, heavy and devouring, his tongue breaching mine like some starving man needing my flavor.

His fingers found their way back down between my legs, and then he slid inside me again. There was no holding back the scream that escaped my lips as my body arched against him, my hands grasping at his shoulders, clutching him desperately as I threw my head back in pleasure. His fingers curled and twisted inside me. He pulled them out just when the pleasure almost became intolerable, leaving me panting. He silently pressed his slick fingers past my lips, and I sucked greedily on them, tasting myself. "Your lips are fucking heaven," he praised.

Damon's hands tugged at my hips, digging deep into my skin while pulling me to the edge of the altar. As I completely submitted to him, my pulse raced, and the ache deep inside me surged in anticipation of what would happen next.

"Are you—" he started, but I managed to cut him off before he got the whole question out.

"Yes, asshole, I'm clean! Are you?"

His smirk extended, eyes darkening with humor. "I was going to ask if you're on any birth control. But, yeah." His words were heavy with sarcasm.

"O-oh," I stammered, feeling my cheeks burn with embarrassment. "Yeah. I'm on birth control."

Damon stepped backward, his eyes never leaving mine while he unzipped his trousers. When he pulled them down, my breath caught in my throat at the revelation of his length springing free, hard and massive. Every ridge, every vein popped out along the sides, making it look even more intimidating, even more tempting.

He's huge! More than I could have ever imagined. Just the thought of him inside me began to make my body tense. *How the hell is he going to fit inside of me?* I swallowed hard, and a gulp of nervousness escaped my throat as I stared at him, unable to pull my gaze away.

Damon caught the doubt on my face and chuckled deeply, clearly impressed with himself.

"Don't you worry," he said in a sultry voice that oozed promise. "You'll be taking every inch. I'll make sure of it." My body ached for him as he stepped closer, his huge cock prepared to claim me.

His hand slid from my hip down the small of my back, pulling me right into him until our bodies slammed against each other. His hard cock leaned against my stomach, insistent, and its mere size had me gulping audibly. He reached between us, his fingers guiding his cock along the slick folds of my pussy, coating himself in my wetness. "Your pussy is so fucking ready for me."

Before I could get a word out, he had the head of his cock at my entrance, circling in teasing motions before pressing inside. The stretch was extreme, bordering on painful. The pressure of him filling me inch by excruciating inch had me moaning. His hand gripped my hip, holding me in place. "Just relax and let me in."

It's not natural to be this fucking full.

I tried to comply, willing myself to relax around his cock. With one determined thrust, the full extent of him was buried deep within my pussy. For a moment, we both paused.

"I wanted to go easy on you, Hilly. But I don't think I can."

He pulled out most of the way before he slammed into me again with a brutish force. It sent shockwaves deep into me, slamming me against the cold stone beneath me. Every thrust was heavier. "Fuck, I can barely fit."

I spread my legs wider, and my stomach tightened as he quickened his pace.

"Oh, my God!" I moaned loudly.

Damon leaned down to the side of my face. "You're crying out for him in the right place," he whispered, out of breath.

The church echoed as his thighs slapped against mine.

He growled as his free hand slid up to cup my breast, his thumb flicking over my erect nipple. "Tell me what you want, beautiful."

"Make me yours, Damon."

"Are you sure?"

"Yes, claim me. Make me yours."

In an instant, Damon's hand clamped around my throat, his fingers pressing into my skin with just the right amount of force. "Eyes on me while I fucking choke you."

His thrusts became frantic, plunging into me with such urgent desperation I actually thought I would lose my mind. His lips captured mine in a dominating kiss, his tongue breaching my mouth just as his dick was breaching my body.

I tried to focus, my vision blurring as he grasped me tighter. My body responded on its own, quivering in his possession. My eyes tried to hold his gaze. Damon pulled back a bit, and I could tell he was trying to fight the urge to come. "D-Da—" I stammered as his hand clenched, shutting off most of my air. He slowed his thrusts, his hips grinding, more deliberate.

The tighter he pressed, the dizzier my head got.

I don't want this to be over.

Damon released his hand from my throat, his body leaning

into me, his voice a growl against my ear. "That's my good fucking girl."

Still buried deep inside me, he lifted me off the altar. My legs instinctively wrapped around his waist. It was hard to hold a moan back as I felt his cock twitch inside.

"Feet down."

I obeyed.

Pulling my legs away from his waist, he placed me on my feet. The moment his cock slipped out of me, my pussy was throbbing for more. I felt an instant ache, already craving the fullness he'd given me.

He sat on the pew, his legs wide apart, that dark smirk playing on his lips. The flash of his eyes gleamed with control, and I loved how easily he took that power over me. "On your hands and knees."

I dropped onto the cold stone floor beneath me without wasting a second. I felt a chill as I placed my hands and knees on the floor.

"Now crawl to me, if you want my cock."

I looked up at him, my eyes locked on his, and I began to crawl toward him, aware of how much of me was on display.

When I reached him, he already had his fingers outstretched for me. He hooked a hand under my chin, swiping it upward so I had no other choice but to continue looking at him. His eyes burned into mine, and without a word, he motioned with his fingers for me to straddle him.

I swallowed hard, my pulse raced as I rose to my feet and swung a leg over him, positioning myself above his lap. He held the base of his cock, ready for my pussy. My knees just barely grazed the edge of the bench.

A whimper tore free from my lips as I lowered myself down onto his erection.

He fisted some of my hair, his eyes never leaving mine.

"Now ride me," he ordered, pulling my hair back and exposing my neck to the cool air. "Ride me like it's the last time you'll ever fuck me."

Last time? No, I never want him to leave my body. I'm his and he's mine.

I moved in circular motions at first, letting myself adjust to the fullness of him, then faster, grinding down against him as I lost myself to the feeling of him stretching me, filling me up completely. Each thrust was laced with a hint of desperation as my body answered his demand. His hands clamped onto my waist, urging me to move harder and faster.

I felt my juices spill out, slickening both of us as I rode him. Damon's hand tangled deeper into my hair, his fist clenching deep and painful, keeping my head in a tight vise that refused to let go. Everything in me wanted to throw my head back, to let go into the riot of pleasure coursing through me and scream, but he wouldn't let me. My entire body was quivering with the need to surrender, but he conquered me and refused to let me break eye contact.

Tears pricked the corners of my eyes, blurring my vision, and his cock hit that spot deep inside me with every thrust. I couldn't help it. The tears slipped free, one after another, each a testament to just how hard he was dominating me.

A low growl rumbled in his throat, and the grip in my hair tightened while he thrust up into me hard to make sure I was feeling all of him.

The hard wood bit into my knees, and the pain was sharp, but I could hardly feel it. All that mattered was pleasing him, giving him anything he asked for. My hands grasped his shoulders to steady myself, my fingers digging into his skin as I rode him, rising up and down on his cock with desperate need.

Reality struck me. There was something sinful, being in an abandoned church and fucking my future stepbrother right in a place meant for worship, and yet it felt so right. *So fucking perfect.*

It was completely taboo. Feeling his body against mine, it was all just so inherently sinful, yet Heaven itself. The only thing I could think about in that moment was the pleasure he was giving me, his hands roaming over my body, gripping me, owning me. It was intoxicating. My mind was a jumbled mess of lust and guilt, and yet I couldn't and wouldn't stop.

As I sank down onto his cock, I felt myself unraveling a little more. I could see it in his eyes, too—the satisfaction, the hunger —as I gave myself completely to him, letting the sinful pleasure consume me. "Look at how well you fucking take me. Every inch of my cock," Damon groaned.

I felt proud, being able to take all of him. I continued grinding on him, lost in the moment, when something to the left of us caught his gaze, and his eyes flicked to the side. Lying on the bench beside us was a set of prayer beads, their dull wood varnish catching the faint moonlight filtering through the stained glass.

Damon's hold on my hip loosened, and he reached for the beads with a smirk, like he had an idea. It was enough to make my heart skitter wildly as he wrapped the beads around his fingers.

Before I could do or say anything, he had them around my throat, the wood almost weightless against my skin. He pulled them taut, enough to make me gasp, reminding me of how much of me he controlled.

"Who's your god, Hilly?" he whispered with lust as he tugged the beads, urging me to move.

My body bucked on its own accord, bearing down and grinding on him. My pussy was getting wetter. I was surprised his cock didn't slip out of me.

Every thrust, every breath became a prayer of its own—a worship of him, of us, of the dark pleasure we were lost in.

"Who's your fucking god?" he repeated with a dark tone.

"You. You're my god!" I dug my fingers deeper into his shoulders, my nails cutting into his skin, the blood oozing out.

My words only seemed to darken his eyes, and a dangerous smirk played on his lips as he growled from between gritted teeth, "Then fucking worship me." He gave the prayer beads a tug, his hand yanking tighter to cut off just enough air that made me feel lightheaded. "Make me come, beautiful."

Our bodies moved in a frenzy, each thrust stronger and stronger than the last. The heat between us was overwhelming. *I wanna make him come. I wanna make him feel so good.*

His cock continued to pound at that sweet spot inside me, wave upon wave of pleasure crashing through me, building toward another orgasm that was almost too much to bear. I felt it coming, tension coiling tighter inside my stomach as I screamed, "Yes! Yes!"

I could feel my pussy tightening around his cock, milking him like it was worshiping him with every muscle. Every pulse, every contraction was exactly as he wanted. Sweating with need, my body seemed to move of its own accord—to please him, to make him feel like the god I'd just named him. "I'm coming!" he breathed.

Finally, Damon let out a deep, low moan, sending an electric current of arousal right through me and making me climax. "Damon, I'm... I'm—"

The tension in the air thickened while his body started shaking. The power of his thrusts softened, slowing but still full of intensity.

His hands fell, loosening the prayer beads at my neck, letting coolness from the air seep into my skin. His strong arms clutched my waist, yanking me into him, pressing our sweat-slicked bodies together.

As I sat draped in his arms, I couldn't help but press a kiss to the top of his head. His cock twitched inside me, the heat of his cum filling me, mixing with my own juices. It was intoxicating.

We kill together, we come together, joined in blood and lust.

I looked up at a painting above us. There was no mistake as to who the figure was, God looming from the heavens. His gaze seemed piercing. I knew by the look that he was condemning both of us to Hell for fucking in a holy place and because of our pasts. Quite honestly, I didn't fucking care. If anything turned me on more. We were lost in sin. There was no escape. We were destined for destruction, and I craved it.

I realized that Hell wasn't something to fear. Hell was being without Damon Northwood.

He snapped me out of my daze with a firm grip on my hips and flipped me onto my back. In one swift motion, I slammed against the hardened surface of the bench. "Don't move, beautiful."

His cock was still inside me, throbbing, and those few seconds it took him to withdraw slowly caused my body to shudder. Every inch that slid out of me left me aching for more.

The instant his cock was out of me, I could feel our cum oozing out in a warm, wet stream to my asshole. The slickness only made me more aware of how full I had been, and how hollow I was now.

Damon leaned over, carefully untangling the beads from my neck.

"What are you doing?" I asked.

A smile curled his lips. "Spread your legs."

I spread myself for him—one leg resting over the top of the bench, the other falling to the floor—my pussy stretched wide open, my folds slick and swollen.

He dangled the prayer beads above my dripping pussy, swinging and taunting me with the promise of what was to come. Slowly, he lowered the beads over my skin, starting up at my clit and dragging them down slowly. He pulled them down further and I could feel our combined juices coating each bead as he ran them over my folds.

The beads glistened with our arousal, and he stopped at my hole, allowing the coolness of the prayer beads just to hover there for a moment, teasing me. It was fucking dirty, so sinful, and I couldn't breathe, completely at his mercy, desiring every twisted second of it.

Damon raised the prayer beads, and I watched, mesmerized, as they glistened in the candlelight. "I want you to taste both of us. Now, open wide."

My lips parted, and I stuck out my tongue eagerly.

As he dropped the beads in my mouth, my lips clamped down, and I started to lick them, not wasting one drop of our mingled juices. The combination of our flavors was more intimate than a kiss. With every passing lick and swirl of my tongue, I wanted more.

Damon really did savor every moment of my submission. He pulled the beads from my mouth, the wet string sensually slipping past my lips. I panted, still tasting us, demanding more of that taboo flavor. He dropped the beads over his head, wet and still leaking our juices. "I'm keeping these." The sight of him wearing the prayer beads, stained with our sin, made my heart race—a crude reminder of what had tied us together, what had just occurred within this holy place.

I sat on the bench, naked, my skin pricking as a chill traced its way along my skin. My body began to shake. Without hesitation, Damon got up and walked toward a dark blue curtain hanging above a door. He pulled it easily off the pole, the cloth falling in his hands. He flung it over his shoulder silently and walked over to a bench with two praying pillows laid neatly.

He picked up the pillows and strode toward the center of the church, where a deep red aisle carpet was, setting the pillows next to each other before he turned back to me. A small smile tugged at the corner of his mouth.

He beckoned me to come over. Completely naked, I stood from the bench and walked towards him. Weirdly, I felt vulnerable yet safe at the same time. I knew his eyes were on me, not just lustful now, but protective. "This will do for the night," he whispered, his voice soft yet sure.

We sank down onto the carpet, and it was so much more comfortable than I expected. I buried my head against the prayer pillow—the fabric was well-worn but still unbelievably soft against my face. Damon settled beside me, placing the deep blue curtain over us. Its warmth instantly banished the chill, and his body shifted and pressed against mine.

There was a moment of silence. His hand wrapped under my neck, his fingers tracing light patterns over my skin. It wasn't just the passion or the heat between us anymore. Something softer, almost fragile, revealed itself.

Under that heavy curtain, it was as if we had created our own world, where nothing else mattered but him and I. He reached out, his fingers brushing my cheek and tucking a strand of hair behind my ear. I was safe, cherished, and completely his.

The moonlight filtered down through the colored glass, bathing us in soft, gentle hues of blue and white. Damon leaned in closer still. "You look so beautiful in the moonlight."

I blushed profusely at his words. He drew me closer, his arms folding around me, making me feel small but treasured in his arms.

But as I burrowed into his chest, my gaze fell to the thin, red lines etched into his skin—the cuts I had inflicted with my nails. Guilt hit me like a wave. "Fuck, I'm sorry." My voice was full of regret as I reached out and delicately touched the marks.

Damon gave a silent chuckle, his chest rumbling against mine. He shrugged it off like it didn't matter. But something about seeing that blood tracing on his skin did something to me. I hated that I'd hurt him, even by accident. Not thinking, I leaned down and pressed my lips against the cuts, kissing softly against the wounds I'd made.

He reached out and lightly pulled my chin. "Hilly, I'm okay."

I stared into his eyes, and suddenly, everything just faded away. It was like looking into the soul of the one person who made me feel truly safe. He was more than just my protector. He was everything. He wasn't just the man who saved me.

"I think I've been waiting for you my whole life," I whispered as tears formed. The words slipped out before I could stop them.

Damon's thumb brushed tenderly over my cheek. "You were always mine, Hilly. Even before you knew it."

I hadn't ever had sex sober, but with Damon, it was different. It was raw, real. I was so present at each and every moment, each touch. I just felt so glad I was with him.

It was intense, super intense.

For the first time, I wasn't running from myself. Damon had seen me at my most vulnerable, and instead of pulling away, he'd only held me tighter.

I laid my head against Damon's chest, the rhythm of his heartbeat steady. It sounded like a silent promise that within his arms, I would be safe. Closing my eyes, I fell deeper into him, and I wanted our souls to stay in that church, wrapped in each other's arms forever.

His fingers danced down my back, grazing over the raised scars etched into my skin. I held my breath, instinctively bracing for his reaction. But Damon didn't flinch. There was no hesitation in his touch.

Every stroke of his hand told me he accepted me, even though it made me feel sick when he touched my scars. I knew they must have felt rough beneath his fingertips, but it didn't faze him at all. He wasn't searching for perfection.

My gaze wandered up to the church ceiling, where intricate details of stone arches were bathed in the soft candlelight. Everything was just so right. I slipped into a haze until Damon's voice snapped me out of it. "Are you okay? You're not sore or anything?"

I smiled through my exhaustion. His eyes were softer, not dark and intense like usual.

"I'm fine," I mumbled as I yawned. "Just really tired."

He slowly leaned down and pressed a soft kiss on the top of my head. I snuggled into his side; he held me close as if he would never let me go again.

My eyelids drooped, and I started to drift off.

I clung to the sound of Damon's heartbeat beneath my cheek. I normally struggled to sleep, but the second my eyes closed, the only thing I could think of was how peaceful I felt and how Damon was my refuge, my calm in the storm. I knew sleeping on his chest was the only place I wanted to be.

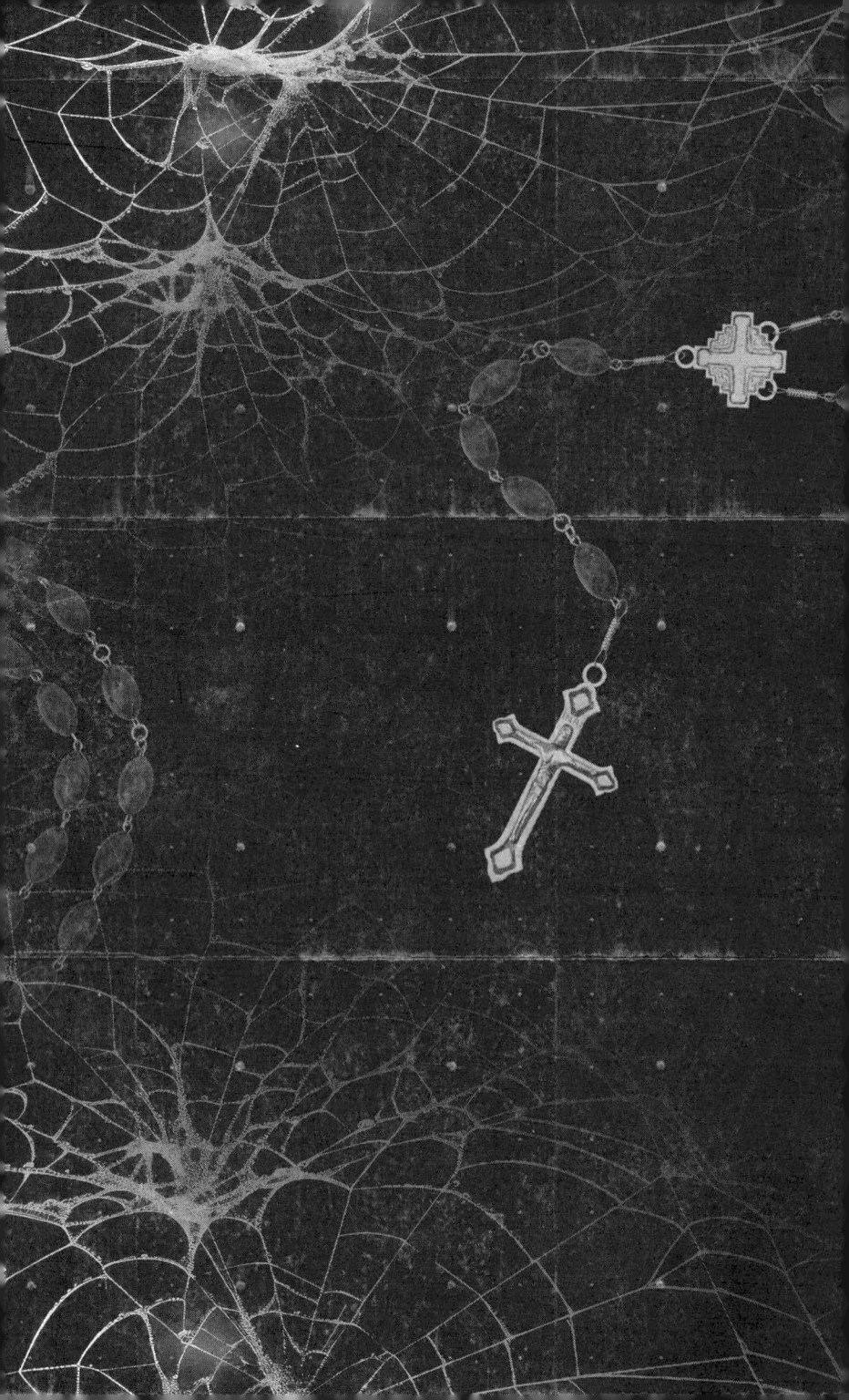

CHAPTER
EIGHTEEN
DAMON

GODDAMN IT, HILLY IS FUCKING PERFECT. I'M OBSESSED. I CRAVE HER existence.

No woman in my life had ever made me come before her. Anytime I'd had sex with someone, my cock would go soft halfway through. The whole thing was a pathetic act. It was like my cock had been waiting for Hilly this whole time.

I just wish she'd come into my life sooner. Maybe I could have saved her from the crap she'd been through. I knew I was all she needed. I was everything she wanted. Her body said it with every moan, every cry of my name, the way she clung to me like I was her salvation. I was hers as much as she was mine.

Hilly was a fighter, but behind all the scars, the fear, and all the walls she had put up, she had so much inner strength. That's what really drew me to her.

The thing is, I am a killer, and I have never denied that part of me, nor am I ever going to. I have learned to deal with it. It's just part of my nature.

But she didn't care. *She knows what I'm capable of, and yet she still wants me.*

She never cowered, never looked at me like I was some

monster. If anything, it felt like my violence, my urge to protect, was something she understood.

As long as I breathed and my heart beat, Hilly would never go to bed feeling lonely again. She'd never lay in the dark staring up at the ceiling, afraid one day, those demons of hers would come slinking back in. I'd make fucking sure of it. She would no longer spend another day without feeling loved, without knowing she had someone there for her—watching, protecting, wanting her.

A loud squawk from outside yanked me from my thoughts. I looked toward the window. A crow was sitting on the stone ledge, his black, round eyes staring at me. *Don't judge me, little fluffy-winged fucker.*

The church seemed so different in the morning light, almost peaceful compared to last night.

I glanced down at Hilly, sleeping in my arms, relaxed, no longer weighted with terror or pain. *She's an angel.*

I brushed a strand of hair off her face. *This was where I was meant to be, with her. Always.*

She stirred, heaving her body a little as she murmured my name in her sleep. I carefully pulled her arm off of me, making sure not to wake her. I slipped under the curtain. I had a plan— a morning surprise my girl wouldn't be prepared for.

It was dark under the heavy cloth, but I didn't really need to see anything. I sucked two of my fingers, still tasting Hilly on them from last night, letting out a moan, and placed my hand between her thighs. She instinctively parted her legs for me, like her body knew exactly what I was going to do. She responded to me so fucking well, even half asleep. Slowly, I slipped my fingers past her lips and inside her. Her pussy constricted tightly around me. I was only able to put my fingers in up to the knuckle.

I splayed my other hand across the lower half of her stomach, applying pressure.

Inside of her, I flicked my fingers up once, hard and fast, hitting her sweet spot. Her body arched, and I heard a loud gasp escape her lips.

"Damon!" Her voice cut through the church, pure pleasure as she ripped the curtain off me.

"Mornin', beautiful," I said with a smirk, starting to work my fingers. The look on her face was priceless. *What a perfect way to start the day.*

I didn't think it was possible to get any harder, but Hilly does wild things to me. My cock pressed against the carpet beneath me as I worked my fingers inside her. Her body reacted to every flick. She then pried her legs further apart, succumbing to the pleasure, and sharp moans fled her mouth as I moved in closer, my face merely inches away from her pussy. My pulse raced at the thought of her juices covering me.

"I'm going to make you squirt and I want you to cover my face. I want to be able to taste you on my lips and fingers for the rest of the day," I growled.

"I've never—"

She fisted her hair, eyes half-lidded as her body arched off the floor.

"Oh, you will," I promised.

My fingers moved quicker, relentlessly and without mercy. Her moans grew louder, more desperate, and her body bucked under the intensity of it all. Her thighs tensed; her hips lifted higher as she let out loud whimpers. I could hear how wet her pussy was getting.

And then, with a final moan, her body let go, her juices spraying past my fingers, across my face, warm and sweet. I couldn't resist licking my lips. *Her taste will forever be my favorite.*

I didn't let up as she trembled, her body riding the waves of her orgasm.

"Fuck, you taste so good in the morning." My fingers slowed but didn't leave her. I wanted to draw out every last drop of pleasure.

I peered up at her, her chest rising and falling as she sprawled out, panting. Her eyes were shut, her lips parted like she was still catching her breath.

"Just look at your pussy, it's all puffy and soaking wet. All for me. *Only me*," I growled, so full of lust, pulling out my slippery fingers slowly, enjoying the wetness coating them. "And it's begging to be fucked again."

Hilly raised her head, fluttering her eyes open, exhausted. It was as if she couldn't take me all over again, her body still quivering. *But I know she can handle me.*

She pleaded with her eyes, but I gave her a smirk, moving in closer, my body right between her spread legs.

My fingers traced up her inner thighs, teasing her swollen lips. I hiked both her legs up, pinned them to her shoulders, slid my cock along her slick folds, and teased her entrance. "Are you gonna take my cock in your tight pussy?" I asked as I pushed inside her inch by slow inch, filling her.

My cock was in Heaven, buried inside her as if her pussy was fucking made just for me. She squeezed me tighter with every thrust.

Her needy voice tore through the air. "I can take you. I want you to fill me up," she cried out, shaking with each of my thrusts.

I held her legs tighter as I leaned forward and started pounding into her. Her wet pussy slapped against me.

She threw her head back, sinking into the prayer pillow beneath her, her mouth open in a silent scream. With each pulse, every desperate gasp, I slammed my hips into her hard.

I grunted louder as I increased the pace, plunging deeper until I could feel my cock hitting her cervix.

"Damon! Damon! Damon!" she kept repeating, attempting to shift away.

Oh, you're not getting away that easy.

"I thought you said you could take it?" I teased in a dark tone, thrusting harder into her as her body squirmed, her legs quivering, her skin slicked with sweat, and her eyes rolled right back into her skull.

The force of every thrust sent her back arching and gasping for air. I watched her dig her fingers into the prayer pillow, her knuckles white as she tried to anchor herself against my furious pace. Her lips fell apart as moans gave way to whimpers.

I watched her totally lose control. Literally, she looked like she was about to pass out.

She couldn't take it anymore, shaking hard as if her body would snap. But I wasn't going to stop. I grunted as I felt myself pushing more into her while her pussy squeezed me tight.

My balls slapped against her as the feeling of pressure built and built in my cock. My breathing quickened.

Slap.

Thrust.

Slap.

Thrust.

Slap.

With every thrust, I felt her getting wetter. The rush of her release ran through me. I could sense my release was coming. I was only a few seconds away from emptying right into her.

"I'm coming... I'm coming," I moaned loudly. Every muscle in my body tightened as I thrust into her one last time, ready to pour my release deep inside her.

I felt my cum fill her, my cock twitching with each pulse as I emptied myself deep inside her. Her pussy was so tight around me, milking me for every last drop. My body wanted to collapse on top of her, to feel her softness beneath me as I came down from my high. But then I looked down—her chest heaving, her eyes half-lidded, and her legs trembling. I might have broken her, at least for a moment. I let her legs drop as I slowly pulled my cock out, still throbbing. Our juices mingled in her there as she laid out of breath with a satisfied smirk.

I sprang up, adrenaline coursing through me, and walked across where I'd thrown my pants. I reached into my pocket and pulled out my pack of cigarettes. I returned, sitting down beside Hilly, and dropped the curtain back over us, wrapping us again in the stillness of the church.

Cigarettes after sex. It's always the best feeling.

I lit one and took a long drag, blowing the smoke out. Hilly looked at me, still trying to catch her breath. I held out the cigarette.

She lifted herself onto her elbows, took the cigarette from me, inhaled deep, and exhaled. "I've been meaning to ask you something," she said, handing it back to me.

A flicker of unease ran across my mind, but I kept my face neutral.

"How'd you know where to find me?"

I wasn't going to lie to her. *I couldn't.* I leaned in closer, and my fingers played with the silver cross around her neck. "The cross..." I paused for a second to check her expression. "It's a tracker."

She stared at me for a moment, digesting my words, then shook her head, emitting a reassuring chuckle. "Any sane person would say you're crazy... but I think it's strangely romantic."

I blinked, slightly narrowing my eyes in confusion. "Really?"

She shrugged. "Yeah. You really were telling the truth when you said you would always protect me?"

"Always."

I put my arm around her shoulder, tugging her against me. My lips were a few inches from hers, but she jerked her face away at the last second. "Oh no, I have morning breath," she teased, though I could tell she was a little embarrassed.

"Really? I have morning pussy breath," I laughed, shaking my head. "After everything we just did, that's what you're worried about?"

She just shrugged and took the cigarette from me.

"Well, I think you might find this romantic... I knew I'd beat you in that maze, so I waited at the exit... with a black rose. A peace offering."

"Well, I'd have beaten you if I hadn't been abducted," she said, squinting up at me. "But I would've loved the rose."

I waved my hand dismissively, knowing full well she never had any chance. "Don't worry. I'll buy you a whole bouquet of black roses, beautiful."

Her cheeks went a rosy color as she blushed. She took a last drag from the cigarette without ever taking her eyes off mine, then stubbed it out on the cold stone floor beside us.

Hilly pulled the curtain off and looked around on the floor for her scattered clothes. I watched her for a moment until my phone buzzed loudly. I went to my pants and fished it from the pocket. The screen lit up. My father.

I answered, pressing the phone to my ear.

"Hello?"

"Good morning, son."

My eyes didn't leave Hilly's as my father spoke, asking me how I was. She slid into her skirt and mesh top. I reached into my shirt pocket, pulling out her panties. I flung them at her, and they fell on her shoulder. She turned around, giggling, and her eyes rolled.

"Yeah, everything is good here, Papa."

Papa was a code, and my father knew exactly what it meant —a situation not to be discussed openly. He wrapped up the call, knowing I would text him the details.

As soon as I hung up, my phone buzzed again.

FATHER:
How many?

ME:
Three.

FATHER:
Locations?

I felt Hilly staring at me, her eyes cutting from the phone to my face, but she knew better than to ask.

I let him know, and within seconds, my phone buzzed again with his response.

FATHER:
I'll send some men, and it'll be sorted.

My father cleaned up "messes" well. Anything he was handed just vanished. We both knew the unspoken rule: you didn't ask any questions. I had my reasons, he had his, and we both respected that. My tendencies were from my father. He was as dark as me. It was a legacy I never asked for but one that I inherited. I watched my father fight dirty to protect the ones he loved and our wealth—even if it meant living with buried secrets.

Like father, like son.

I reached for my clothes, but I just wanted to stay in that church naked and curled up with Hilly forever.

"Will you lace my corset?" she asked, holding it in place. I moved closer, and my fingers started to feed the laces through the loops, tugging the corset tight upon her body. "Damon... what about Mitch?"

I knew that question was coming at some point.

"You don't have to worry, beautiful. It's all being sorted."

She hesitated but understood not to ask any questions.

"There. You're all laced up." I leaned forward to tie the last knot, my breath whispering across her neck as I caught her intoxicating scent. I wanted to stay that way a little longer and savor the moment.

We stood in silence for a moment. The time had come for both of us to leave the church. So I took her hand in mine, and I pulled her lightly toward the door. We knew it was like a gateway back into reality.

Stepping outside, the sun cut through clouds. Fresh air and flowers filled my lungs. The sun shone through the nearby trees, lighting the green grass around the gravestones. Crows sat on the branches, their black, glossy feathers shining in the light as their beady eyes seemed to follow us intently.

Hilly stopped, looking back. It seemed like the church didn't want us to leave.

"Hey," I drew her attention back to me. I lifted our hands to my lips, pressing a kiss against her knuckles. "We can come back... This place will always be our sanctuary."

Hope flickered in her eyes and a slight smile broke through. At that moment, we both knew we were stepping into a new chapter of our lives.

We took one deep breath together. I led her away from the church as our fingers remained intertwined, knowing whatever happened after, the church will always hold a special place in both our lives. It's where we both allowed ourselves to be unrelentingly authentic to ourselves and each other. The stories that the old church held will always be a part of this place's history, and now Hilly and I have added to that. Our story lies here, forever holding our secrets.

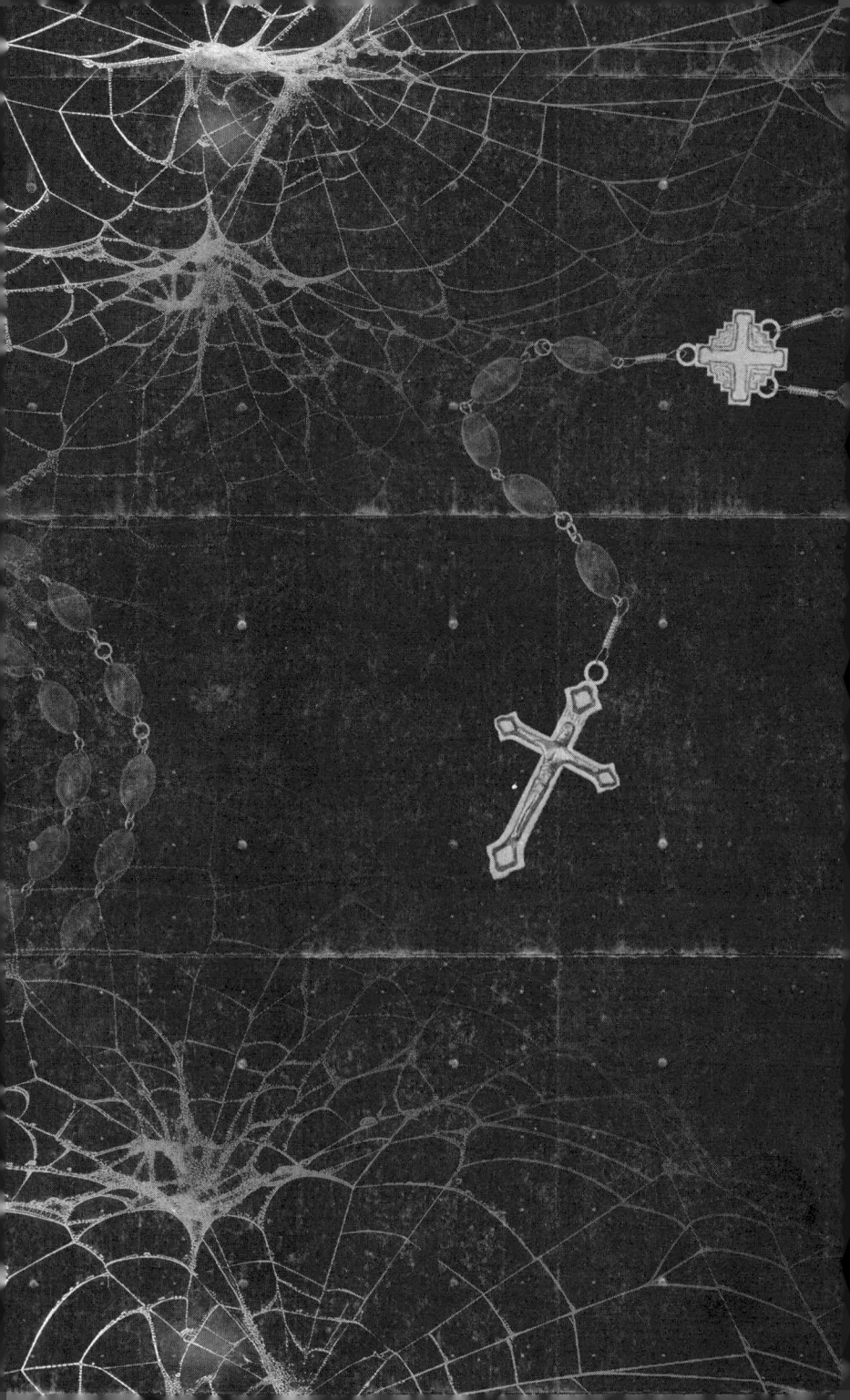

I SAT IN THE PASSENGER SIDE OF HIS CAR AND WATCHED OUT THE window as the world blurred by. My body ached in ways I hadn't anticipated, every strained muscle reminding me of what had taken place last night and this morning. It wasn't just the bruises left by Mitch. It was everything—the roller coaster of emotions, the intensity of being with Damon.

Questions swirled around my mind. *What's going to happen now? Do we tell our parents? What would they say if they finally knew the truth? How would they even react?*

Part of me could really not give a rat's ass about their reactions, but the more cautious side of me was terrified of the fallout.

But all those thoughts got drowned out by one thing: Damon. Literally every inch of my mind was full of him, as if he'd become the center of my universe. Everything outside of him didn't matter. It was thrilling and terrifying.

I looked at him, his eyes stuck on the road, the muscles in his jaw clenched, hands clasped on the wheel. So calm, so in control, but my head wouldn't stop with what possibly could be going through his mind.

THE HALLOWEEN DECORATIONS WERE STILL UP—COBWEBS DRAPED over stairs, skeletons lining the windows, jack-o'-lanterns flickering with fake candles in the fading daylight. Yet somehow, all of that felt different now.

Damon and I walked into the kitchen, where Mom and Richard sat at the island, eating breakfast. Immediately, the rich smell of coffee and toast wafted to my nostrils, and my stomach growled despite all that was on my mind.

The moment my mom laid eyes on me, alarm registered. In an instant, she rose from her stool and rushed over. "Oh my gosh, Hilly, what happened to you?"

"Uh..."

Fuck. What do I say?

Damon took control, stepping forward. "It's okay, Ruth. We were just on a ghost ride, and an animatronic felt on her. Trust me, the employees heard all about it.."

Richard shot a glance at him. I knew it was some sort of signal passed between them.

But Mom wasn't buying it for a second. She leaned forward and took my chin in her hand for a closer look at the bruises. "Hilly, are you sure you're all right?"

"It looks worse than it is. Trust me, it's just a couple of bruises and cuts," I assured her with a forced, weak smile. "Really, I'm fine." I was just hoping she wouldn't press further.

She seemed to accept that.. Sighing heavily, she let her hand fall from my chin and resumed her seat at the island.

Richard shifted on his stool, eyes flickering from me to Damon and back again as he brushed a piece of fluff off his sweater. "Apart from the ride incident, did you guys have fun?"

Mom sipped her coffee, and I could tell she felt more at ease. "Oh yeah, how was the night?"

I stuttered for one second, catching the heat of Damon's amused stare without even turning in his direction. "Yeah," I finally said, trying to sound as nonchalant as possible. "Last night was... fun. Had a little dance and went in the scare maze—"

"I had an excellent night," Damon interrupted.

I wanted to glare at him so fucking badly, but I knew I couldn't.

Richard and Mom smiled warmly, but the corner of my mouth twitched as I caught the curve of Damon's lips—he was holding back a smirk, undoubtedly thinking of the real reason last night had been so memorable.

"Well," I started, "I really need a long shower. I smell like an ashtray and fog machines."

And Damon's cum.

Turning for the stairs, I assumed Damon would follow, but I realized he didn't move. He stood by the counter, arms across his chest, with a smug, knowing glint in his eye.

Our eyes met for a second, and it felt like he was telling me something. But he stayed put. So I shrugged it off, going up on my own, my body yearning for the warmth of the shower and quiet space to think about everything.

Before turning on the shower, I stood at the window and looked out onto the grounds. Lined up across the edge of the garden were cosmos flowers, with their deep maroon petals that seemed almost black, adding to the gothic allure. Beyond the garden was the forest, stretching to the horizon, thick and shadowed as if the trees held secrets of their own.

My eyes dropped to the cross necklace. I didn't even care that it was a tracker. It meant Damon would always know where I was. It was a reminder that I was never truly alone. I wrapped my fingers around it and pictured Damon and I, living at the mansion, waking up in each other's arms, watching the sunrise.

I closed the blinds and lit a few fancy candles that sat untouched on the bathroom shelf, their wax a little dusty. The room instantly smelled of a rich, floral orange blossom. The room was dark apart from the flickering candles.

Showers had always been a sanctuary, a place where I felt like I could rinse away everything. Each time my body had been used, each time a man left his marks on me, that was where I went to scrub it all off. The sins, the pain, the memories—it all seemed to flow down the drain with the water. I could let my guard down in the shower. I would sit on the floor, the hot water cascading over me, and I would just... cry.

I let out a sigh as I stood under the stream, feeling the warmth slide across my skin. It was a sensation I welcomed. Cleansing was needed.

I looked down, and my gaze caught something. A little trickle of brownish water swirling towards the drain. *Blood.*

Still clinging to my skin after everything that had happened. My breath hitched in my throat.

I watched the water turn clear, but the thought of that blood remained vivid in my mind. I wanted anything related to Mitch to wash away with the water.

I leaned my forehead against the cool tile, letting the steam envelop me. But no matter how hard I tried, I couldn't scrub away what I was feeling inside.

Suddenly, a shadow flickered over the bathroom walls. Before I could even react, the shower door swung open. My heart leaped in my chest as I instinctively tried to cover myself, my hands moving to shield my body. "Damon! Fucking hell, you scared me!"

He was completely unfazed by my reaction, starting to undress, his eyes never leaving mine. The sight of him peeling off his clothes made me freeze, watching as his tattoos came into view, dark and intricate against his skin. His body was a canvas of strength and secrets.

"W-wait, Damon," I stammered. "Our parents?"

"It's okay. They've gone for a walk."

He didn't hesitate, joining me in the shower. The space felt much more constricted as heat emanated from his body toward mine, and immediately, the water drenched him, making his toned body glisten.

He was a god. His dark hair was plastered to his forehead, slick and wild. Every vein in his arms was bulging. We were both naked and vulnerable, but the fact that he didn't have an erection told me this was something more, something deeper and more intimate.

"I thought we could save water and shower together," Damon said with a grin and winked.

I couldn't take my eyes off him. The water ran down his body, highlighting every dip and curve of his muscles.

The world outside the shower no longer existed—just him and I in the steam.

He pulled me against him and his arms wrapped around me as our slick skin slid without friction against each other in the water. Damon reached up and tucked my wet hair behind my ear. Everything felt so intimate.

His hands wandered down my back, tracing over my scars with his fingertips. My body stiffened, my thoughts flooding with my insecurity. "Ugh, the scars are just reminders of my demons. I wish they weren't there. They must look ugly. "

He pinched my chin, lifting my face so our eyes met, his intense gaze locking onto mine. "There's nothing ugly about you, Hilly," he said insistently. "Your scars will never bother me. They're part of your past, but you're mine now. All that matters is our future... together."

Our future. The words felt heavy. I couldn't help but chew the inside of my cheek, lost in thoughts.

How will we face this new life together?

He must have seen the uncertain look on my face.

"We'll take it one day at a time. But no matter how hard you try to push me away, you can't. I'm not going anywhere. You're mine. Every part of you belongs to me, and I'll claim you through every fight. I'll protect what's ours, and I'll fight for you, for us. Always," he whispered. Before I could utter one word, his lips claimed mine in a kiss that robbed the air from my lungs.

His lips never left mine as he pressed me against the cool glass panel of the shower. His hands slid up my sides, and his chest pressed firmly against mine. The water poured down like it was cleansing us. Our fears, doubts, and the past.

"Alright, beautiful. Let's get you cleaned up." He spun me around and pushed my front onto the cold panes of glass. As soon as my boobs touched the surface, my nipples immediately hardened. I could see the foggy outline of the two of us in the misted glass.

Damon spread my legs apart with his knee. I caught him out of the corner of my eye, leaning down and reaching for the body wash and loofa. Fresh citrus scents filled the air. He squeezed the soap into his hand and worked it into a rich lather before pressing the loofa to my skin.

His hands started to work the scrub up my thighs. As he reached my pussy, the strokes became even more deliberately slow, as if he was almost savoring the moment.

I bit my lip as the heat spread through my body. The touch of his hands was intimate and sensual, like each stroke reminded me I was his. He was taking care of me in every possible way.

"Such a fucking pity that I have to clean my dry cum from your pussy..."

His words made me feel weak, and I could feel him right at my opening. He leaned in and started using the loofa on my pussy softly.

God, how I wanted his mouth there instead, his tongue tracing a slow path behind the loofa. My body actually ached for him.

I bit my lip and fought a groan while he continued. Each pass was like a tease, like he knew just what I was wanting.

I could not help myself, pressing my ass back into him, wanting more.

He bent down, his hot breath teasing my neck. "Patience." The word fell from his lips like a pledge, and I was left breathing heavily. "There's a surprise waiting on your bed."

I turned around and ran my hands up his hard chest. "How did I get so lucky, Damon?"

He leaned into me and kissed the top of my head. His hands came to rest upon my waist, tugging me closer until no space existed between us.

"No, no..." he whispered. "I'm the lucky one, Hilly. There's nothing in this life I crave more than you. You're everything I need."

His words dissolved into me as I leaned into him. My hands slid up to his neck, and my fingers tangled softly in his hair. "Same here, Damon. I don't want to spend another day without you. You've saved me and now I'm yours completely. I don't care what happens, as long as it's with you." My voice shook just a little, overwhelmed.

He didn't say a word as he tightened his grip around me. I didn't need him to say anything; it was how he held me. Damon made me feel safe, cherished, and loved.

Love.

It terrified me, yet there it was, heavy in my chest. I've never really felt love, and I wasn't sure if I even knew what it felt like. But Damon made me feel things I didn't know I could feel, which scared me more than anything. I've never had feelings like this for anyone.

BEFORE WE GOT OUT OF THE SHOWER, HE WASHED MY HAIR. DAMON wasn't just a dark and dangerous man. He had layers, and with each layer that I managed to peel back came something else to make me fall for him more.

I opened the door to my bedroom, but I stopped dead on the threshold. On my bed laid the most beautiful arrangement— thirty black roses, their deep, velvety petals complemented by tiny white flowers sprinkled in between. They were stunning.

Beside the roses was a small, black box. My heart jumped into my throat as I opened it. Inside lay some painkillers and a big bar of chocolate. I giggled softly. That was so Damon, equal parts sweet and practical. I reached in and lifted them out, and as I did, a small note fluttered from the box onto the bed.

I had these delivered just for my beautiful girl.

I know you're sore from last night... Every ache is a reminder that you're mine.

And the chocolate? Well, that's just to sweeten the pain...

Of course, he knew I would be sore. I smiled, running my fingers over the note. It wasn't the flowers or the gifts that meant so much. He paid attention to the little things that mattered.

I sat on the edge of the bed, holding the note close to my heart, feeling so lucky to have someone like him who understood me.

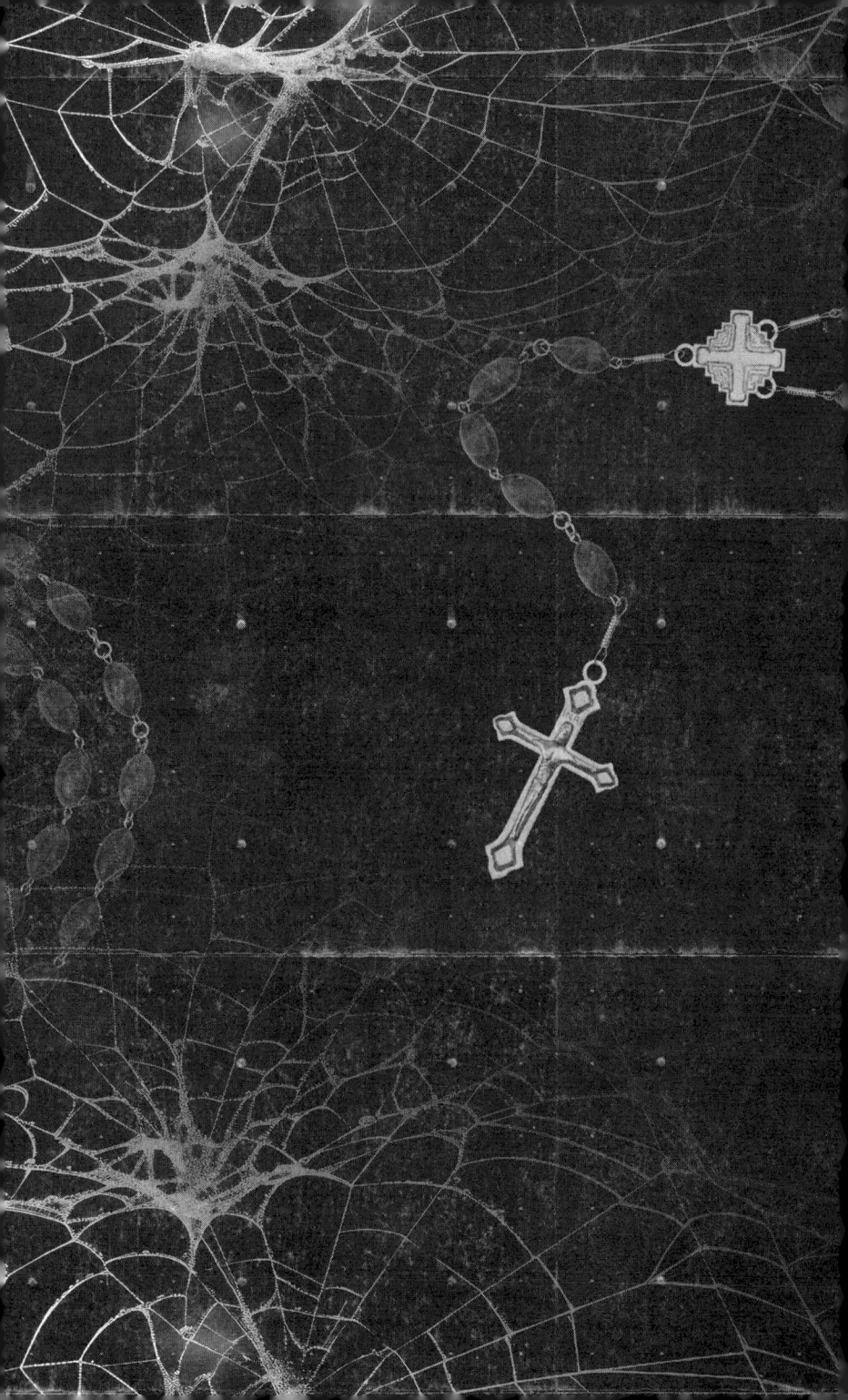

TWENTY

DAMON

FOR THE REST OF THE DAY, NOTHING MUCH HAPPENED. WE SAT DOWN for dinner, and then we came together to watch a movie. Hilly sat next to her mother on the couch, probably because she knew that if she sat next to me, I wouldn't be able to keep my hands off her, even in front of our parents.

When the movie finished, Hilly and Ruth went to bed. I figured Hilly would be tired after everything.

Finally, I had time alone with my father. We stepped outside onto the patio. The night air had a chill. I leaned on the rail while he lit a cigar. "It's all sorted." His voice was reassuring. "No questions, no loose ends." There was an unspoken understanding between us, an acknowledgment of the darkness we both carried.

I was about to head back inside when my father's voice stopped me. "Damon."

I turned back. He was surrounded in smoke, his cigar glowing in the dark. He puffed on it, narrowing his eyes.

"I know there's something going on between you and Hilly. I don't want Ruth finding out... *yet.*" His voice had an edge, a hint of the brutality we both shared.

I nodded, giving a half-serious salute. With one last look, I turned and slipped inside.

I HAD PROMISED MYSELF THAT I WOULD NEVER LET HILLY SLEEP ALONE, and I couldn't shake the need to be beside her. *I'm seriously infatuated and obsessed with her.*

The guest bed was hard as a brick and much too small for the two of us, but I had a plan.

I slipped into her bedroom and saw her fast asleep, her chest rising and falling. She looked so peaceful, almost angelic.

I slowly reached under her, lifting her off the bed. She didn't even flinch.

Dammit, Hilly, you would be easy to kidnap.

I pulled her against me, tucked her head under my shoulder, and carried her down the hall into my room. I put her in my bed and fluffed pillows around her to ensure she was comfortable. Her face relaxed into the softness, and that made me smile.

I pulled the blankets over her, tucking her in. A stray hair had fallen across her forehead, and I gently brushed it off, my fingers lingering. She needed to be right here, exactly where I could protect her. I sat on a chair opposite the bed, where I could keep my eyes on her. She lay still, all mine, even when asleep.

I had a plan for when she woke up—something special. This was where she was meant to be, and I would make sure she felt it, too.

HILLY

I blinked, feeling groggy. The warmth of an orange lamp cast a shadow on a wall I didn't recognize.

Fuck! I'm not in my room!

In an instant, my heart jolted, and before a scream could escape my lips, a hand clamped firmly down on my mouth. "Shhh, beautiful," Damon whispered in my ear. "We're in my room. We wouldn't want to wake up our parents, would we?"

It was as if the instant I heard his voice, my panic fled. His hand fell away, and he sat on the edge of the bed, watching me with that intent stare that so often made me feel like I was the only thing he saw. I rubbed my eyes, and my eyes unblurred. "How'd I get here?"

"I promised myself I'd never let you sleep alone. Do you realize how vulnerable you are when you're asleep? It makes me want to keep you close at all times so I can protect you from anyone trying to take you away from me."

I shook my head as my eyes dropped to his lap, where a black knife sinisterly gleamed under the lamplight. It lay there, razor sharp, as if it had been ready for this moment. Damon watched where my gaze went and reached up to cup my face with such softness.

"Hilly." His thumb traced along my cheekbone. "I want you to forget about your past scars and for us to make new ones together. I want you to cut, claim, and leave your mark on me."

His desire felt raw, offering me a piece of him that was both dangerous and vulnerable. The very idea of marking him, leaving something permanent on his skin, was thrilling. But I didn't want to hurt him.

It was as if the silent vow in his eyes told me this was far more than a moment. This was a testimony to our connection. He beckoned me farther into his darkness, asking me to trust him. He cocked his head to one side, waiting and watching for my reaction—almost daring me to jump deeper into the shadows with him.

"I don't want to hurt you, Damon..."

He shook his head as he pressed the blade lightly against my throat, sending a chill through me.

"You'll be claiming me as yours. I want you to have some power back. I want you to take control. You fucking need this."

As he leaned in closer, with the blade against my throat, there was a reminder of the boundaries we were crossing. He kissed me deeply, claiming my lips. At that moment, I knew how entwined he and I were.

He put the knife in my trembling hand and then peeled off his T-shirt, revealing the chiseled contours of his tattooed chest. The mere thought that I was about to scar his perfect chest made my heart start racing. "I can't, Damon," I sobbed.

"Look at me..." He grasped my face, his fingers tight as he wrenched me toward him, his eyes dark. "Fucking look at me." Tears welled up in my eyes as I held his gaze. "You need to do this! You need to feel powerful."

With the knife firm in my hand, he set his hand over mine and drew it onto his chest. Underneath the blade, I felt the pulse of my heartbeat. He gave me a nod of approval as his jaw clenched. "Go on. Show me just how bad you want to mark and claim me. Make me fucking yours."

I felt an intoxicating mixture of fear and desire, the knife becoming an extension of our connection.

His hand squeezed harder as I pressed the sharp blade to his chest. I felt my tears stream down my cheeks. It was a surreal moment, yet he was right. I felt powerful. I stopped breathing as my trembling hand started to drag the blade across his skin.

Finally, it broke the surface, and small beads of crimson welled up and dripped down his chest. A grunt escaped his lips as his eyes glanced down at the wound, shining with satisfaction and need.

I finally released a breath I hadn't realized I was holding. "That's my fucking girl," he whispered, wiping away my tears. "I am so proud of you."

In that second, we crossed the line between pain and pleasure, just two souls entwined in an act that felt like a ritual.

The knife kissed my skin before I could fathom what was happening, the flat edge of the blade tracing along my lips. The metallic taste of blood started seeping into my mouth.

He laid the knife on the bed and paused for a moment. I felt his eyes stare at my face as his thumb circled around the seal of my lips, painting my skin with his blood. Then he pried my lips open with his thumb.

Two fingers slipped in, taking over my mouth. Instinct kicked in. My lips wrapped over his fingers, sucking and savoring the trace of iron. My tongue danced around them. *Even his blood tastes amazing.*

"Fuck, Hilly," he groaned. His eyes were full of pride, satisfaction, and something dark.

Slowly, he drew his fingers out of my mouth. His skin was clean because my tongue had laved up every last bit. I could feel the blood on my face start to dry, tugging at my skin as it began to tighten and flake off in small bits.

Without warning, he yanked my arms up in one swift movement, peeling my T-shirt off.

His eyes went dark as he traced his finger over the fresh cut on his chest, anointing crimson across his fingertips. A wicked smirk tugged at his lips, and he leaned in, tracing the line of blood along my chest, down my breasts. The feel of his warm, slick finger tracing my skin stirred something raw and primal inside.

My heart was racing as I looked down, realizing what he

was doing. With each careful stroke, *mine'* was spelled in his blood. I was his, and he knew it. Every part of me belonged to him—body, mind, and soul. I craved him fiercely, and he thrived on that desire.

It sent a rush of possessiveness through him, and I could see the satisfaction in his eyes. "You look so beautiful, coated in my blood."

Damon's lips swooped down, and our tongues met, fighting each other. The taste of blood lingered as I reached around the bed with one hand, my fingers closing over the hard handle of the knife. I picked it up, pressing it against his side, feeling it dig into his skin.

He drew back from the kiss. "What are you doing?"

"Mark me, Damon," I panted. I had a thirst for him to claim me. "I want your initials carved into my skin."

His eyes darkened, and he took his time digesting my words. A predator's smile spread on his lips. "You really want that, Hilly?"

I nodded desperately as my hand trembled, holding out the knife.

He took it from me, and I pulled my leggings down, showing him the top of my thigh.

"Hold still, beautiful." He pressed the blade into my skin, his hand firm. A wave of fear and excitement crashed inside of me as he made the knife dance across my skin.

A small whimper escaped my lips, and he pressed his free hand against my mouth. The blade felt like it was burning me. Every cut felt like a promise, and I could feel his eyes searing into me as he claimed me.

He stopped and pressed his lips over the freshly made mark, sealing it with a kiss.

I looked down, my breath catching at the sight of the new markings across my thigh.

DN

It was red and raw. Blood trickled down my leg like ink across a wet page. Damon sat back, his eyes meeting mine, my blood on his lips. I could tell he was proud. "Look at my initials... It makes me want to claim every inch of you, mark you so everyone can see you're mine."

A part of me wished he would have carved his initials into every inch of my skin. It was just intoxicating, being so utterly claimed, his mark in blood and scar. It wasn't the knife or the blood, it was him. The way he looked at me like I was his unfinished art masterpiece.

He tugged my leggings and panties off, flinging them across the room.

"You trust me, don't you?" he asked, twirling the blade between his fingers.

"Always."

Completely and utterly.

"Now spread your legs, beautiful."

With an evil grin, he pressed the blunt side of the blade to my skin, drawing it down from chin to stomach, relishing each inch. The cold steel caused goosebumps on my body.

I spread my legs wider, and my breathing came in quick gasps.

"Look at you... You really are obedient, aren't you?"

He ran the knife up my inner thigh; the touch made my body jolt. A whimper escaped my lips as my body silently pleaded for more. "Beg," he growled, the blade dancing along my thigh.

"I want this. More than anything. Please..."

"You can do better than that, beautiful," he ordered.

I swallowed hard as the weight of his demand hit me. "Please, Damon. Use me... I need you." I fully surrendered.

"I'm just gonna put the knife right here, okay?" He started tracing the dull edge upward, teasing the edges of my pussy.

I nodded desperately, my body aching for his touch. "O-okay," I panted.

I felt our blood dripping from the knife onto my pussy as he brought the blade closer. He started to work the dull edge on my clit, moving it side to side with slow precision, teasing with the faintest pressure.

I threw my head back into the pillow and let out a moan.

His finger pressed on my lips. "Shh.".

I was completely at his mercy; every move deepened our dark connection.

I dug my fingers into one of his arms. "Don't stop..."

"Oh, I won't," he said. "Not until you're screaming my name."

I couldn't help bucking my hips against the knife.

He increased the pressure just a little bit more. "Take it... Take what you need, beautiful. Take it all."

I could feel my clit swelling under the blade. I knew I was close. *So fucking close.*

My moans began filling the room. Like he predicted, I reached for the pillow beside me, and pressed it firmly over my face in an attempt to dampen the sounds. Damon continued to move the blade faster over my clit. I bit hard onto the pillow.

Just as I was getting ready to climax, he stopped. He pulled the blade away and placed it on the bedside table. I threw the pillow across the room, glaring at him in frustration, but his eyes only sparkled with dark humor. He leaned in closer, the smug smirk playing on his lips. "Not yet, beautiful."

I hate him for keeping me on the edge! Every fucking time!

I knew that he wouldn't let me orgasm until *he* decided it was time.

I looked down at my pussy, and it was covered in a mixture of our blood. I didn't care.

He wasted no time burrowing between my thighs. His hot breath grazed my skin, and dizziness hit me. I didn't get any time to get my head around what was happening before his tongue darted out onto my pussy, licking in one continuous stroke that was torturing me from my entrance up to my clit. It felt like an electric shock, sending ripples of this sensation spreading in my body. My legs quivered involuntarily, almost at the edge of an orgasm.

My breath caught in my throat, my chest tight, as my body bucked under him. His tongue was voracious, every teasing flick bringing me closer to the brink.

He paused for a moment. "Damn, our blood tastes so good mixed together."

I looked down, and he stared up at me, smiling, his perfect teeth shined bright, lips and chin smeared with our blood, like a vampire who had just feasted. The way the blood clung to him felt ceremonial, like some unholy ritual.

"You looked stunning in your Halloween outfit. But black is not your color... I think red is."

Blood dripped down his chin.

How fucking festive.

He started licking my pussy again. I bit my bottom lip hard, as though it would hold me and not allow me to fall apart. I dug my nails into anything that would keep me attached.

His fingers sank into my thighs, and his tongue danced around my clit with such precision that it left words tumbling incoherently. I could hardly articulate any thoughts.. "Damon. I'm going to—"

My voice threw him into a frenzy; his tongue moved furiously, with a speed and insistence beyond anything before. As the pressure spiraled beyond my control, every muscle in my body tensed. I knew I had to let go, and the orgasm raged through me.

I shook, barely able to breathe, while his mouth continued to devour me, his hands wrapping tighter onto my thighs with each contraction of my orgasm, making sure every drop of that pleasure coursed through my shaking body and rendered me helpless.

My fingers moved their own accord, lacing into his hair, tugging on the roots, desperately drawing his head from my numb pussy.

Low laughter rumbled from his chest. He crawled silently up my body, his hands skating along my hips, up my waist. His warm breath danced across my face.

His lips landed on mine in a raw, deep, and altogether demanding kiss. I could taste the metallic tang of our mingled blood. He seemed to seal everything that had happened with one kiss.

He got off the bed and looked down at me. "Your pussy is such a beautiful shade of pink. I just want my lips on it all the time, pleasuring you..."

I smirked as he undressed himself from the waist down. His erection sprang up ready, thick and veiny. He stood at the edge of the bed and beckoned me. "Now, come here."

I got on all fours and crawled to the edge, feeling the cover under me.

Damon's fingers stroked across my lips. He paused for a moment before he pressed, easing my mouth open. He watched in great detail as my lips parted. His thumb outlined my lower lip. "You're gonna take every inch of me in your mouth. I want my cock to hit the back of your throat. Do you understand?"

"Mhm."

I stuck out my tongue and a drip of saliva dropped onto the

bed. His eyes flashed as he stared at me, his breathing hitched at the sight of my submission.

I reached between us and wrapped my hand around the base of his cock, hard between my fingers. I worked my mouth and spat on the tip so it glistened in the light. I licked his shaft, my tongue working its way across every vein, every ridge, worshiping him with my mouth. *I want to please him so badly.*

Damon let a low groan escape between his lips as his hips jerked forward. "That's it, beautiful. Now I want you to open that pretty mouth wider and take all of me."

I obeyed, taking the head of his cock in. My lips sealed around the shaft of his penis, my tongue working the underside as I took him deeper. "You can take more of me."

The pressure built up in the back of my throat, the resistance making my eyes water, but I pressed on, wanting to please him.

"Fuck, yes. Just like that," He fisted my hair. "Take it all. Don't stop... Don't you dare fucking stop."

His cock hit the back of my throat, making me gag a little. I breathed in deep through my nose.

Each thrust of his hips brought his cock deeper into my mouth. He pulled on my hair as his other hand reached down to cup my chin. Tears of pleasure and submission filled my eyes. His thumb brushed across my cheek, wiping away a tear before he thrust forward again, burying himself to the hilt.

I could feel him lose some control. His thrusts started slowing down as he tried to restrain himself. I could taste precum mixed in with my saliva. *Fuck, he tastes incredible.*

He let my hair go and slid his cock out of my mouth with a low groan. Breathing raggedly, his chest rose and fell as he took a backward step to collect himself. "I need to hold off. I don't wanna come just yet." He reached down and ran his hand along my jawline, his thumb grazing my lips. "You did so fucking good, beautiful. Now, I want you to turn around and press your face into the mattress," he commanded.

My body responded instinctively to his every word. I arched my back and presented myself to him.

I heard him stir behind me, the soft creak of the floor as he leaned for something. "Oh, look what we have here..."

I threw a sideways look over my shoulder; he was standing there, smirking, fingers interlaced through the long strand of prayer beads. They looked almost innocent in his hands, but his expression betrayed their true purpose. He ran his fingers along them as if savoring each one before locking eyes with me. "These are going to remind you who you belong to. Now ass up."

"Damon..." I whispered.

"Shh. You don't have to say a word."

His hands traced over my back, falling between my ass cheeks. I moaned as his fingers settled against my asshole and touched me.

"Relax," he growled. "Let me inside, beautiful."

Damon spit on his fingers, then he moved them back to my ass—circling, teasing, pushing just slightly inside before withdrawing.

I whimpered, my body trembling. The sensation was amazing but painful, and I couldn't help but push back against his hand, seeking more.

"You're so eager to please. Are you my own cum whore, Hilly?" Damon chuckled darkly, his breath hot against my ear. "Greedy little thing, aren't you?"

I heard him spit again; it landed on my asshole, oozing down into my pussy. It was an odd feeling, yet so fucking arousing. My body tensed at the thought, my muscles clamping around nothing.

My pussy pounded with my need. The saliva dripped from

my pussy onto the mattress. I felt it mix with my own juices, running down my thighs and making them sticky.

I burrowed my face into the mattress. He took it as a sign, pushing the first of the prayer beads up my ass. I moaned.

He waited for me to get used to the feeling of it. The bead stretched me in ways I'd never felt. It burned as he threaded one after another, each adding to the intensity. He worked the fifth bead inside me, and my hips bucked against the bed.. Firmly, Damon held me still as he worked the sixth bead. "Damon!"

He jammed my head firmly into the mattress, his hand tangling into my hair, his weight pinning me in place. I obliged, breathing ragged as I let go to him. My ass was so full. "You take the beads so fucking well."

I felt the prayer beads dangle from me, swaying slightly with each movement. Damon's fingers traced a path down my spine before gripping my hip. His other hand reached between my legs, spreading my folds open.

"You like feeling exposed, don't you?"

I let out a moan, unable to form words. His cock pressed against my entrance, the thick head slick with precum, teasing me, coaxing me to open wider. He pushed the tip inside, and I gasped, my body arching just for him.

His fingers dug into my hip as he inched into me. My pussy clenched around him, desperate to pull him deeper, but he held back, relishing every fucking second. The beads in my ass twitched with each movement. It felt like I was being split inch by inch. I'd never felt so consumed.

"You're so tight and wet for me." Finally, he was buried to the hilt. At first, he was slow, but soon enough, his thrusts went hard and fast, every one of them pushing me closer to the edge.

He reached up with one hand, fisting my hair, and yanked my head back, baring my neck. "Let's see how much you can handle."

My head felt like it was on fire as he kept a tight grip.

I gasped, my voice husky. "Harder, Damon. Fuck me harder."

His thrusts became relentless, each one pounding into me so much that the beads shifted inside my asshole, adding to the sensation. My hands scrabble at the bedsheets, but there is nothing to hold on to, nothing to anchor me.

Every movement took what little breath I had in my lungs. I was starving for air, for release. I felt every inch of him. Instinctively, my hips moved to the rhythm of his as he desperately pounded into me, seeking my sweet spot.

"You like me taking you, owning you," he growled.

Yes, I did love it. I loved how he took control and made me feel so utterly consumed by him. It was intoxicating, addicting.

He leaned into me. I whimpered as his hands found my clit, his touch hard and unforgiving. He started rubbing, his thumb circling with precision. I could barely endure the sensation. Every nerve in my body was ablaze. Every muscle was taut with the need to orgasm again.

"I want you to come all over my cock. I need you to milk me."

It hit me like a flood all at once, and I cried his name. I didn't care if I woke our parents.

He didn't let up or give me time to recover. Instead, he continued to pump into me. "Let me feel every last fucking spasm."

I did, surrendering entirely to the waves of pleasure that washed over me. My vision blurred, my senses overwhelmed, until there was nothing left but the sensation of him inside me, claiming me, owning me.

He swiftly took his cock out of my pussy and turned me around on the bed. My breath escaped in a series of rapid gasps as I struggled to process. *I don't think I can handle anymore.*

"I wanna hit that fucking G-spot. You're gonna squirt on my cock. Do you understand?"

Fuck. Fuck! All I could do was nod.

He lifted my legs and laid them over his broad shoulders, then pressed his chest onto me so that I could feel his heartbeat synchronize with mine. His warm breath danced across my neck as his hands made their way up my arms. The prayer beads still hung out of my ass, adding to the sensation.

Damon didn't waste a second, reaching for my wrists and hauling them above my head, pinning them to the mattress. His body was on top of mine. His cock nudged my pussy, and in one move, he filled me again. His hips began a rhythmic motion, each thrust hitting my G-spot. *There's no way I can orgasm again?*

I arched beneath him, my back rising off the mattress, striving to press closer, but his grip held me down firmly, leaving me immobile. His relenting cock hit my G-spot over and over. I could feel the bed moving under us.

The room was filled with the sounds of our bodies moving together—his deep, guttural grunts mixing with my breathless gasps.

The deeper and harder he thrust himself into my G-spot, the wetter my pussy was getting.

An uncontrollable pressure built up within me.

I moaned. "Damon... Damon..."

"I'm going to count to three, and you're going to squirt for me."

I couldn't help but let a little whimper.

"One..."

He let out a deep breath.

"Two..."

I was so fucking ready.

"Three."

My pussy gave in, and a gush of liquid erupted from me, my

juices smothering his cock, dripping down on the sheets beneath us. "That's my fucking girl."

He still didn't stop, thrusting harder into me, his cock diving deep into the wet mess I'd created. My legs wrapped tightly around his shoulders, leaving me to quiver beneath him.

I wanted him to come so badly, but not in my pussy.

"Damon, I want you to come on my face," I told him, out of breath.

He froze, his face full of satisfaction. Slowing, he removed his cock from me and let go of my wrists, easing the tight grip on them. My skin felt hot and flushed. I twitched my fingers, feeling them as the circulation returned to them.

My trembling, weak legs slid down from his broad shoulders to the bed.

He hovered over me for a second or two, his eyes inspecting my face, as if he wanted to make sure he remembered every second of this moment. There was pride shining in his eyes.

"Choke me," I demanded.

"Fuck, Hilly."

He slid beside me, kneeling. His fingers curled around my throat in a firm, teasing hold. My heart was racing, with a mix of fear and something darker. His other hand began to move over his shaft. "I need you to tell me that you're mine."

I tried to swallow, the words trembling on my lips. "I'm yours," I whisper, barely above a breath.

His grip tightened on my throat. I thought I could see stars. "Say it louder. Make me fucking believe it."

"I'm yours!" I repeated in a broken voice. "I'm fucking yours, Damon. Every part of me."

My head spun as his fingers clutched my throat; the pressure was intoxicating. I wanted to let go, succumb totally to his darkness, and surround myself with it like some heavy cloak.

"You wear my hand like a pretty necklace."

His cock was just inches from my face, and the tip glistened with precum. He threw his head back and his eyes shut as he continued to stroke his hand over the tip.

"I-I'm..." My words faltered.

"What is it?"

"I'm scared to lose you," I whispered, little more than a murmur, as if the admission tumbled from me in some kind of confession.

He opened his eyes, and the look he gave me was fierce and possessive, like he had been waiting for me to say that. A shiver ran down my spine as he let out a moan, coming on my face, spilling over my skin like a mark of ownership. I wanted to pass out from the sensation of it all.

He leaned down, claiming my mouth with his. He didn't care that his cum laced my lips as his mouth moved against mine, leaving me panting.

"You'll never lose me. I'm fucking obsessed with you, Hilly," he murmured against my lips. "I'm yours. Always and forever."

In an instant, all those moments of doubt and fear vanished. Damon Northwood owned me. I was all his, and he was all mine. A promise that sealed our fates.

DAMON CLAIMED ME IN WAYS NOBODY ELSE COULD. IT WAS LIKE HIS fingers ran through the knots of my soul. It wasn't just my scars or my past that he accepted. It was more that he embraced them, every fucked up piece of me, even the dark and sinful shadows I carried. Our dark souls were intertwined. He'd kill for me, and I knew it. With Damon, I was safe and completely fucking his.

That's when it hit me.

I had pulled my angel cards prior to meeting him. *Blessing in disguise.* I had remembered it but had never grasped its meaning until then. I knew it was about him. Damon was my unlikely savior. The realization swelled up within my heart. Its weight hit me like a tidal wave. I wish I had met him sooner. He had been my salvation, my blessing in disguise.

We laid in bed, covered in dried blood, naked and out of breath. His arms clutched my body, hugging me into an intimate fortress.

Damon's fingers danced along my stomach and arm, giving me goosebumps as I twiddled with the cross that hung from my neck. I burrowed my head into his chest, inhaling his scent. The beating of his heart soothed me.

I looked up at him with a mischievous grin. "So, now that Halloween is marked off, how about Christmas?" I teased.

Damon chuckled and looked over at the knife on the side table. "Christmas, eh? I can already tell it's gonna be a wild one..."

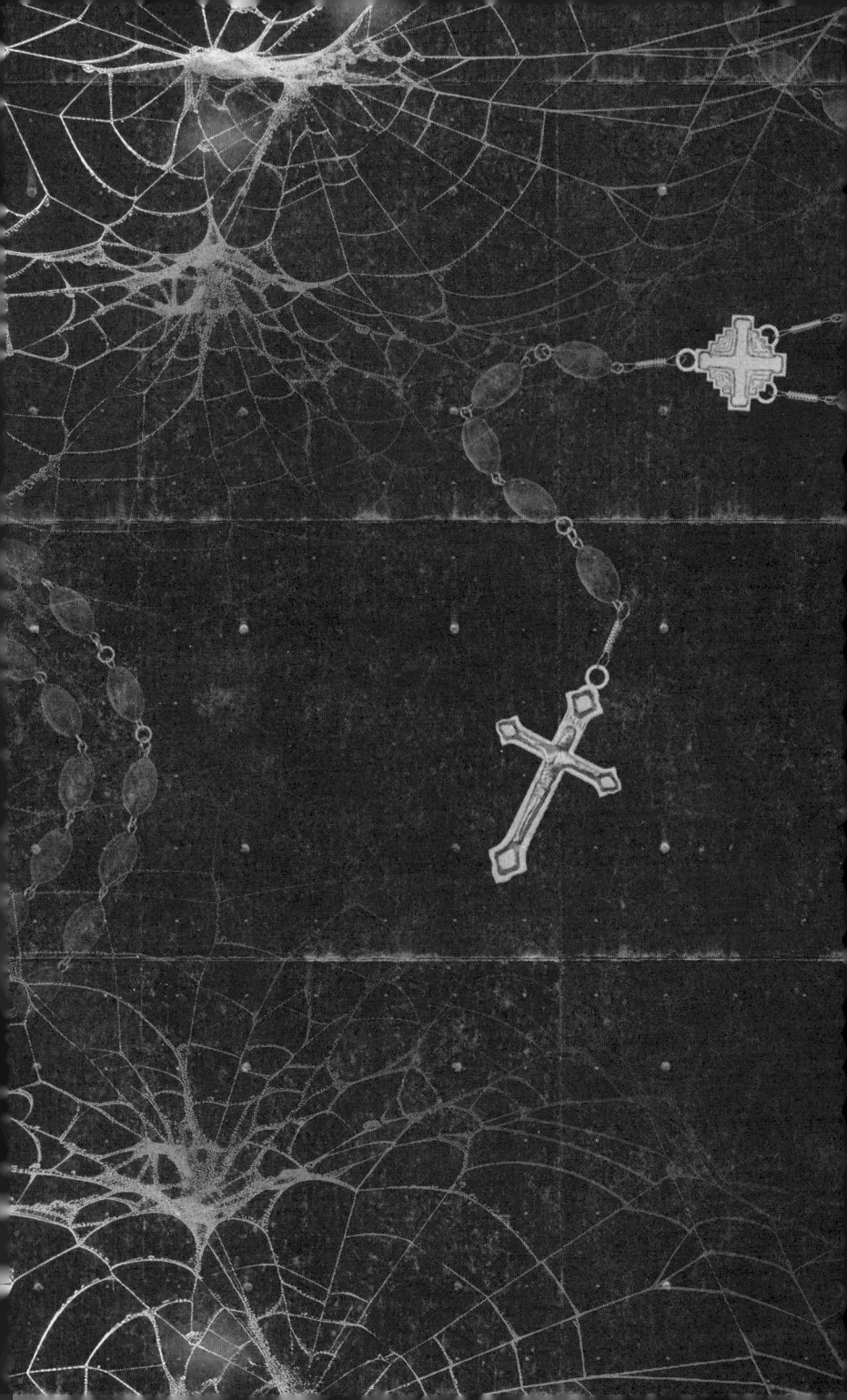

Acknowledgments

Readers
I appreciate you dedicating your time to reading my book.
Second book? Hmm. More Damon Northwood? Maybe!
I look forward to sharing more of my work with you in the
future. Thank you for your continued support and for allowing
me to share my passion for writing with you.

Disturbed Valkyrie Designs
From day one you have been my rock.
I appreciate your patience and understanding in dealing with
me. Your exceptional qualities and skills are truly admirable.
You go above and beyond for me. Thank you!

Havoc Archives
I want to express my gratitude for all your help.
Thank you for being such an incredible asset and making my
book come alive.

Beta & ARC Readers
Your unwavering support has been incredible. Your
encouragement and motivation have pushed me to reach new
heights. Thank you from the bottom of my heart. You mean the
world to me.

Nadine
Thank you for being my alpha reader.

You have given me constant motivation, and I appreciate your encouragement.

J.D. Midnight

Yo, my dude. Thanks for helping me with the blurb and so much more.
How you put up with me I'll never know.

Brandon F

Dude... Thanks for getting me through the hard times.

Daisy & Rachel

I love you.

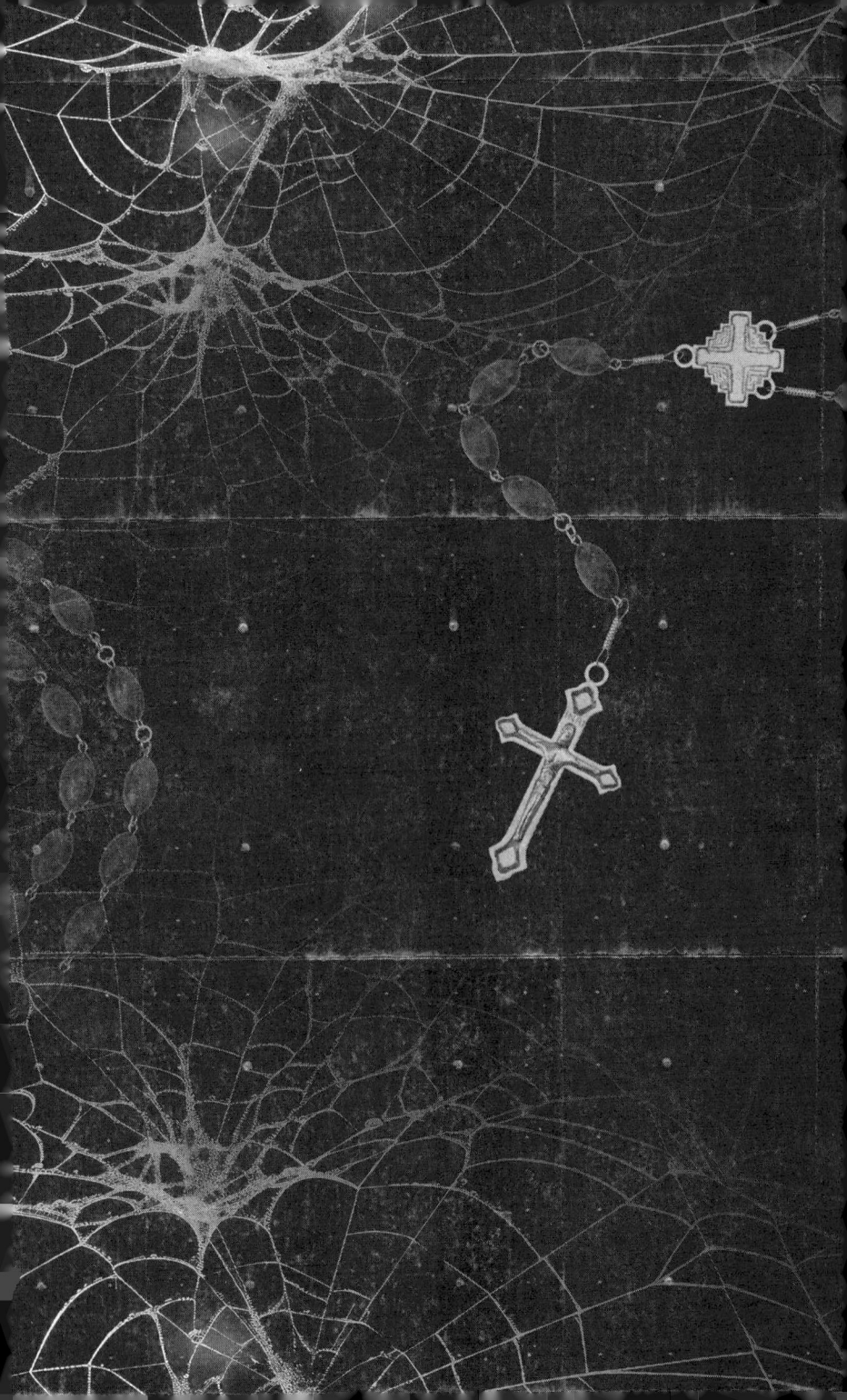

GET IN CONTACT

Jade always enjoys hearing from her readers. If you would like to get in touch with her, you can find her on social media platforms. Alternatively, you can also reach out to her through email at jadewauthor@gmail.com

tiktok.com/@jadewbook

instrgram.com/jadewbook

www.jadewilkesauthor.com

Printed in Great Britain
by Amazon

50498904R00144